Hi Emmett,

A mad, bad

Best wishes,
James

DYSTOPIA

A THRILLER

JAMES ROWLINS

Dystopia

Published by The Conrad Press in the United Kingdom 2023

Tel: +44(0)1227 472 874
www.theconradpress.com
info@theconradpress.com

ISBN 978-1-915494-59-7

Typesetting and Cover Design by:
Charlotte Mouncey, www.bookstyle.co.uk

The Conrad Press logo was designed by Maria Priestley.

Printed and bound in Great Britain by Clays Ltd, Elcograf S.p.A.

PROLOGUE

I COULDN'T BELIEVE MY EYES. A moment ago, there was just one woman. Now there were two.

They were standing either side of a window that opened onto the balcony, shrouded in an aura of mystery. Sunlight obscured their features, but I could see they were very similar – the same blanche complexion, the same jet-black hair. They wore identical dresses, one white and the other black.

A white swan and a black swan. I was drawn towards them as if by a magical force. They were not human but godlike in their perfection, and this unsettled me most of all. One was Venus, Mary Magdalene, Ophelia. The other was Medusa, Jezebel, Lady Macbeth. One was good and the other was evil.

They locked eyes on me. One radiated kindness, the other wrath. I looked for the mirror or projector that had created the illusion. The drugs meant I could be seeing things, but it somehow made sense on a deep, unconscious level. It was the answer to a mystery that had frustrated me for an eternity.

'Ellis, *mon amour*. I love you. I am truly sorry,' said the woman in white, tears streaming down her cheek. The woman in black scowled but said nothing. I reached out a hand to touch the crying lady, but my vision was clouding over and I was going under fast.

Blank.

PART ONE

ONE

THIS IS NOT A POEM, dream or fantasy. It is a factual account of events from the first encounter with my foes, up to my final escape and current captivity. It is a true story.

You guys aren't into stream-of-consciousness narratives. You want a linear and reliable report. I disagree. A story should have a start, middle and end, but not necessarily in that order. But I am tired of the interrogations and the torture, so to hell with it, I will give you your goddamn start, middle and end. A 'once upon a time' tale with a Hollywood ending.

I had never been inside Brighton Police Station before, although I had often walked past its oblique modern facade. Inside, it is cramped and squalid. Desks are piled together in large, anonymous office spaces adorned with family photos and children's drawings. It was deserted at such an early hour of the morning.

I had been read my rights – it was just like it was in any number of films, though I wasn't asked if I wanted to make a phone call to my lawyer. As I was naked at the time of my arrest, I had been given prison-issue clothes to wear – a cheap polo shirt, some supermarket-brand jeans and white trainers. This upset me more than anything.

The cell was cold and empty – a Spartan affair with a plastic-covered bench and hard pillow. There was a spy camera on the ceiling, but anyone could see through the iron-barred door. There was no toilet. I thought about pissing between the bars and imagined a castrating blade falling from above.

A few officers passed by without paying me any attention. A strange balding man stopped to look at me. He was strangely familiar. Was he a neighbour?

There was no toilet so I assumed I wouldn't be held long. I needed water and aspirin, but it was too much effort to ask. This hangover would take days to clear, argh. I vowed to give up drinking but knew even in my condition that wasn't likely. Instead, I solemnly promised never to drink that much ever again.

I had no memory of the night before – I must have passed out on the street. I had done that before but never been arrested, so there is a first for everything. I thought back to when I was suspended from school for beating up a boy who called me 'Tory tosspot.' I was terrified of how father would deal with me. Things weren't so different ten years on.

At nine o'clock I was taken into an office on the fourth floor with impressive views of the Brighton cityscape and introduced to Chief Constable Williams and Deputy Chief Constable Edwards of Sussex Police, both dressed in impeccable uniforms. The latter was a few shades greyer and blander than the first, but otherwise they were identical.

I thought it odd that I was brought before such senior police-men for such a minor offence. Had news of my arrest leaked to the press? I pictured hordes of journalists and photographers camped outside, waiting for my release. That wouldn't help my job hunt. I've always distrusted the police, but I reminded myself to be polite.

'Can I go now, please?'

'Mr Ellis, we are here to make you understand the gravity of your situation. We are at an early stage of our inquiry, but charges will likely be brought against you.'

I looked blankly at the Deputy Chief. My brain was scrambled and it was hard to get my words out.

'Charges?'

'Tell us about last night. What do you remember about the party?'

A party, yes, I had been at a party last night. And something had gone wrong – terribly, terribly wrong. Something gut-wrenching awful had happened. But at that precise moment, I could not remember for the life of me what it was. I tried to say something that would sound credible.

'Look here, something bad happened… at this party. But what has it got to do with me?'

I had my first flashback and paled visibly.

'Oh my God,' I muttered. 'I've been framed.'

A long silence ensued. A shrill noise raged inside my head and I felt nauseous.

'Do you know who my father is?' I asked at last.

'Yes, yes, Mr Ellis, we know who your father is. Bail is never an option when it's a question of murder,' said the Chief Constable.

'Daddy can't help his little boy,' chimed in the Deputy Chief.

I stood up in rage.

'What the hell is going on?'

The interrogation went on forever. The Chief and Deputy Constables wanted to know all about my dealings with Bigboy. When did we first meet? How often did we 'party'? What drugs did we do? How did I get a job on his promo team? Who was this Judy I was raving about in my cell?

I tried to give answers, but no sooner had I uttered a word I was bombarded with more questions. Did I deal drugs for a living? Could I explain the giant deposits on my account? How long had I been seeing Angie Hammond? Did I supply her? Was I an abusive boyfriend? Why did I do those awful things to her?

The interview was called to an end. Alone in my cell, I tried to formulate answers to the policemen's questions. I had to make sense of this madness, for my own sake. I kept coming back to one question – and one question alone. How had my ordinary life got so screwed up?

I shut my eyes and waited for memories to fill the void.

TWO

A few months earlier.

'Thank God!'

First a din, then a hum and a waft of stale air, then a tube whistling around the bend at a speed strictly prohibited by EU transport directive 456A. It was Victoria underground station at 8.43 am and the sexually smooth tones of the announcer heralded the arrival of the northbound Circle Line tube. London's finest paced up and down, late.

'Bloody hell!'

An unkempt man was tottering near the edge of the platform. If he wasn't a tramp, he was down on his luck.

'Christ Almighty!'

One glance at the torn Reeboks, the ripped shirt and filthy overcoat confirmed that he was a member of London's homeless community.

'Oh my God!'

The tramp skidded on a puddle of vomit, possibly his own, making his bottle veer off the platform onto the track. Petrified at losing his treasured commodity, the man followed. Only those near the far end of the platform saw him fall and nobody actually saw the collision, which happened at the speed of light. But the thud was heard by all.

Later that morning investigators would unpick the remains

of the tramp's charred body from his meth-soaked coat. The severed hands and feet, riddled with moles and verrucas, were scattered over several metres of track. The police pathologist was given ten minutes to photograph and prepare the body for transfer, and in the rush left a finger and two toes on the track.

The tube driver had a split second to react – not that he would have done so. Asked by the *Evening Standard* how he felt about the incident, Albert Smith said that 'there was one less homeless person to worry about' – adding that track deaths were 'regular nuisance.' The Sun fêted him as a 'have-a-go hero' and he was the toast of punters across the land.

The incident caused a furore in *The Guardian*, who revealed that Albert Smith was a member of Britain First. This fuelled rumours on anarchist websites about a 'homeless elimination programme' where drifters were murdered and their deaths made to look like accidents.

Commuters were upset by the tramp's violent death. A lonely woman shed a tear. But alarm soon turned into rage. Who was this guy to screw up their morning? A benefits scrounger or failed artist, no doubt.

'No mobile coverage in the London underground, bloody unbelievable!'

There was a dash to find Wi-Fi hotspots to get the word out that meetings would have to begin without the Head of Strategy or Risk Analyst. But they were *not* to worry – they were fine, and would they please leave all major items until their arrival? Yes, especially that.

They consoled themselves that it was a good story to tell down the pub. The shrewdest began to spin their part in the tragedy to prove their humanity – how they didn't want to talk about it, it was too raw, but if pushed, how they called out to the tramp to bring him back from the brink. Yeah, that was good. Could even be pillow talk.

I was also late – not for work but for an assessment centre. As I searched for the number to call, my iPhone ran out of charge. Damn. I scoured the station for cafés with power sockets before realising I didn't have the cable so gave up on the whole idea.

As I exited the station, I caught my reflection in a blank billboard. The day before I had gone to the hairdressers just as they were closing.

'Yup Richie, I can squeeze you in. And talking about squeezes, I must tell you about my new beau!'

'I'm all ears.'

Half an hour later I was just that, as my normally foppish, dirty blond hair was cut short, making my very English blue-green eyes, fair skin and square jaw stand out. It wasn't my favourite look, but I was tall and thin enough to pull it off. In a suit, I looked like a successful young Englishman of my times. I could almost believe it was true.

After the morning stress, I was in dire need of a drink to calm me down. I knew that if I had alcohol I may as well not go to the test centre at all, so I settled for a large chai latte from a street vendor. Not having any cash, I waved a bank card at the elderly black man who shrugged and said I could pay next time. That made me feel better.

I decided to walk. I knew London, at least Mayfair, well enough to find it. I headed up Buckingham Palace Road, taking a left at the Palace. I gave a mock salute to Her Majesty – I was, after all, about to embark on her service. The invitation letter screamed secrecy – no heading, number or even name.

It simply gave a date, time and place at which I should present myself, and was signed *S.S.* in blue ink.

I thought it was a hoax at first, but as a matter of fact, I had replied to an ad in *The Times* for the Secret Intelligence Service. I had also applied to three national broadsheets, six investment banks, eight public relations firms, twelve advertising agencies and fifteen blue chip companies, so I hadn't exactly been waiting for MI6 to get on the phone.

Green Park was looking splendidly autumnal. I crossed Piccadilly and headed up Half Moon Street, whose name is more evocative than the street itself, and passed the Hilton where a married woman had once invited me for a tryst. I admired the elegant Mayfair medley of Georgian and Regency townhouses on Curzon Street, noticing how many were home to minor Arab embassies and banks.

I'd read online that MI5 had moved out of Leconfield House in the 1970s, so I was intrigued that they maintained an operation here. I was greeted by a bespectacled receptionist.

'Sorry I'm late. I'm here for an assessment…'

'Name and ID. Leave your bag at the counter and come this way.'

I was taken in the lift to the sixth floor and led through an endless maze of doors, corridors and offices until we reached a windowless room filled with computer terminals. I was acquainted with the computer and told that if I needed something or wanted to leave the room, I had to press the intercom button by the door. She left me and shut the door behind her.

The computer took my photo and scanned my fingerprint. It then made me read through a long statement promising not to disclose any information about the test centre or questions.

This was rather different from my other test centre experiences, where as a rule they tried not to freak out their future employees.

I was finally allowed to commence the test. It was time-limited, but I stared blankly at the screen for some moments and doodled on rough paper. I looked at what my hands had done – a train entering a dark tunnel with human body parts scattered across the tracks. I pulled myself together and got to work.

It began with maths, logic and verbal reasoning conundrums. The questions got harder, which probably meant I wasn't doing badly. Next were the psychometric tests. Was I more responsible than honest? Was I more of a team player or a leader? More of a freethinker or a problem solver? The first ten questions or so were predictable, but the rest were mind-bending. Was I more subversive or hedonistic? More Machiavellian or patriotic?

The programme asked me about my politics. This too was unusual, to say the least. Were my ideas more left or right-wing? How did I feel about the USA? And Europe? Truth be told, I didn't know how to answer. What the hell, I would be a pro-European centrist for the duration of the test.

In the last section, I had to write an essay on the 'greatest national security threat faced by Britain in the 21st century.' A model answer would demonstrate 'strong analytical skills and refer to issues such as Islamic fundamentalism, European federalisation and the prospect of Brexit.' The suggestions were odd – was European integration on a par with jihadism?

Fine, whatever. I figured that I may as well indulge in some journalistic polemic. The idea of taking control of our borders to stop the bogeymen was a lie. Leaving Europe would have major national security implications. Sharing intelligence was the most effective way to prevent terrorist attacks on British soil and leaving the EU would inevitably lead to all kinds of security mishaps.

There would be other consequences. Living in isolation will foster our island mentality and British nationalist tendencies – homegrown terrorists liable to attack immigrants, minorities and anyone outside of the norm. What's more, leaving the single market will damage the British economy, making us weaker and less able to defend ourselves.

The problem with the EU was with the body politic, I argued, not Europe itself. We were fed a daily diet of stories about the wasteful, corrupt and incompetent European Union and its mishandling of every major crisis, but it was absurd to believe Britain was a lost cause because of EU bureaucrats and politicians. If only the EU looked and sounded more like the UK itself.

I didn't like what I had written. For someone who thought of himself as completely apolitical, I'd written a lot and gone off-topic. Worst of all, it sounded just like one of father's speeches. That wasn't good at all. But I couldn't face rewriting it and I was running out of time.

The test took three hours. I sighed with relief when it was over. Talking politics felt dirty. As I logged off, the computer asked for my permission for my dossier to be forwarded to ESIS – the European Secret Intelligence Service, currently recruiting. I clicked on 'no' and the screen froze, then the secretary arrived to escort me off the premises.

I got back to Brighton at six that evening. At home, I poured myself a glass of Macallan single malt and charged my phone. I had four messages. Father, demanding a serious talk about money. Oh, and not to forget his visit next weekend. Next was a message from my bank manager, inviting me in for a friendly chat. I poured myself another scotch.

The third message was curious indeed.

'Hello Ellis, Bigboy, your neighbour, would just *lurve* you to give me a ring back on 07739664569.'

Smooth bastard, I thought, using his celebrity name and talking in the third person. The call was especially odd as we had only met once on the landing and hadn't exchanged numbers. And how did he know that my friends call me by my surname, Ellis?

Having a famous neighbour is like having an unusual nationality. It counts for sweet FA, but everyone tends to remember you for it. I turned on the news. Scientists had identified the same gene in the DNA of famous psychopaths and serial killers, from Jack the Ripper, the Yorkshire Ripper, Fred West, Dr Shipman and Ian Huntley. Jack the Ripper? I poured myself a third scotch.

The last message was stranger still. It was from a cockney shouting down a crackly telephone line.

'Alrighty Ellis, geaser, be round la'er on! Lookin' forward to gettin' to knaw you, is I. Your number's up mate!'

I tried to figure out which of my friends was high as a kite in Thailand.

THREE

A new watch has always marked a fresh start in my life.

Casino digital – primary school, boredom, sleepovers. Grandpa's vintage analogue – homework, afterschool rugby, first crushes. That one got smashed in a school fight. A platinum Mont Blanc for my eighteenth – acne, A-levels, first car, clumsy sex, copious drinking. I lost that one in freshers' week at Oxford.

I mention this as I left my 1970s 'KGB' Poljot chronograph at the test centre in London. It was a great piece of machinery – mineral anti-scratch glass and near-atomic precision, so long as you wound it up every two days, which I invariably forgot to do. It was a graduation present from mother.

Watch buying is a serious business, as every GQ reader will tell you. I spent a few hours circling the main shopping mall and Lanes' jewellery shops before narrowing down my choices to a Cartier with lots of chrome and lots of leather, and an Omega with elegant Roman numerals and a steel strap.

The Cartier was three hundred pounds cheaper, but the Omega was far more stylish and I refused to be a victim of my dire finances.

'Shoo, I'd like to claim the impeccable taste reduction,' I said in a Sean Connery voice.

The sales assistant was a pretty brunette with big cleavage

and gothic makeup. She rolled her eyes back till all I could see was the whites.

'Watch your back. Times are dangerous, my friend. Expect the unexpected. Beware the Ides, beware the tides,' she howled in a husky voice.

I stepped back in fright.

'Z'alright mate, just 'avin a larf! Doing drama at uni, yer see.'

'Oh.'

'Take it eazy, won't yer!'

'Okay.'

Back in the flat, I stared out to sea and tried to work out if I was bound for success or a failure. I told myself that I was doing alright. I was living in a large top-floor Regency apartment on Brighton's seafront – a plaque on the door testifies to Oscar Wilde having stayed there.

It had a balcony and with a damned cool view, about the best in the city. To the east, you could see the bulky arms of the Brighton Marina, with its ebb and flow of luxury yachts. To the west were the gaudy lights of the Brighton Pier. If you craned your neck, you could make out the sad spectre of the West Pier, abandoned to the sea, and the latest addition to the city skyline, the i360 'cock and ring.'

The flat used to be Lady Elaine Stamford's before she passed away in the early 80s. Gran was a waif-like woman with an elegant demeanour and austere eyes. As a teen, I believed her ghost lingered in this flat. One day while I was listening to Pulp's *Different Class* and spending some quality time on internet porn, I had a strong premonition the old lady was staring at me in disgust.

My girlfriend at the time was Debs. I nicknamed her Sam

Cam II. She was an above-averagely-fit brunette with an above-average figure. She was always chipper. A posh girl at heart – Daddy saw to it that she went to the right schools – she did her best to cultivate some 'attitude.' She had a small flower tattoo on her lower back and got drunk once a week.

As Head of Corporate Sponsorship at American Express, she had an above-average income, but her tastes were simple. She enjoyed 1980s club nights, girlie gossip, weekends away and Hollywood movies. We met at Baxter's birthday party, a school friend of mine whose parties were legendary among Brighton's hip urban crowd.

We snogged and had sex that same night. Truth be told, it was a bit rough. We had both been through bad breakups and were hammered. At God-knows-what-time in the morning, I offered to drive her home, to my home that is.

'Shalla giveyer a litfsh darlin'? No obligations. Just an honest shag.'

I was beyond suaveness. Not that she was in a state to care. She threw up in Baxter's fishpond, killing a Shubunkin. Our host thought this was hilarious and promised to freeze the fish and to do something dreadful with it on our wedding night. Baxter now lives in HM Prison Belmarsh, doing ten for dealing.

I suspected that Debs was on E because she was hyper and horny. When we were finally in the car driving to my place, she unzipped my fly and buried her head in my lap. I was pretty turned on myself at this point. I remember telling her not to bite and got flashed by a speed camera doing sixty-three miles per hour in town.

I used to drive a 1989 Porsche Carrera 964 with a rear-mounted 6-cylinder 3.6-litre engine with an acceleration of

0-60 mph in 5.2 seconds. The spoiler raised automatically when you hit 50 mph. *European Car* magazine described it as providing 'a driving experience like no other,' which doesn't do it justice. The car is a drivable penis – sex on wheels.

I had to let it go a while back to pay off some debts, so enough of the success bullshit. If I faced the facts, and I tried hard not to, I was in trouble. I didn't have a job, and aside from a fast-diminishing inheritance, I was dependent on my misery father. Stepfather, that is. One of the many irksome conditions of his marriage to mother was that I call him 'father.' I was four at the time and it felt wrong even then, but it stuck by force of habit.

A high-school dunce, John R. Goodman knew from an early age that he could rely on his gift-of-the-gab to make the grade in other ways. His parents, working-class Londoners, were killed in a bus accident when he was young. Penniless, he had no trouble persuading one of his many girlfriends to invest in small-time ventures, some of which paid off. His most lasting and profitable investment was Lady Jane Stamford – a.k.a. mother.

The rest was plain sailing. In the 1980s, father applied himself to making money – loads and loads of it. He was in on every 'get rich quick' scheme on offer in Thatcherite Britain –stocks, shares, sell-offs, the works. Once in the big league, he acquired influential friends in the Conservative party and was even invited to run for parliament. He declined. Why twiddle your thumbs when there was so much money to be made?

In the early 90s, after the economic bubble had burst, he changed his mind and got himself elected as Member of Parliament for Arundel, one of the safest Tory seats in England.

It looked like a blunder after the Major government began unravelling, and like he was on the wrong side of history when New Labour routed the Tories in 1997. I know for a fact he came close to jumping ship.

To make matters worse, Goodman's pro-European politics put him at odds with his party, whose Eurosceptic right-wing had taken over. He went back to his business ventures while his party was in the electoral doghouse, making back the fortune he'd lost during the recession. He went unnoticed by the political world, although he did build up a sizable grassroots following and a reputation for being a good MP.

He came back to the big table as soon as his party's fortunes were on the up. The two decades in parliament earned him the job of Deputy Chief Whip in the 2010 coalition government, followed by Junior Minister in the Foreign Office. His pro-Euro stance was a problem for some, but this was overlooked in the light of his strong business skills.

The Tories beat Labour in 2015, wiping out the Lib Dems in one fell swoop. Everyone was surprised except father, who had predicted exactly that. In the victory euphoria, the Prime Minister promoted him to the Cabinet as Minister of State for Business, Industry and Enterprise. After that, the press often referred to him as a 'serious contender' for the Tory Leadership.

I know rather little about my real father. Anthony Ellis (I go by Ellis to honour his memory) was a poet of talent, though unpublished. I know that he was a devoted family man who loved my mother. He was a committed socialist, despite coming from privilege. The Poljot watch had been his, which is why I was so upset about its loss.

Mother tells me that I am his spitting image, which I think

accounts for why she is so distant with me. I only have one picture of him – a grainy Polaroid taken a few weeks before he died in a boat accident in the Lake District. I have never been able to find out what happened – mother never talked about it and my therapist advised me not to dig deeper.

Enough about fathers. I left home at eighteen to go up to Oxford, where I read PPE – Philosophy, Politics and Economics, the ultimate 'I-want-a-great-career-but-not-sure-in-what' degree. Back then I thought that I had got to Oxford on merit, that I was the embodiment of the whole classless society thing and the future was there to be seized.

In my last year at Oxford, I received an anonymous letter setting out father's financial contributions to my college over the past ten years. I was devastated. I threatened to drop out a week before my finals, but some friends staged a kind of intervention and talked me out of it.

I regret that now.

FOUR

SHE CAN'T HAVE BEEN THE first thing I saw when I opened the door.

It must have been the wafts of weed, and the techno remix of *Love in the 90s* that was pumping out of ultra-sleek Bowers & Wilkins Nautilus speakers. A Stanton vinyl mixer had pride of place on the central coffee table from The Conran Shop. An Aspen sofa, ultra-streamlined with metal ski legs and lilac cushions, a Saarinen white marble dining table and five metal chairs adorned the varnished parquet floor.

All the furniture had sharp edges and funky designs, and I thought to myself that you can attain a level of cool with well-chosen high street labels. And I must have almost walked into the huge stuffed tiger shark in a glass tank of formaldehyde, which I recognised as Damien Hirst's *The Physical Impossibility of Death in the Mind of Someone Living*. I doubted it was the original, which had famously been bought by Saatchi for seven million pounds.

I saw the Ultra HD TV which took up much of the north-facing wall. I remember that the news was on – a report about a young fashion model stabbed on her doorstep. I noticed that the walls and ceilings were sound-proofed and that the perimeter of the French Bay windows was wired with some kind of hi-tech security system. I wondered why a minor celebrity needed that kind of protection.

But all I really saw was her. She was sitting on one of the metal chairs in the middle of the room. She was lovely. She had a naturally pale complexion, firm cheekbones, and straight long dark hair. She was tall. She exuded Englishness in her complexion, was French in her demure and Japanese in her hair arrangement. She had Irish eyes, an American smile and erotic lips.

As cliché as it sounds, it was love at first sight. Truly, madly, deeply. She was strong and confident with a dose of vulnerability. She was aware of her beauty but didn't flaunt it. She had gone everywhere worth going, read everything worth reading, seen everything worth seeing, but she still had a lust for life. She had savoir faire without being elitist.

I knew for sure she possessed these qualities and she was everything I had ever wanted, the perfect companion. It's amazing what you can tell in a fleeting moment. Part of me knew it was fantasy, but I believed it all the same, and that she would feel the same about me too. Love exists in your mind, anyway, so who needs the other?

I had visions of Pygmalion's muse and Edgar Allan Poe's painter capturing his wife's eternal beauty. And Scottie in *Vertigo* chasing Kim Novak playing, what was her name…?

'Bollocks!'

I snapped out of my reverie. Bigboy was standing behind the cocktail bar speaking on two phones, one clasped to each ear while shaking a cocktail mixer. He had a spliff clenched between his teeth, was wearing oversized Dolce and Gabbana sunglasses and a bathrobe with 'Shag for England' on the backside.

He motioned me to sit by waiving a baguette-sized spliff towards the sofa. Ash fell into the cocktail mixer leading to another tirade. Through the thick weed-haze I made out two others in the room sat on a bench in an alcove. The man was short and podgy and dressed in a patchwork quilt jacket. His friend, who from the look of her lips was an addict, wore a sexy nurse's outfit with a stethoscope dangling from her bra.

Bigboy had finished his calls and stood with his backside to my face.

'One for Gaz and one for Shaz.'

'If there's skunk in mine, I'll bloody kill ya!' bellowed Gaz. 'Ellis, right?'

'Alrighty there Ellis!' chimed in Gaz.

I replied in my best public school voice that my name was Richard, no smile. Bigboy finally turned around.

'I know people, Ellis m'boy, who know people, who tell me that you are my neighbour and that you is a writer.'

It was a bad Michael Caine impression. I noticed he had two gold teeth.

'Ever done the promo for a kick-ass music tour, Ellis m'boy?'

'I'm between jobs right now, so there might be…'

He wasn't listening. He rattled off some people I should talk to. Madeleine – this was her name – was to be my writing partner. Details to follow. He got back behind the cocktail bar and rummaged through shelves made of vinyl.

'How can you make a fucking Malibu Mango Cosmo fucking bloody mango?'

It was one-thirty in the afternoon and he was as high as a kite. As I stood up to leave, my eyes met fleetingly with

Madeleine's and I felt the same tremor go down my spine. Some unknown force, no doubt fear, stopped me from speaking to her.

As I was heading out the door, Gaz exploded in a fit of giggles.

'Alrighty then Denis! Be seein' ya 'round, I will!'

His whiny voice betrayed a hint of menace. It sounded familiar – then I remember the message. What a weirdo, I thought.

FIVE

I DON'T KNOW WHY I wasn't turned on, I was excited. Was it the wafts of weed in Bigboy's flat? I have never been a fan of the magic dragon. I was also bothered by that geezer, Gaz.

But that wasn't it. The girl's beauty was so neutralising – so deeply intoxicating – that it seemed wrong tossing off while thinking about her. That is not a feeling I have often.

I went over every detail of our encounter. She hadn't said a single word, but she *had* smiled. That was fine – we had yet to exchange our first words. Then I wondered if it wasn't a little odd. What if she was a bit simple? *I* would be fine with that, but you know, mates, parents, etc. It dawned on me that I was being stupid. Her gaze told me that she was highly intelligent.

I showered and lay naked on my bed, picturing the beautiful stranger. Madeleine – that is a lovely name. I was only half aware of a tongue working its way up my legs to my buttocks. I knew it was Debs, of course. She was wearing a Victoria's Secret décolletage with a black mini skirt. I gave her some 'nice to see you' kisses, pulled her skirt off and got to work. Wham, bam, thank you ma'am. Seconds after coming, I remembered about my parents.

'You think I wanna be shagging your brains out in front of your father? Not my thing hun.'

They had texted her to say we were meeting at the restaurant.

I scrambled to find some clean clothes.

'Didn't you hear the bell?'

'Uhh, what's that Debs?'

'Delivery guy. I had to sign something saying I was legally responsible for handling secretive materials, or some bollocks like that.'

'On a Saturday night? Must be for father!'

We arrived half an hour late to *Donatello's* in Brighton's North Lane. It had been one of father's favourite haunts since the Prime Minister dined there during the party conference. It was the perfect place for politicians to pretend to be like everyone else. We sat under a large-framed photograph of the PM himself.

'Donatello always remembers us,' said father as the head waiter sat us down.

He had arrived in his new ministerial car, a black Jaguar XJ Sentinel, with driver and three-man detachment. I knew it would please him to talk about the new trappings, so I didn't. The officer in charge sat at the table nearest to us. He was a lean, balding man in his fifties and didn't look like a security agent.

My parents greeted Debs warmly – they loved her, which I blamed for my doubts about our relationship. Everyone looked the picture of respectability – father in a cream polo-neck shirt and tweed jacket, mother in a no-frills black dress and cardigan and Debs in an Oasis and Zara ensemble. I was the hipster of the crowd, wearing an army shirt, skinny Levi's and Chelsea boots.

We ordered and mother and father talked with Debs at cross-purposes.

'Isn't this the best Italian in town?'

'There are so many Italians in Brighton these days – more than French.'

'And less Polish, fortunat…'

'How was your weekend in Tuscany?'

'Oh, didn't Richie tell you? We found a last-minute to the Dordogne, saved a bloody fortune on the gîte.'

'Spent it all on duty-free though, didn't we darling?'

'The cave is burgeoning now, ready for a Big Day, nudge, nudge, hint, hint.'

It was all so predictable. I gave the 'you know, keep talking' smile and rearranged the salt, pepper and knife into a transsexual sculpture. I thought about making small talk about the day's news. A young woman had been found dead in the tip with her lips and genitals removed. A man was on trial for raping an eighty-year-old woman and giving her AIDS.

I went to the toilet instead to do a line of coke. I exhaled loudly and rolled my eyes, thinking of the scandal it would cause if I were caught. On my way out I decided to take a slash. I was mid-piss when father walked in, went to the next urinal next to mine and undid his fly. He whistled loudly and finished off quickly so that we were both washing our hands together.

'Son.'

No other one-syllable word inspired more loathing in me.

'I know a man who knows a man who says you have a job lined up.'

'Huh?'

'Just don't screw up, will you son?'

At that, he walked through the swing doors without waiting for me. Confused, I went back to the cubicle to do another line and loitered in the toilet riding the high.

The agent looked me up and down like he knew what I had been doing. *Arsehole*, I muttered. I was sure I had seen him before, but I couldn't say where. No one else was bothered by my absence. Debs was sipping wine and speaking to one of her girlfriends on the phone. *Yah*, sure, she could do a few drinks in the *Funky Fish*.

Mother was staring bleakly at her steak, looking upset. I gave her a peck on the cheek, and she clasped my hands and burst into tears. This was more than I could handle. My high was turning into low, and I knew from experience this could take me to a dark place. I muttered something about needing air and left.

The Peace and Quiet is a dive bar off St James's Street, a few streets from my house. Its patrons – queers, lesbians, trannies and drag queens – are about as far removed from my usual social set as is possible, which is why I love it. You never have to worry about making conversation – you can just sit on a barstool and Lucy, Jemima or Monique will bitch their hearts out. Or you can hide in a corner and be sure that no one will bother you.

I had a few vodka shots and a bottle of wine. Outside, the streetlamps blurred into one bright light, which was a fair indication that I was wasted. I hauled myself up three flights of stairs and fumbled for the key. A short, fat man in a woollen sports jacket, striped shirt and garish pink cravat was sitting on my doormat.

He sprang up so quickly I thought he was going to deck me, and I readied my fists. He roared a belly laugh.

'Been waitin' for you I ave. Where you been my luv?'

'What the hell are you doing on my doorstep?'

'Ooh, touchy! Doing you a fava, and that's the fanks I get?'

Gaz slid his hands in my trouser pockets. If I hadn't been so startled, I would have punched him.

'Message from Daddy. Being seeing ya, babushka!'

He shot me a toothy grin and sauntered off down the stairway.

It was a major relief to be home. I tore off my clothes and got in the shower, picking up the letter Debs had signed for earlier in the evening. It was addressed to me, not father, and was almost identical to the one inviting me to Leconfield House – blank header and a London PO Box with no sender's address.

Following my recent application and aptitude tests, I was accepted onto the ESIS Training Scheme at 'Camp Lutetia.' More details forthcoming, etc. I had been selected from hundreds of applicants, blah blah blah, and the organisation was confident that I would be delighted, etc. I was to reply in writing to the PO Box. Signed 'B.S.O.C. Scarlet.'

I ripped the letter into small pieces and dropped them into the toilet.

SIX

I woke up at midday and took three aspirins. I couldn't remember what I had done the night before apart from drinking. Ah yes, the Peace and Quiet.

I spent a lazy Sunday. I had nuts and Macallan for dinner and caught *Vertigo* on TMC. Kim Novak's character was Madeleine. Though in fact, Scottie never actually met her, only the imposter. I'd seen it countless times but could only remember it being about love and death and there being an uncanny prescience that haunted the film.

I drifted off mid-evening on my sofa. Around 2 a.m., on the way to the bathroom, I saw a note sticking out of the left pocket of my trousers lying on the floor. The message was scribbled in block letters on Brighton & Hove Albion football team stationery:

ELLIS. WORK 8.30 MONDAY MORNING. LOOK SMART THE PART. OFFICES IN CONCORDE II COMPLEX OPPOSITE OUR HOUSE. BUZZ MADEIRA DRIVE VICTORIAN LIFT, YEP – THE 'BROKEN' ONE. PEACE. BB.

It didn't make any sense to me until I remembered Gaz's visit to my flat. What a bunch of jackasses. Monday morning was only a few hours away. Shit. I set my alarm and tried to sleep.

I fell out of bed at 8.07 a.m. I was out of coffee. I thought about bolting the door but feared Bigboy's wanker-in-residence would come to fetch me. I grabbed a pair of grey Kenneth Cole jeans, put on a white shirt and flew down the stairs. I cursed the traffic that wouldn't let me cross Marine Parade and stood solemnly in front of the Victorian lift.

'Waitin for ya, sir!'

I stepped inside. The one-legged attendant hauled the doors shut, blocking out all the light. I froze to the spot, panicked. Seconds later the mechanism clunked into action, making an unearthly screeching sound. Two minutes later – yes, it always did take an age – the whining gave way to a thud, the lift stopped and the doors opened.

When my eyes adapted to the light, I made out a lobby leading to an open plan office and some meeting rooms. A reception desk was decked out with corporate trophies and clocks showing the time in London, New York and Tokyo. Three people – Bigboy, Gaz and Shaz were standing in front of a large CCTV monitor.

They were laughing so hard their faces were grotesquely distorted. I tried not to look fazed as the threesome staggered around, sniggering and guffawing. They had clearly been up all night and reeked of booze. I got a soft punch in the stomach from Bigboy. Shaz was wailing, or sobbing. Gaz went to give me a peck on the cheek, but he thought better of it.

'Gawd, you crack me up you do, gorgeous! A big barrel o' laffs is you!'

The party was over and the three jokers stumbled into the lift. I was glad they didn't bring me along, but it was odd being alone.

'Hello? Anyone here…?'

I opened a door and discovered my writing partner sitting at a desk.

'Madeleine?'

'It's Judy.'

'Oh, I thought you were…'

'Madeleine is… a bad joke.'

Our first words. I looked at her with a blank expression. I wasn't sure she was the same person I had met the other day. There was no doubting she was beautiful, but she was different from the girl I'd fantasised about. Maybe it was the name – Madeleine is elegant and full of grace, but Judy is common. 'A bad joke' – what did that mean?

She had gone back to her MacBook.

'Ellis. Pleasure to meet you.'

'Yup.'

'I need coffee.'

'Down the hall, fire exit door – give it a yank. There's a kettle and some instant.'

'Would you like some?'

'No.'

I was strangely blasé about being in a complex inside a cliff. It probably helped that I was tired and hungover. I made coffee and walked around the office, idly opening draws and picking up folders to learn about where I was.

On my return I was given a bunch of materials to read through, contracts and legal documents, to prepare for the job at hand.

I set about the readings, but it was hard to concentrate. I kept looking at her through the corner of my eye. Her cheeks were blanched and spotted with delicate freckles. Her fragile skin contrasted with her jet-black hair, tied into an Audrey Hepburn beehive. She caught me looking at her and scowled.

I tried to start a normal conversation about an hour later.

'So, where are you from?'

'Around.'

'So you're, err, this is, uhm, your line of work?'

'That's right.'

I couldn't place her accent. She was well-spoken in a way almost nobody is these days, as if she had learned English at a finishing school overseas. In any case, she didn't give a damn about being friendly. I wasn't looking for a fight, but if she carried on being so rude, that is what she would get.

This was all bitterly disappointing. Judy was about as far from my fantasy as possible. I barely wanted to spend the day with her, let alone a lifetime. I wondered how my intuition had been so wrong. Was it the weed in Bigboy's flat? I felt that our relationship was tarnished and sensed that things could get a lot worse.

'Can we go over my duties and the deadlines?'

'No, let's have sex.'

SEVEN

Deadlines exist even in the world of celebrity stoners. Bigboy's European Definitive Tour was due to kick off in a month and tickets went on sale in six days, but there was no sales or marketing strategy in place.

There had been a dramatic falling out – lawyers were suing other lawyers, etc. It had got messy and nasty. The priority was to devise a marketing campaign for Bigboy's tour to be sent out to the European agencies promoting the gig. A modified version was needed for the sponsors. If the tour was cancelled, or seriously undersold, Bigboy stood to lose hundreds of thousands of pounds.

Judy had said 'checks' – not sex. We spent a dull half hour going over the paperwork. We were joined by execs from the music industry representing the major parties involved in the fiasco. It was strange seeing such ordinary people in the grotto – my nickname for the office – but they were not fazed in the slightest and seemed familiar with the layout.

I didn't have much time for idle observations. As Executive Media Coordinator, my main job was to assemble a press kit for the tour and a short pitch for booking websites. It sounded simple enough. No questions were asked about my experience, which was fine as I didn't have any. I was told success would have a positive effect on my bank balance, which was an offer I couldn't refuse.

If I failed, on the other hand, there would be no bonanza – I might not even get paid. The suits made it clear that Bigboy's agents were screaming for the materials and that the threat to pull the plug the tour was legally grounded. Judy was to oversee my work, come up with a marketing strategy to stave off disaster and to do PR with the Euro reps, insurance companies and sponsors.

'Lunchtime. Follow me.'

This was welcome news – I longed to be outside again after falling down the rabbit hole. I was led up a damp stairway that resurfaced through a door on the underpass just below the Victorian lift.

Lunch at Alfresco seafront restaurant was remarkable for its dullness. I learned that she likes her caesar salad with extra fresh parmesan but without the dressing.

'Calorie counting?'

She didn't answer and took a phone call. It was odd seeing her next to the Brighton types – the hippy-hipster with piercings and vegetarian shoes, the gays from every walk of life, the elderly foreigners who had come to visit and never left. The woman sitting opposite was a perfect outsider.

I arranged the salt, pepper and cutlery into naked people, but she didn't notice. She was eventually done with her phone call.

'Is that what you call an uncomfortable silence?' I ventured at last.

She looked me squarely in the eyes.

'I don't know what that was,' she replied in a decent Uma Thurman voice.

Phew, I thought – hallelujah! She likes films! The ice is broken!

'Isn't that when you know you found somebody special? When you can just shut the fuck up and comfortably enjoy the silence,' I said suavely.

'So shut the fuck up,' she said abruptly. 'Lunch is over.'

She fired up her MacBook back at the ghetto and ploughed through hundreds of emails. I was beginning to feel stressed – Judy and the execs would be checking on my progress tomorrow morning. How could I write a life-saving pitch for Bigboy when I couldn't talk to the person next to me?

She was being called nonstop by frantic events organisers, CEOs of record labels, PR outfits, music journalists and clubs such as the 'Right to Rave Outdoors' and 'Gays & Lesbians Luv Bigboy.' She spoke to the European Cultural Exchanges Bureau in perfect French – her accent was so good I wondered if she was half-French.

I got fed up with hearing the same pleasantries and petitions over and over again. She kept non-business banter to a minimum, but when she had a hard time she became coquettish and flirted. She always got her way and seemed to relish the banter and thrill of the chase. By mid-afternoon, I could take it no more.

'Can I work in a separate office?'

She pointed to the door. Alone in the adjacent office, I idly listened to Bigboy music on my phone. I walked back into her office at six o'clock.

'I'm heading out for some dinner,' I said. 'Fancy a bite?'

She said 'no' with a sleight of hand. I left the office without further ado.

Nobody had mentioned working hours, and besides, creatives don't work nine to five. This was a results-based task and I was calling it a day.

I ranted under my breath on the way home. What an arrogant bitch. I bet she worked for some bigwig PR outfit in London, big bloody deal. Back in my flat, I heated up a microwave meal, finished off the bottle of Macallan and opened a bottle of Chianti. I fought against the urge to go the Peace and Quiet.

I lounged on my sofa, fell asleep and had a vivid dream about spies and underground lairs. I then had an altogether different dream – more like an old memory. I was twelve years old and on holiday in Paris with mother and father, who had only been married a year or so. I was in the way, a nuisance, and I understood for the first time that father hated me.

We stayed in a five-star hotel, a bit like a film set, with butlers, rich and famous guests, endless corridors, posh sofas and strange sculptures. It was exciting at first, but it soon got boring. I was left alone for hours on end while mother and father went out to museums, cabarets and restaurants.

I spent the time doing detailed sketches of the Eiffel Tower from the balcony. I added cracks and splinters, as if it were toppling, and a series of wild paintings of what looked like an exploding top covering Paris with a toxic substance. I heard girls giggling in a neighbouring room but couldn't see them through drawn curtains.

One night, father came home drunk and abusive. Mother locked herself in the bathroom, but he barged in. I heard loud sobbing and a familiar thud, thud. I decided to run away. I packed a bag with toothbrush, a map of Paris, a fistful of father's credit cards and stepped into the corridor. The door to the suite opposite was ajar and I poked my head in out of curiosity. Two girls, identical twins about my age, sat on the bed.

I felt sure I'd seen them before but couldn't say where or when. One was dressed in black leather and wore dark makeup. She looked worldly and grownup beyond her years – I'd never seen a girl so fierce. Her twin appeared more kindly. She wore a light Floral dress and was reading a book.

The fierce girl made a come-hither motion to me. My instincts told me to get away.

'*Es-tu Ellis? Tu es gentil. Je suis…*' said the nice girl.

'Don't talk to him! He's not allowed to be here!' said the mean one.

She leapt at me with a pocketknife in her hand.

'If you tell anyone about us, I will kill you!'

'*Non, arrête!*'

'You retard, you spaz!'

The girls began to fight, scratching at one another. The fierce girl cut her sister's arm with the knife.

Father stormed in and grabbed me by my shirt collar.

'Doing a bunk, huh? You've let me down good and proper and this time you won't get away with it!'

I woke up in a cold sweat at 5 a.m.

EIGHT

JUDY WAS ALREADY AT HER desk in the grotto at 6 a.m. We exchanged curt 'good mornings' and got to work.

I deduced that she was staying at the Grand Hotel from the napkins on her desk. She was wearing a business suit from Jaeger and silk red top with a high-collar and had arranged her hair into an oriental-style bun with a kanzashi hairpiece. She was a tad blancher than yesterday, but otherwise immaculate.

I stayed in the office in the vain hope of rebooting our relationship but regretted that decision when the phone started ringing around 7:15 a.m. The suits checked on our progress mid-morning. Judy's reports were rapid-fire exercises in brevity that left the execs intimidated. Mine were a mess.

'Yes, uhm, I'm going to flaunt Bigboy's populist credentials, at the same time, err, trying to, you know, produce something witty, a bit clever-clever, a bit camp, uhh, upbeat maybe…'

'Mr Ellis, this isn't your homework,' said a suit.

I clawed at the desk and sloped back to work. I punched in words all morning then deleted them one by one. I looked through promo packs from previous tours, doodling on the glossy pages and made coffee every forty minutes.

Morning turned into afternoon. I went on the BBC news website. The prime suspects in the case of the woman whose body had been found dumped minus her lips and genitals were members of her own family. A Cambridge-educated banker was suspected of torturing and murdering two sex workers in Hong Kong after a decapitated corpse was found in a suitcase in his flat.

I clicked on the magazine section. Metrosexuals were yesterday's freaks – eighty per cent of women polled preferred the machismo of Burberry-clad 'chav' to the charms of effeminate sophisticates. For a long time, chavs had been depicted in the press as nothing more than morons and social cases – the curse of the nineties and early noughties. But attitudes towards them were changing. The chav was a rogue and a loser, but a lovable one. The article reported that retro chav nightclubs would soon be all the range in London and beyond.

This gave me the beginnings of an idea. There was no getting away from the fact in the public's mind Bigboy was linked with 'chav culture' – a phenomenon that he had a personal hand in creating. It was time for Bigboy to capitalize on this tie. Of course, his fan base might not actually see themselves as chavs, so the connection needed to be made ironically.

I started writing sentences that didn't get deleted. Judy noticed that I was working well and shot me a few probing glances.

'Have you had lunch?' she asked.

'Uh?'

I tried to conceal my surprise at her question. At this rate, I would be finished by the evening and could sleep off the stress or drink it away. I made a note to call Debs later – I was beginning to miss her.

Sentences turned into paragraphs and a body of text emerged. Judy, meanwhile, seemed distracted. She stumbled a few times on the telephone, shot me evil stares and played five finger filler with a paperknife.

'Shit!' she yelled as she hit her thumb.

She stood up abruptly and marched over to my desk.

'Is it done?'

Her body language said, 'Come on then, you tosser.'

'Almost,' I replied calmly.

She shrugged and mumbled something about working as a team. I nodded and carried on writing. I read out loud parts of my text in French, Italian and German accents, fully aware of how annoying this must be.

Judy kept looking at me over her shoulder and tapping her foot anxiously. She was clearly furious and kept shooting me filthy looks. It wasn't long before she erupted.

'Stop being a tosser, Ellis.'

She slammed the door.

Touché. So she was human after all. I didn't feel triumphant or guilty – I had simply given as good as I had got.

I read through the marketing pitch a few last times and made some minor changes. I was more or less satisfied with the body of the text, but the ending wasn't quite right. At seven o'clock, the lights dimmed and the air-ventilation system faded to silence. I took this as a hint that I should pack up and work on the ending at home.

I peered through the door of Judy's office. Her jacket was still on her chair and her laptop was on, but there was no sign of her. Just as I was about to exit the grotto, she came out of a door I thought was a cupboard. I braced myself for an angry outburst but instead, she put her hands up to signal a truce.

'*Elise. Sorri about ze bover.*'

I looked at her, not understanding. I said the words back to myself and this gave me an idea for the finishing touches to my pitch. In the excitement, it barely registered that she was speaking with a strong French accent. Was it a joke?

'Give me five minutes and let me read you my text.'

'Okay.'

We sat next to each other, the office lit only by our laptops and an emergency exit sign.

Chavs, chavettes and the Burberry elite! Come together to celebrate the master of machismo and music maestro – BIGBOY IS BACK AND BIGGER THAN EVER! The boutique that never shut is coming to Europe, and it ain't missing a beat. The drum fest of the Big Beat Revolution is in full swing and Bigboy is leading from the front.

Why bover? Because DJs are the new rock stars and Bigboy's unique musical blend of vaudeville and vodka has the sweat dripping off the club ceilings from Brighton to Budapest, Paris to Prague, Seville to Sarajevo. Bigboy has taken dance music from the clubs into the living room via four acclaimed albums – 'Better Living through Biology,' 'You've Come a Wee Way, Baby,' 'Halfway between the Sewer and the Stars,' and 'Balookaville.' He's worked with no less than the best, sold a few records too (ten million) and won some awards (Brits, MTV Videos and Grammys). He's come a more than a wee way, baby. But Bigboy is much more than the sum of his musical parts. Under the Hawaiian shirt is a man with a mission – to bring the beat back to the clubs, Euro-style! So get ready to be grabbed by the short and curlies and hurled onto the dance floor. Bover baby, cos' it ain't gettin' hotter than this!

'It's fine,' Judy said. 'Look *Elise*, I'm *so-rri* about being so *sheety* with you.'

'Don't mention it.'

'No, I was bad. You're… nice.'

I accepted the apology and considered saying sorry too, but I blamed myself for being taken in so easily. She obviously still needed me for something. *Whatever*. All I wanted to do is go home and call Debs. I made for the door.

'Ellis, wait. I want to make it up to you.'

'It's okay, really…'

She left the room and came back with something behind her back. I stared at her sexy legs as she walked towards me. She slid one hand in between her inner thigh and pulled out an uncorked bottle of Moët & Chardon.

'Gosh, was it that good?'

I saw vulnerability and anxiety in her eyes. This sudden change in attitude was utterly perplexing. I don't know what made me want to run, but it wasn't the fear of being unfaithful to Debs. It was a gut feeling this was plain wrong.

She poured the champagne. It was odd that she had only brought one flute, but I didn't think to ask why. She held it up to my lips and I took a sip, then another. She sat on my lap, her skirt rising up her legs.

'*Embrasse-moi.*'

She began kissing my neck, icily at first, then more tenderly. She worked her way from my forehead towards my lips while her hands pulled at my trousers and fondled my crotch. I was dizzy, as if my hands were tied to the back of the chair.

I took a mental snapshot of the scene as it was unfolding – her tangled bra and blouse, her naked upper body and pear-shaped breasts. She was a goddess of physical perfection, except for a cross-shaped mole on her right breast. Her mouth locked onto mine and we kissed deeply. She slid off her panties and pushed me inside her.

The chair began to make an 'eek, eek' sound – the kind that usually gets a smile during sex, but not here, not now. Sensing that I couldn't hold on for long, she stopped kissing me and pushed my head against her breasts. I glimpsed a frenzy in her eyes as I came.

'Don't move,' she whimpered.

We held this position for an age. She was panting, her hands gripping the chair and her gaze fixed at the ceiling. She said something that I didn't hear because she was sobbing.

'*So-rri, Elise.*'

'It's okay,' I replied lamely.

NINE

GAZ HAD MADE HIMSELF SCARCE since that morning I arrived in the grotto and I had almost forgotten about his pitiful existence.

I had heard him speaking outside our office on one occasion and mimicked his accent, which got a rare smile from Judy. I caught a brief glimpse of him later that day playing around with CCTV footage on a laptop.

After our tryst, the door handle slowly turned and he burst into the office.

'Oh, gosh! Oh, I *doooh* apologize, *excusez-moi!*' he said.

I was dazed and needed the toilet. Judy was sitting on the desk and still staring at the ceiling. She had put her skirt and top back on, but her panties were still lying on the floor.

'Alrighty Ellis! Time's up, innit darlin'? Gonna miss you I am. So's she, 'n all. Ain't that right…?'

He pecked her on the cheek.

'She'll be alright though,' he blabbered. 'Always be alright, lookin' like that, the little hoe.'

He got out a multi-coloured feather duster and swept the desk, computer and chair where we had just been going at it. Shaz then made an appearance, dressed as a French maid. She was carrying an aerosol that smelt of gasoline. They were dancing around me – spraying and waving the duster in my face, giggling.

The scene was so surreal that I didn't react. I shut my eyes and breathed deeply, wishing them away. I opened them again and they were all gone – as if I had imagined the whole thing. Back on the street, I felt better but shaken. I vowed never to enter the grotto again.

I got home, turned on the television and opened a beer. I had to get my life back on track. After a day of hardly checking my phone, I had one missed call and voicemail. I guessed it was Debs, upset with me.

When I heard a young lady with a cut-glass accent, my curiosity was piqued.

'Ellis. It has been such a long time! Things are dapper, the modelling is taking off, yah. I've just done a shoot with Kate, she's a babe. Anyway, it was stellar to hear from you, a lovely surprise. Oh, it's Angie by the way. But *d'oh*, you knew that!'

I racked my brain for Angies. Angie Hammond. We went to high school together – a posh and pretty girl who gave up Oxford to launch a modelling career. We were close at seventeen, but I hadn't heard from her since then and we weren't even Facebook friends. This was way too much weirdness for one day.

I turned out the lights and looked out at the moon shimmering on the sea. I loved that view. I thought of Hemmingway's moon, running away from wicked mankind. I didn't blame her – she should go where she is wanted. I turned towards the city and slept the sleep of the just.

Two fire engines were parked directly opposite my building. Damp smoke was rising from the hole that used to house the old Victorian lift. The whole area was cordoned off with yellow police tape. I couldn't believe it – what could have happened? Bleary-eyed, I went back to bed, not getting up until five in the afternoon.

In my dreams, I was imprisoned by Al-Qaeda, fell from an aeroplane without a parachute and set fire to Parliament. It was a relief to be awake. It dawned on me that I had slept for close to seventeen hours and that this definitely wasn't normal. An internet search told me that I suffered from hypersomnia.

I pottered about, finding a piece of paper that had been shoved under my door. I expected a break-up letter from Debs or a summons from the bank.

Dear Ellis,

Thanks for writing me such a nice piece, like. Come over to mine, Friday at 9.00 p.m., for the pre-tour party.

Love BB xx

I was starving but had run out of milk and bread, so I went out to the local Tesco. A uniformed policeman was on my doorstep.

'Do you have authorisation to access this building, sir?'

'Uhh?'

'I need to see ID and proof of residency, sir.'

I dangled my door keys. A second policeman repeated what the first had said.

'Get out of my frickin' way!'

I brushed past them, muttering 'bloody joke' under my breath. I had overreacted, but it felt good. I assumed it was because of the fire. It wasn't the first time this had happened – father had the place listed as an official residence so any minor incident in the city brought out the boys in blue.

In the store, I scanned *The Argus* for stories about the fire but couldn't see any. Surely it had made the news – or had I dreamt it up? The front-page headline read 'Angie, Pick Up the Phone!' It was an appeal from the parents of a model who had been abducted over the weekend. Awful business.

I remembered about my money troubles. I loathed having to contact anyone working on the *Definitive Tour* – and if the fire had gutted the grotto, they had a new disaster on their hands. Still, it was a pressing matter. I dug out a business card from my back pocket.

I had left my iPhone at home. Shit. I started to worry that I would forget to make the call when I caught sight of a solitary red phone box on St James's Street. What kind of losers still used these?

I scanned the penis graffiti and dodgy ads inside the piss-scented booth.

INTERNATIONAL HIGH-CLASS HOOKER MAKES YOUR DREAMS COME TRUE. ALL THINGS TO ALL PEOPLE.

'Oh, hello, err, are you Ron Miller? I'm phoning about my paycheque.'

'Yes.'

'I'm just checking in on how much basically… when I can expect the payment, that kind of thing.'

'Hold the line please.'

The line went dead. I sighed, feeling lethargy creep over me – I was ready to sleep more and to miss the party. I suddenly got a sense of how strange the past few days had been and how affected I was by a brief encounter with Judy.

She might be at the party. I wasn't sure if that was a good

or bad thing.

TEN

I OPENED THE DOOR TO Bigboy's around nine-thirty. I'd tried to stay away, but I was overcome by the need to see her.

The party was full of execs. In a casual suit and Lacoste shirt, I looked much sharper than the balding businessmen. But nobody looked more out of place than Bigboy, dressed in a bright blue Hawaiian shirt. He was regaling suits with show biz banter, but it wasn't working. One was showing him hefty legal documents that required his signature.

As business was on the cards, I tried my luck.

'I say, Bigboy, I was wondering about my fee!'

'Ellis m'boy! Glad you could swing by – get yourself drink,' he said without looking at me.

The party took a different turn once the suits left around ten. A group of teenage girls in micro-skirts and 'Lolita' tops with bare midriffs wandered in, pulling at a lingering exec's tie like he was a doll. They seemed to know the place well by the way they headed to the bar and spread themselves over the luxury armchairs.

Next came two guys wearing Marilyn Manson mascara and dressed from head to toe in black. They touched each other's crotches in an oops-a-daisy kind of way. A big black man entered the room with a petite jockey whose bony head was covered in tattoos. A bouncer with Schwarzenegger-sized biceps manned the door.

I clung to my vodka tonic like it was my only friend. Bigboy was on better form now, playing master of ceremonies in the freak circus of his living room. A gang of lesbian bikers entered the room to raucous laughter and butt-slapping. An old man in a skimpy pink top bent down in front of me and kissed my hand.

Bigboy was floating between posies, the toast of all. He took off his Hawaiian shirt and waved it around his head as he did the 'chimp's lap of honour.' I hid in a corner next to the bartender, who shot me a 'you-look-ready-for-a-refill' look. I downed my third vodka and make my way to the door.

I saw her. She was chatting with the only exec left in the room. I don't know how long she had been there. She looked fantastic – an emblem of beauty and style in the depths of hell. There was something soft and sensual in her face that made my heart race and my stomach sink.

I got stuck behind the black guy and his beau who were having a tiff. We finally stood in front of one another.

'Ellis.'

'Judy.'

'Ellis.'

There was still anxiety and vulnerability in her eyes – I hadn't been mistaken. We edged closer, buffeted by passing freaks, then kissed, coolly. We stopped, then began again – this time passionately. It felt good.

Bigboy had crept up behind us and was gawping. He put his arms around our shoulders and jumped up and down on the spot like a wild ape.

'A pair of star-crossed lovers take their life.'

He stood there grinning.

'Learnt that at school, I did. Anyways, I fink you're in need of a Bigboy special, m'boy!'

I said that I'd had enough and that we were leaving, but he told me *I had to*.

I sipped and things began to fade away.

I'm being held by the hand and led into a bedroom that is not my own. I lie down on the bed and fall asleep.

A dream. A woman covered from head to toe enters the grotto. I am startled when she performs the dance of the seven veils. On the verge of showing her breasts, she produces a knife and lunges at me. I rip the veil from off her face to reveal that it is father. I escape to the beach but am blown by storm winds into the rough sea.

Another dream. I'm auditioning for a part and have a meeting with the producer and director. This turns out to be Gaz and Bigboy. I'm naked and everyone is laughing at me. They tell me I have to appear on a reality television show where I commit acts of torture. Gaz waves a contract in my face and tells me 'my number's up' – then they start to burn me all over with a giant spliff.

The clock says 4.30 a.m. I reach for my quilt but can't find it. My head hurts like hell and I'm naked. I fumble for a light switch and look for the toilet. It occurs to me, little by little, that this is not my flat.

I have a flashback – to the party and seeing Judy across the dance floor. There is a bar in the living room, but it has no furniture apart from a plasma TV, so I figure this cannot be

Bigboy's flat. I am troubled about not knowing where I am and try hard to remember the party, but my memory is blank.

I want to be sick but haven't found the toilet, so I go to a window. I yank it hard and set off an alarm – a shrill noise that I want to stop very badly. I need to get out of here quickly, but I'm still going to be sick any second now, so I carry on hunting for the toilet, which I find near the entrance hall. I lift the seat in the dark and vomit.

As I reach for the sink I brush against a damp and rubbery material with a jagged edge which makes me pull my hand away sharply and stand up straight. I hit against the light switch. My eyes are slow to filter the horrors before me and I cling to the hope that I am dreaming or that it is an optical illusion.

A decapitated body is in the bathtub with a kitchen knife protruding from its left breast. The head is wedged between the legs, its eyes rolled back as if in the grips of pleasure. The arm is also detached from the body at the elbow and is lying in the sink. This is what I touched, the elbow part, with splintered bone sticking out of ragged crimson flesh.

I cannot breathe. I stumble out of the toilet, crashing into every surface and leaving red stains on the wall. Seeing the blood dripping from my hand, I think I've been stabbed. I can no longer put one leg in front of the other and collapse on the living room floor, choking and hyperventilating.

The television comes to life. I can barely make out the grainy CCTV images, but they appear to be forensic photos of the corpse in the bathroom. *Iron Maiden* blares out from the speakers, producing an appalling cacophony with the alarm, and my head feels like it is going to explode.

A TV news report comes on. It is about a recent spate of

murders of young fashion models. The latest victim was stabbed on her doorstep and carted away in a limousine. The item is from next week's news. I fail to understand why I am being shown this and what the hell is going on.

The screen returns to grainy CCTV footage of the grotto. I am sitting on an office chair, working on my laptop. A young woman with blonde hair and a leather miniskirt is sitting at Judy's desk. I can tell that it is not Judy, even in my current state, although she bears a passing resemblance and is uncannily familiar.

The woman walks to my desk and gives me a glass of champagne, which I drink. I am saying something to her while she performs a striptease in front of me. The screen goes fuzzy and suddenly we are on the chair, having sex. I look away in shame, even though I know this isn't real.

In the next clip, a man is pacing up and down in the grotto lobby. He is about my height and build, wearing a dark hoodie and holding a large canister. He douses the desks, chairs and carpet with a liquid that appears to be gasoline. The man lights a cigarette as he makes for the exit.

A black screen appears and I'm watching myself asleep. It is filmed using night-vision technology that displays everything in a sickly green. The camera pans to the wall above the bed where newspaper cuttings are stuck on a large bulletin board. The headlines include the words 'model,' 'evil,' 'horror,' 'pervert' and 'psycho killer.'

Close-ups of the articles tell of missing students, au pairs, escort girls and prostitutes. They were all blonde and beautiful, and they were all mutilated and decapitated. The last clipping is from *The Argus* – 'Angie, Pick up the Phone!' ANGIE

HAMMOND is scrawled in red ink below.

I am experiencing a deep malaise and have a violent need to get out. The alarm masks a soft thudding and the words 'police' and 'open up.' The officers who break down the door find me clawing at the floor and sobbing.

ELEVEN

A CELL INSIDE BRIGHTON POLICE STATION, where I began, if you recall.

Chief Constable Williams and Deputy Chief Constable Edwards were relentless. They asked a question. I told them I didn't know. They asked it again. I told them again that I didn't know, but I hesitated before answering. I demanded to see a lawyer. They said no. It went on and on like this until I was certain of nothing at all.

First, they wanted to know where I had been on a string of dates stretching back years and about my relationship with dozens of women. Going by their names – Brandy Randy, Destiny Rose, Angel Delight – they were escorts or street girls. I told them I had never met or heard of these women.

They changed tack in the next session. My blood sample had just come back from the narcotics lab with traces of cannabis, crystalline tropane, diacetylmorphine and methyl amphetamines.

'Are you out of your mind?' I asked.

They looked at me sternly.

'Bigboy smokes weed. My drink at the party was spiked.'

'That was yesterday. These drugs have been in your system for months.'

They kept going back over the night of the party.

'Sweet Jesus. Look here. I turned up at nine-thirty. I live next door. I was doing a job for him… there are witnesses.'

'Who?'

'Music industry executives – Ron, err. Judy, a colleague.'

The Chief Constable wrote down 'Ron' and 'Judy' in a note-pad and looked at me with suspicion.

'You have a contract to prove this, of course.'

'No, there wasn't time. It was an oral agreement.'

He jotted down 'oral agreement' and a large question mark.

'When did you say you got in touch with Angie Hammond?'

'I didn't.'

'But you did speak to her on the phone?'

'Yes. I mean, err, no. She left a message.'

'Why did you make Angie your next victim? When did you lure her into the abandoned lift and office? Why did you torch the place and leave so many clues? You wanted to get caught, huh? To put an end to this… this nightmare.'

The Deputy Chief Constable put a DVD on the table labelled 'video evidence.' I knew what was on it.

'It's an edit job – stand-ins and CGI.'

I remembered Gaz editing a film on his laptop. I tried to figure out how to tell them about him without sounding insane.

'Where did we arrest you up, Mr Ellis?'

I stayed silent.

'We picked you up an empty apartment. Bigboy has never lived there. Besides, he's been in Ibiza for the past three weeks. The *Definitive Tour* began last weekend.'

This was the strangest news of all.

'None of what you've told us is true. Why are you lying?'

'I'm not lying. I don't know anything. I DON'T KNOW

ANYTHING!'

I sunk into the chair and clasped my head in my hands. I was trembling and sweating. It was strange being told by persons in authority that you are lying. I knew it was a stitch-up or some kind of test, but in the face of their evidence, I felt unsure of my innocence.

All I knew for sure was that I was heading for disaster.

Heavy footsteps and the clunk of a key turning the lock. I had finally fallen asleep in my cell – the first time in more than a day, and it took the stern hand of a woman police constable to wake me. I called her 'bitch' in my delirium, which earned me a smack around the ear and handcuffs.

It was early evening. In the back of a police van, the constable told me that I was being taken to HM Lewes Prison – about ten miles away. I groaned as this meant I wasn't being released on bail. In the van, I tried to find a soft place for my head but only found a harsh metal bar.

Less than fifteen minutes later we pulled up onto some gravel. I cursed the driver for getting us here so quickly – in normal traffic, it takes thirty minutes. I was taken out of the van and uncuffed by the constable. I waited like an obedient prisoner to be led inside, wondering if the strip-search would be as brutal as in the movies.

The officers got back in the van and drove away, leaving me standing there. I looked around, at a loss for what to do. Had father secured my release? Had they dumped me here to avoid the press? Surely there were protocols to follow. I pottered around to get my bearings.

In front of me stood a scruffy modernist building, a derelict hotel. There was a dim light inside – just enough to see art deco mouldings and all manner of broken statues and furniture. The front door was unlocked, so I went inside hoping to find a builder or security guard to ask where I was.

On the curved reception desk, there was an envelope with my name on it. I seriously wondered if I was tripping. I picked up the letter with trepidation – inside was a key for room 310. The lift was cordoned off, so I navigated the splendid spiral staircase. Looking down from the third floor I felt vertiginous and had a premonition of danger.

I exited onto a dusty corridor and made my way to the room. I put the key in the lock and opened the door, nervous about what to expect. It was surprisingly clean and decorated as a luxury cabin. There were toiletries in the large bathroom and pyjamas and clothes – my own – on the king-sized bed. I ripped off the prison wares and fell asleep.

I woke up at midday. I could smell the fresh sea air through a hub-shaped window that was ajar. Seagull squawking had never been so enchanting. I looked out the window at the east Brighton seascape and the rolling Sussex hills which I recognised as Saltdean. I was inside what used to be the Ocean Hotel.

This was all too real to be a trip. I tried to enjoy the newfound freedom and not to think about the weirdness. It was obvious that father had wielded some influence and had got me out of this sticky situation. This was lucky for me, but I dreaded the conversation that awaited.

In the corridor, there was a note on a breakfast tray saying that my 'presence was requested and required' in room 312 at 14.00. I had a bath and got dressed. I figured that whatever they had in store for me, it couldn't be as bad as being accused of drugs, arson and murder.

I lingered in the corridor before knocking.

'Enter!'

The room identical to mine except for a large oak table instead of a bed. Facing me were two men almost identical to the policemen I had met with the other day – the only difference being that British Secret Service Special Ops Chief Scarlet and Deputy Chief Black were suited and dapper.

These men were friendlier too and keen to assure me that they were here to help. No demands, no threats. I was 'in a jam' now that the police were pressing charges. They had the report on the desk, which Chief Scarlet summarised for my benefit. Drugs, more drugs, arson, suspected homicides. Deputy Black shook his head and tutted.

'Not a good position to be in, Mr Ellis.'

I didn't protest. Newspapers, tabloids and broadsheets were scattered around the room. Father's photogenic smile across them and I strained to read the headlines.

'Your family's had quite the week,' said Deputy Black, throwing me a handful of papers.

'Goodman appointed to Foreign Office,' read the headline in *The Times*. The editorial, 'A Good Man to Represent the UK,' agreed that he was the best candidate for the job but questioned the PM's judgment in promoting a rival to such a high-profile position with the Brexit vote only six months away.

The Guardian reported Goodman would also preside over the Britain Stronger in Europe group, making him de facto leader of the Remain campaign. If the UK voted to stay in the European Union, the status quo would be maintained. Goodman would be the man of the hour and Conservative

Eurosceptics would lose their grip on the levers of power.

The Telegraph explored a different hypothesis. The Prime Minister was suspected of being a closet Eurosceptic. If Leave. EU prevailed, the Europhile wing of the party – a perennial thorn in its flesh – would be eliminated, along with Goodman, who would be made to shoulder the blame. Losing the referendum could be a masterful gambit and the Prime Minister's best chance of clinging to power.

'Prime Minister stakes all,' read the *Daily Mail* headline. The article cut to the chase. If Remain won, Goodman would likely topple the Prime Minister, but if Leave triumphed, Goodman and his Europhile cronies would be done for.

The newspapers were dated Sunday 15 December. I knew for sure it wasn't this close to Christmas, and that it was Friday, but when I started to scrutinise them more carefully Deputy Black took them away. I tried to formulate a question, but matters were swiftly brought to a head.

I was to be kept out of sight until this 'all blew over.' In Paris, as it happened. I was to train at Camp Lutetia as an intelligence operative for the European Secret Intelligence Service (ESIS) – a new security service responsible for EU member states' security. Yes, that's right, the letter was real.

I would be consigned to Camp Commander Eric W. Roper, and his deputy, Special Agent Michael O'Reilly. Roper would take very good care of me as he was very, very nice. Chief Scarlet winked at Deputy Black. I clearly wasn't privy to a private joke. And if I was lucky, they chuckled, I would spend time with Dr Europa, Director of Studies.

Scarlet and Black told me, not without pride, that ESIS will one day rival the CIA. The investigation into 'that funny business' would be put on hold, for now. It was made clear to me that this 'request' was not voluntary. More than a few arms had been twisted so that I could be admitted, and I was to do my country, and my father, proud.

I left for France that evening. There was no time to reflect on the absurdity of how I got there. As the train whistled through Kent, I saw fields burning in the distant horizon, making the sky blood red. At Ashford, there was a delay of half an hour as immigrants were pulled out from underneath a Eurostar and taken into custody. A motley crowd of Brexiteer activists looked on in anger.

I shut my eyes and saw flashes of the dead body, its severed arm pointing at me, accusing me. I felt sick to the pit of my stomach. I kept asking, *why me? This was not meant to be, this was not meant to be.* I thought of mother and Debs, and all the women I had ever loved. I wanted to be comforted by them and shed a tear for the unspeakable loneliness of life.

PART TWO

TWELVE

My arrival at the Gare du Nord was smooth. I was met at the gate by a tall man in a dark overcoat and leather gloves who told me to follow him without making small talk.

A gust of cold wind blew onto my face and I put on my Ray Bans to hide my bloodshot eyes. In a black Armani shirt, Levi's jeans and Burberry coat, I looked more like a rock star than a trainee spy – I had been given an hour to pack under police escort so had grabbed all my best stuff. I was ushered into a black Citroën C6 with tinted windows that ducked and weaved into empty taxi lanes and ran a red light.

We skirted down the Boulevard de Magenta until we hit the Place de la République, then headed towards the Bastille. Frozen partygoers huddled around the central plaza. We sped down the Rue St Antoine towards the Rue de Rivoli and arrived at the Place de la Concorde in no time at all. The Assemblée National stood aloof, lit up in red, white and blue.

We drove across the bridge onto the Rive Gauche. From the Boulevard St Germain we turned right onto the Boulevard Raspail, and right again onto the Rue de Sèvres. It was warm and relaxing in the back of the car, but my anxiety heightened as we turned into a maze of side streets.

'*Monsieur, nous sommes arrivés.*'

I was led into the posh lobby of a Parisian residential building and a cramped lift. On the sixth floor, there were three identical brown doors, one of which was mine. It was a dingy one-bedroom flat with salmon pink walls, Matisse and Picasso prints on the walls and a solitary houseplant.

An empty cupboard sat next to a table in the bedroom with a retro alarm clock and old-fashioned telephone. Inside the drawers were thick documents, toiletries and boxes of pills. I collapsed onto the bare mattress without bothering to fit the sheets and fell fast asleep.

The phone rang at 9.15 a.m., at 9.16 a.m. and again at 9.18 a.m.

'Uhh?'

'Mr Ellis? Camp Commander Roper here from E-S-I-S-H-Q.'

I awoke from turbulent dreams and grunted. I had no idea where I was. Back at school? I was in some kind of trouble, by the sound of things.

'You were meant to be at the British Embassy at eight forty-five and *en route* to Camp Lutetia for orientation by now.'

The voice was effeminate and put stress on the words 'camp' and 'orientation.' Had I hooked up with a guy?

'This isn't the best of starts – are you unwell?'

He told me to locate a folder in the second draw of my bedside table. On pages four and five there were instructions for cases like this. Could I turn to it now to make sure the page wasn't missing? He told me to get to the Embassy by midday and Camp Lutetia by two o'clock. I said yes – anything to end the call.

Light was streaming into the living room through venetian blinds, which made it look more pleasant than at night. A narrow hallway led to the bathroom and kitchenette – it was functional and clean. The best feature was the balcony. I was taken aback by the nearness of the Eiffel Tower and the Hotel des Invalides, whose golden dome shone brightly in the sea of grey.

Towards the west, across elegant gardens, stood Bon Marché department store. Directly opposite was an elegant turn-of-the-century building with wrought-iron balconies and bow windows. I didn't recognise it at first as part of the front was covered in scaffolding. A sign above the ground floor restaurant told me it was the Hotel Lutetia.

A gust of freezing air blew into my face, so I went back in, showered and tried to figure out what the hell it was I was late for, how to get to the British Embassy and where this 'Camp Lutetia' was. As I left the flat, I had a strange feeling of freedom – it was the first time in days that I had been alone.

The streets at lunchtime were packed and people were going about their business. I had been left some change in euros, so I took a detour towards the bistros and bakeries across the street.

'*Oui Monsieur?*'

I was jolted into ordering a ham baguette. I had difficulty getting the money out of the plastic wallet, causing the man behind to curse me under his breath.

In the metro, I was kicked in the back by a fare-dodging teenager as he pushed through the guillotine-style doors. Two ticket inspectors were lying in wait around the corner.

'*Votre billet, monsieur?*'

The youth had given them the slip and they were looking for someone to vent their anger on.

'*You mus' no' let ze people pass ze door…*'

I was allowed on my way. The metro had not come for

some time and the hoards were impatient. It made me think of London. I had to push to get in when it arrived, and a man who reeked of alcohol shoved himself in as the doors shut and began telling a tale of woe to the carriage.

At the next stop, more people crammed into the wagon. A woman in high heels trod on my toes and I could hear stomachs rumbling. The man next to me, dressed in a tweed jacket and a bowtie like a university professor looked at me like I might be one of his students. I felt an urgent need to get out of the subway.

I alighted at the next stop and joined the throngs moving like droids down the long underground passages. On the platform, I overheard an English woman who sounded like Debs, but I couldn't see who the voice belonged to. Carried along by the crowd I failed to see that I was heading towards the exit.

I sat down on a station bench. I was at Madeleine station, one stop away from where I was meant to be. I was more affected by the last few days than I'd realised and shouldn't just pretend everything was fine. The spooks had said I could come home when it 'all blew over.' When would that be?

It was a given, despite the smiles, that they didn't have my best interests at heart. How could they simply make those charges go away? Because they had made them up in the first place. *I knew I had been framed* – I shouldn't lose sight of that. The secret services had concocted the scene in Bigboy's flat and cooked up all the other evidence.

But why? And was I right in seeing the hand of MI5? I was plausibly a victim of the dark political powers that advised father. The wayward son was a liability and it had been decided that I must be out of the picture while father made a bid for the top job. It was hard to believe this kind of dirty tricks went on and I vowed to get back to the UK as soon as possible to uncover the truth.

I got up and headed towards the connecting train. The bottom line was that they couldn't force me to be here against my will – a few weeks, a month at most. I still had my passport. I was glad for this chat with myself as the refusal to deal with recent events was weighing on me.

A train pulled into the station. That's when it happened. I saw her. I couldn't believe it. She was inside a metro carriage on a fold-down chair, only two metres from me. The same pale complexion, firm cheekbones and long straight dark hair. It was unmistakably the girl I had made love to only a few days ago.

I drew a sharp breath and my vision went misty. I observed her through the corner of my eye – she was reading from an iPad and didn't look in my direction. The metro doors snapped shut and she disappeared from view.

THIRTEEN

THE SHOCK OF SEEING HER left me in a bad way. I stumbled out of the metro and vomited in the street.

I sat on a bench and closed my eyes, beholding the La Madeleine church when I opened them. I stared at its temple-like roof and the clear blue sky in search of answers. Had the woman simply born a resemblance to Judy? Had I hallucinated? I had to admit it was possible, yet I still believed it was her.

I went inside the church. Its stone steps and neo-classical columns gave a sense of grandeur to my predicament. I studied a fresco above the altar of Christian saints with Napoleon in the centre and sat in front of Mary Magdalene being lifted by the angles. I said a silent prayer to my future self that my life would get back on track.

I went on my way, chiding myself for being so absurd. I was later than ever now, although fortunately the British Embassy at 35 Rue du Faubourg Saint-Honoré was only a short walk away. I gave my name and passport in return for instructions on how to get to Camp Lutetia.

'And my passport?'

'We'll keep hold of it until your carte de séjour is issued... It takes two to three weeks.'

The Camp was indeed inside the Lutetia hotel. The instructions seemed to be clear, but when I got there, I couldn't figure them out at all. Access to the hotel along the Rue de Sèvres and Boulevard Raspail was blocked off by scaffolding. You could enter the Lutetia restaurant from the main road, but that was it.

I paced back and forth. There was a makeshift door covered in fake green foliage. I opened it timidly, expecting to be told off by the site manager. A temporary gangway led to the main hotel entrance, which to my surprise was open. I had a flashback to the Grand Ocean Hotel and contemplated turning around without going in. What was it with these people and disused hotels?

The lobby was eerily deserted, and the air was stale as if no one had been there for years. Deco candle lights and lamps sat on dusty black and white tiles. Paintings and statues with auction numbers pinned to them were hidden behind pillars and red velvet drapes. It had all the appearances of a ghost hotel.

A man sprung out from behind a backdoor. He had the demeanour of the Wizard of Oz.

'Eric Roper. We meet at last!'

We shook hands. He looked me up and down, like he was inspecting a new purchase, and patted me down from head to foot. He pressed down on my chest, almost massaging my pecs and abs, then bent down to inspect my groin area.

'Security check,' he said softly.

He wore rimmed glasses and a striped suit – dubious choices for a man not yet forty. He had a thin mouth with thin lips and swept-back hair that made him look like Clark Kent from the old movies.

He had taken a step backwards, no doubt smelling the sick on my clothes. His permasmile was waning, but he congratulated me on figuring out the instructions.

'The makings of a good operative – daring and determined.'

We set out on a tour of the premises and telling me in detail about the hotel. The French government had done a deal with the owners of the hotel, Israeli property group Alrov, so that ESIS could use it for a year.

'They're not over the moon about it, but your word is your bond.'

He spoke like an American trying to pass himself off as British. I tripped on the uneven floor and he put his arm around my shoulder to steady me.

'Fascinating history, don't you know? Hotel Lutetia was commissioned in the 1900s as an Art Nouveau *pièce de résistance*. Before World War II it was made into a centre for Europe's displaced – Jews, writers, artists and musicians. And during the Occupation it was the heart of swinging Paris.'

We walked down an endless hallway full of glass cabinets and discarded artefacts. Rectangular floor tiles gave way to triangles as we headed to the lounge, where circular lamps, tables, chairs and mirrors sat below deco chandeliers and mouldings. A grand piano had pride of place next to a statue of a child musician.

'The furniture you see now is authentic deco, added in a 1980s makeover.'

Roper was standing so close to me I could see the pimples on his cheeks. This struck me as odd, given the room was so large. We took a lift to the first floor and walked down a long dingy corridor with deco wall lamps and mahogany doors.

'You'll attend seminars here. The rooms are all named after famous guests of the hotel. Picasso, De Gaulle, James Joyce, André Gide, Rudy de Mérode.'

'De Mérode?'

'A French resistance fighter.'

At the end of the hallway, there was a wood-panelled bar. It was well stocked with spirits and pedigree wines and with its soft lighting appeared like a set from a film noir. Above the counter there was a plaque that read: 'N'oubliez pas le 14 juin.'

'What's the significance?'

'14 June 1940,' Roper lectured, 'is the day the Nazis invaded Paris. Lutetia became the headquarters to the Abwehr – the German military intelligence. Officers were charged with rounding up the Jews and repatriating them to the camps. They found a few right on their doorstep!'

He gave me a sinister smile. It dawned on me that the name 'Camp Lutetia' was ill-advised given that Jews had been sent to their deaths from this very site. Why hadn't anyone from ESIS spotted this?

I was taken to the lower level and the main lecture theatre. It used to be the hotel ballroom and was decorated in lavish golden drapes and a lush red carpet.

'After the war, the Allies used the hotel as an administrative centre. Taittinger bought it and ran it for decades but sold to the Israelis in 2010. Ironic, wouldn't you say?'

I wasn't sure what was ironic. In the whole tour, we hadn't met anybody else belonging to the training programme and I was beginning to feel like I was on the set of *The Shining*.

At last, some men and women about my age came out of a seminar carrying coffees and pastries. Roper called one over to me.

'Dick, meet Mick. Mickie and Dickie – gosh, a naughty double act!'

He let out a guffawing noise that went 'hump' and introduced

Special Agent Michael 'Mickie' O'Reilly as having been with the firm for a number of years. He was an Irishman in his late thirties with closely cropped grey hair. Roper went on at length about the projects they had worked on using a string of acronyms while Mickie eyed me with unmistakable hatred.

'Mickie is aware of the delicacies surrounding your posting here, which I think you'll agree is helpful,' Roper whispered into my ear.

'Aye, we've don sum time, t'e boss 'n aie,' Mickie said at last.

Mickie would brief me on the morning's lecture that had been delivered by no lesser person than the British Ambassador himself. It was a real shame I had missed it – it had been inspiring. But if one is poorly, one is poorly.

I had a strong sense of déjà vu and the feeling that something traumatic was about to happen. It came in waves – first the familiar sound of heels, then a scent. I cast my eyes downwards and when I looked up, she was in front of me, as if back from the dead.

'Madeleine, have you met Richard Ellis?'

'I don't believe so,' she said coolly.

FOURTEEN

Survival was my watchword those first few days. Looking back, it's a miracle I made it through.

My dreams were full of unimaginable horrors. I was often in situations that were impossible to escape from – trapped in a house on fire, locked inside a suitcase, behind the wheel of an out-of-control car, and on trial for multiple murders. I was tied naked to a tree and set on by rabid dogs and injected with giant syringes by insane scientists.

I woke up and the sheets were drenched in sweat, so I ripped them off and slept on the mattress. New sheets still found their way back onto the bed by the evening, and the bathroom was cleaned too. I figured that a kind of room service came during the day without giving it much thought.

There was no television or Wi-Fi in the apartment, and I was not allowed an iPad or laptop. I had been issued with a Samsung Galaxy phone. I've always hated these iPhone knock-offs. This one was particularly useless – the mobile data had been disabled and only the standard apps had been installed.

But the bloody thing was a telephone and I used it to try to place calls to the UK, first to my mother, then to Debs. I dialled the number and it switched to a French dial tone.

'E-S-I-S-H-Q, Roper speaking.'

I hung up and dialled a random local number – Roper picked

up again. Christ. It was nothing more than a baby monitor.

I wasn't ever on time, needless to say, for the morning seminars. Crawling out of bed was excruciating, but the biggest ordeal was getting from flat to seminar. A security protocol required me to call an intercom outside the lobby, in the lounge to call the lift and again outside the room itself. It took at least fifteen minutes every time.

There were twenty-eight students including myself at the Camp. I didn't grasp the significance of the number at first, although I did notice that no two students were from the same country. There were slightly more men than women, though it was roughly even. All the trainees spoke excellent English with those from Scandinavia and Eastern Europe having the best accents.

I had already missed the first week and no-one came up to introduce themselves to me. I didn't blame them, or care. I used my daily food allowance to buy wine from Bon Marché and lived in an alcoholic haze from midday onwards. In the evening, I shook off the hangovers and napped.

The shock of seeing *her* hadn't worn off. But as I hadn't seen her since, it began to seem like a dream. I shut my eyes and relived the episode in my mind. There could be no doubt that it was her. Why the charade? Why call herself Madeleine? Did they think I was so out of it that I wouldn't recognise her?

I somehow got to the end of the first week. At the weekend I holed up in the flat. I slept fourteen hours on Friday, sixteen on Saturday and eighteen on Sunday. I was more tired than ever on Monday morning and it was a colossal effort to drag myself across the street. I buzzed the intercom but wasn't admitted.

'*C'est Noël! Pas de séminaires.*'

The days merged into one. I sat on the balcony and stared across the bleak cityscape for hours on end. I started taking the unlabelled pills in the bedside drawer – tranquilizers of some kind that gave me a high then made me mellow. I nicknamed them soma.

I don't know why I took them willingly. Maybe soma wasn't such a bad thing and there was a thrill, deep down, in not knowing what they would do to me, of abandoning myself to fate. In truth, I was ready to take anything that might get me off my head.

I only wore a light shirt outside despite the cold, but I was oblivious to the pain. Loud shrieking and fireworks interrupted my meditations one night. The Eiffel Tower glittered and shone as the old year ended and the new one began. I went inside, shut the blinds and began a dreamless sleep.

The lectures started up again. 'Recent Political History of the European Union' was about the formation of the EU – how the big two became the big six, nine, twelve, fifteen and then twenty-seven. The major European treaties were analysed in detail, with a particular focus on the Treaties of Rome, Maastricht and Nice.

I slept through most of the sessions. I couldn't even get an erection from my daydreams – such was the tedium. The speakers seemed bored too, and ill at ease about giving lectures to well-dressed students in the bowls of a disused hotel. Accessing the complex was exceedingly tricky for them – even going to the toilet required that they use the intercom and wait to be escorted by a security employee.

One academic with a long list of letters after her name had heated words with her security guard. It wasn't clear what the problem was, but the word 'fascist' was picked up by the microphone. Another speaker asked us how we felt about being under constant surveillance. Moments later he was led away by security. He came back half an hour later and retracted his 'groundless allegations.'

I had my first encounters with my fellow trainees. I sat next to a blond German named Hans wearing a striped sports jacket with corduroy elbow patches. I put a foot on his leather satchel, causing him to kick it off.

'*Deutsche scheisse*,' I growled.

'By what authority do you pronounce this slur on my race?' he asked, eyes ablaze.

Only one of the women was attractive. Athena, a dark-haired Mediterranean from Greece, was the only other one to insult me in front of the group. It happened after I had my first drink of the day – she brushed past me, knocking over the bottle of wine hidden in a brown bag. I stooped to pick it up and she hissed that I was a 'messed up alchie' who should 'piss off to rehab.' It was harsh, but I didn't react.

I had no inkling that these sessions were about to change. It was Friday morning, I was drained and my liver was throbbing. I arrived wearing the same coffee-stained shirt and undone tie that I had been wearing all week. But even I couldn't miss the buzz of anticipation in the air.

I dug out the crumpled programme from the bottom of my bag. The morning's session, 'Noble Intent, Grave Errors,' was to be delivered by a Dr Europa, no affiliation given. The man who confidently strode up to the lectern had handsome chiselled looks, salt and pepper hair and wore a dapper silver suit.

'I admire your patience!' he began. 'To speak frankly, you

have not heard from Europe's finest minds… yet. The European Union, as you well know, began its life as a defence mechanism against autocracy and plutocracy. In its current state, it is a haven of wasteful, incompetent bureaucracy, and worst of all, world-class mediocrity. This must change. This, my friends, is our vocation.'

His charisma made it impossible not to listen. Like Roper, his accent perplexed me – he was over-articulate and used too many idioms, as if English wasn't his native language. I soon gathered that he was not just any ESIS insider, but Chair of the Executive Council.

FIFTEEN

I BADLY NEEDED A DRINK after Europa's lecture. In the evening I roamed the streets to clear my head.

The weeks of alcohol abuse were taking a toll. I was suffering from hallucinations and having a hard time discerning between reality and fantasy. The regulations said I couldn't leave Paris – but they didn't say I had to stay at home at all hours. If I went for an excursion, I figured the worst they would do was to give me a huge ticking off.

I found myself heading north, crossing the Seine and wandering aimlessly in the vicinity of La Madeleine. That place had a strange hold over me. I walked into an empty bistro nearby and ordered a whisky. In between visits to the pissoir, I caught sight of the barmaid's cleavage and felt horny. My libido had all but dried up in those alcoholic days of purgatory, and its return hit me hard. I was on a mission to have a sexual experience.

I first had to lie to myself about my circumstances. I was living in Bohemia of my own free will. I had rented a flat in Paris while writing a novel. My first book had won a few prizes, and I had a fat advance to finish the second. I did actually have some money – about a hundred and fifty euros saved up from the Lutetia food allowance.

I took the metro towards Porte de la Chapelle, the nearest stop to Pigalle. The businessmen all left the carriage at St

Lazarre station to go back home to their wives and kids, and I was alone with the lonely and downtrodden. I walked down a labyrinth of crusty escalators onto the street level, where a coachload of Germans had gathered outside the Moulin Rouge.

I strolled down the Boulevard de Clichy on the hunt for my night angel. I browsed a few sex magazines on the street corner without any concern for who saw me. Ladies of the night of all shapes, sizes and colours were being touted, but first you had to deal with pimps outside each of the clubs.

I didn't have the stomach for that, so I went into Cochran's Irish Pub and ordered a double whisky. The alcohol felt good as it flowed through my veins. 'Come as you are' blared out of the speakers, followed by 'Losing my religion' and 'Creep.' I let myself be taken to a better place by these old-school classics and left the pub on a high.

I passed the gaudy Sexodrome and quickened my pace until I got to a crummy street corner where a gang of hoodies were loitering. To avoid them I took a right down a seedy alleyway, Rue des Martyrs. It was a narrow street with a few cafés and massage parlours.

An old man hailed me from over the road.

'Lovely ladies! Young man, this way if you please!'

He wasn't like the other pimps, with his bowtie, portly stature and cane. I crossed the road to get a closer look at the bar which had a red Chinese lantern outside and was styled like a belle-époque bordello. The man put his hand on my shoulder and ushered me inside.

'You will not regret, *mon ami.*'

A madam escorted me to a dark booth.

'*Merci Papi,*' she said.

'Tell me the girl you would like to invite for champagne.'

Four ladies were sitting around a bar beneath a dusty 1920s chandelier. In the poor light, they seemed highly desirable and I felt sure that I had come to the right place. The excitement was only spoiled by worry about the lack of money in my pocket – now only a hundred and twenty euros.

I set to work as discreetly as possible. A French blonde in her mid-twenties wore ripped jeans and a crop top revealing a giant tattoo of a cross on her midriff. A brunette with very long legs was dressed in a golden evening dress and her hair in an elaborate braid. A black girl in a shimmering miniskirt and top that barely covered her breasts was crossing and uncrossing her legs.

The fourth girl was partly hidden by champagne bottles. She was chatting with the barman and checking her phone. Her hair was thick and dark, and her skin was pale. I saw her smile in the wall mirror – she had beautiful lips and delicate features. I couldn't see her eyes, but I was intrigued.

I fantasized about being a Montmartre artist and depicting her as Eve – no, her face was more innocent – as Eurydice in Hades, or maybe Ophelia in the lake. She made me think of Pre-Raphaelite paintings of fallen woman. We would have a torrid love affair and find fame and fortune. She was the one.

The girl with the tattooed midriff came to sit with me. I don't know what I said but she didn't stay. The madam asked me which girl I wanted.

'I don't have money.'

'We talk money after,' she cut me off.

She whispered into the girl's ear and she nodded, but she didn't leave her seat and carried on chatting with the barman. I fretted that she wouldn't come.

Eventually she joined me. I still couldn't see her eyes because she was looking downwards. She seemed nervous and I got the impression she was new to this. I put my hand on her leg under the table and told her she looked like the last girl I was in love with.

'A beautiful woman then,' she said hesitantly in good English.

I was going to ask her name but thought better of it. A single flute was placed on the table and the champagne was served. I waited for the second glass, but none came.

'I don't drink,' she said by way of an explanation as she lifted the glass to my lips.

This was the first moment something felt wrong. A voice in my head told me it would be a good idea to leave fast.

'Time to go upstairs,' she said.

I swooned as I tried to stand up. I did my best to follow her to the back of the bar and up some dark stairs and into a room that was more like a dentist's surgery than a Pigalle bordello, with a large reclining massage chair, sofa and coffee tables. I was relieved to sit down and took off my shirt. I didn't want sex anymore, only to get away.

She left me there for what seemed like a very long time and returned wearing only lace underwear. Her hair obscured her face, making her look like a wild goddess. She undid her bra and caressed my upper body.

'Relax, Ellis, relax.'

I didn't remember telling her my name. There was an ice bucket and cocktail shaker nearby, and she proceeded to pour sickly green liquid into a glass and served it to me. It was sweet with a vile aftertaste – a cheap kind of absinthe.

My head started spinning violently. I breathed deeply to

stave off nausea, but it didn't work. The girl could see I was suffering but carried on with the massage, pulling and pinching at my flesh. I focused on her breasts to null the pain – perfect pears except for a birthmark above the left nipple.

Things were very wrong. Acting on an impulse, I tried to clear her hair away from her eyes, but she brushed off my hands.

'Who are you?'

'I already told you,' she said harshly.

That was when the second woman put her head through the door. She was very similar in appearance to my girl and for a moment I thought I was seeing double.

This girl was angry with my girl. She said something that upset my girl and they began screaming at each other at the top of their voices – the French was too fast for me to follow, but they were fighting over me. The girl at the door repeatedly said '*arrête*' and something that sounded like '*empoisonné.*'

I begged them to calm down, but the row only escalated. My girl picked up a vase and hurled it at the door, scattering shards of glass everywhere. Her twin beat a hasty retreat. The wild girl stomped back to me and shoved the cocktail shaker into my mouth, forcing the green liquid down my throat.

I pushed it away angrily. I tried to get up, but my legs wouldn't obey.

I fight my way through the crowds at Concorde métro station and board a half-empty carriage.

The train enters the tunnel and I look at the other passengers. An elegant woman in black, her face obscured by a large hat, is crying quietly. A young lady in an identical outfit, but in red, lights up a cigarette and puffs smoke. She is scowling at a tramp who, bottle in hand, is telling his woes to the carriage.

The train rattles and screeches to a halt. The silence is interrupted by a kerfuffle and screaming. The lights flicker and cut out. When they come back on, I see the tramp thrashing about on the floor. His throat has been slashed and a meat cleaver is buried in his groin, blood gushing everywhere. The lady in red pushes her cigarette deep into the gash.

I run up and down the carriage, hysterical. I grab hold of the lady in black and beg her to help before realising, to my horror, that she is identical to the lady in red and concealing a large butcher's knife behind her back. I look at the tramp and see that he is me.

I woke up near dawn in an alleyway slumped against a wall and between two rubbish bins. My nose was clogged with blood. I was wearing my trousers and shoes but no socks, and my shirt was drenched with vomit and sweat. My wallet and keys were gone. I was in pain. My head felt like it had been run over by a truck and stitched back together.

I struggled to my feet and walked, oblivious to the cold. After hours of roaming, I made it to the Opéra and sat down among the army of homeless men sleeping on the marble stairs. I used the Eiffel Tower to guide me south towards the Place de la Concorde and navigated backstreets to the Rue de Sèvres.

There was a suited man outside my building dressed in a dark overcoat and eating an apple. He spoke into a radio phone, opened the front door and escorted me to my flat.

'Apples are tasty,' he said, 'but don't fall into the barrel.'

SIXTEEN

EUROPA'S TALK REPLAYED IN MY HEAD. It had been as inspiring as it was disturbing. Plans were afoot to turn the EU into a Federation. A European intelligence service was a key part of this 'new deal,' but he didn't give much away other than a few broad strokes. A second keynote address – '21st Century Europe: In Varietate Concordia' – would reveal more.

My mind was alert, but my body felt like lead. I had no idea what time of day it was – a shoe sat on top of the alarm clock. I was wearing the other one. I lurched to one side and a pang of pain shot up from my neck into my lungs and stomach. I lay back onto the bed in agony.

I stayed like this for a very long time, groaning loudly enough to make someone on the landing think I was having some kind of attack (*'Ay-oh, ça va? Je téléphone aux urgences?'*). In time the need to vomit overpowered me and I spewed over the carpet as I crawled towards the bathroom.

I took a long shower, drank five cups of water, brewed coffee and finished a bottle of soma pills. I had no memory of the night before, other than a vague relocation of an interminable walk through the city. My keys and wallet were in a sealed plastic bag marked: 'Return to Lutetia Intern R.E. (UK).' A half-eaten apple lay next to them.

The baby monitor told me I had a new voice message.

'Roper here. There are one or two matters we have to discuss urgently. Come to my office on Wednesday.'

I stepped out onto the balcony where the fresh air and drizzle hit me like a slap in the face. Why was this bleak city said to be the most romantic place on earth? It was more the city of death than of love. I went back inside and slept for the rest of the day.

I hauled myself into Camp Lutetia on Monday, a human wreck. Any hope that the seminars would improve after Dr Europa's dramatic talk was soon lost. The talks were delivered by crackpot professors with little grasp of what they were meant to do other than lecture foreign students.

The week's theme was 'Political Philosophy and the European Union.' A lecturer from the Paris Institute of Political Studies claimed that Montaigne, Montesquieu, Rousseau, Péguy, Tocqueville and Victor Hugo all shared the same vision of a strong, united Europe. It seemed farfetched, but I wasn't really listening.

An Austrian professor argued that prominent nineteenth-century European philosophers and scientists, including Nietzsche, Schopenhauer, Heidegger and Darwin, were closer to Hitler's ideals than is generally accepted. He gave a long list of writers and artists who were enthusiastic about German National Socialism, as if he were righting a terrible wrong.

A woman from the Sorbonne gave a dull lecture on Karl Marx and the failure of Communism in Europe. Sensing that she had lost her audience, she put down her notes and changed tracks.

'The layout of this room is perfect proof of the inequalities of the bourgeois state. The lectern rules over the tables, the tables over chairs. Marx wanted to turn the tables.'

The interns looked at her in bewilderment.

I gathered that I had neglected to do some assignments – five essays of four thousand words apiece. I supposed this paled with the bollocking I was going to get for the night-time escapade in Pigalle. It was odd they hadn't called me in sooner. If they were going to lock me up, wouldn't they have done so already?

Roper's office was on the fourth floor. I hadn't yet been to this part of the building and a security agent had to escort me. The room had not been fully converted and Roper's desk sat in a large closet.

He told me to sit down.

'I have to talk to you frankly.'

He took a sip of water and did his best to look intimidating.

'I'm going to say things as they are. There are a great many people invested in you and they have grave concerns.'

If this was the speech that unleashed the trap door, it was going to be torture.

'I hope you are listening to what I have to say attentively. I only have your best interests at heart.'

I sensed he was building up to it.

'You really shouldn't have done it! It's a serious breach of employee protocol, you must understand!'

He was rummaging around his desk, on the brink of hysteria. I braced myself for lurid photos of Pigalle. Instead, he pulled out a printout with a list of telephone numbers.

'If you had taken the time to read the Manual of Civic Comportment for Camp Lutetia Interns, you could not have failed to note that contact with friends, families or outsiders was strictly prohibited for the duration of the camp unless prior permission was granted. It is written in black and white, as clear as can be.'

He ploughed on with his sermon. 'Intelligence' from my phone led him to conclude that I had neglectfully or wilfully broken the rules. So that was it. I didn't protest, as it was true. It didn't take a genius to figure out that I had hung up on him twice when my calls home had been diverted.

He droned on and on, about trust and responsibilities. I had behaved badly at the training seminars. Mickie – Special Agent O'Reilly – had warned that I was 'bad news' and advised that I shouldn't be shown leniency. Roper had a high opinion of Mickie's judgement and was loath to disagree with him. But he knew in his heart of hearts these were isolated incidents – lapses – triggered by 'difficult circumstances.'

I was still waiting for him to talk about Pigalle. Did it even happen? He finally ran out of steam and I got up to leave, thinking I had got off lightly.

'Camp Commanders have decided,' he stuttered, 'that you will be taken out of the seminars and put to work.'

A concentration camp came to mind. But no. I was to draft a press release for journalists about ESIS and Camp Lutetia. He would see to it, though, that I was given leave from my duties to attend keynote talks at the camp. I was sure to be blown away by the next speaker.

'You'll be working under Madeleine's supervision. Do you remember her?'

SEVENTEEN

CHILLED WHITE WINE AND A shared cigarette on the château terrace. The spring sun warms my body and I take off my jacket. There is a hubbub of excitement all around.

Sauntering down the marble staircase from the Louis XVI suite to the restaurant is the only strenuous thing I have done this morning. The *pizza au saumon à la crème de basilic* is a long time coming, but time is something we have. I sip my wine and close my eyes. A toe rubs against my foot and pokes my ankle.

Two nimble hands take off my Wayfarers Ray-Bans and cover my eyes. I feel her breasts brush against my neck as her deft tongue burrows its way deep into my mouth and her body collapses onto mine. I can tell that she is not wearing panties under her Chanel miniskirt. I open my eyes and make a serious face and she smiles back sexily.

Madeleine was waiting outside Roper's office after my session with Roper.

'Saturday. Bombardier at Panthéon. Nine o'clock,' she whispered.

That was it. I vowed not to pay her any attention. But curiosity got the better of me. That evening I walked into a nearby boutique hotel and used a computer terminal with free internet. There was an English pub named the Bombardier in the

Latin Quarter. Interesting. But I still wasn't going.

I had almost got over the internet withdrawal symptoms, but I couldn't resist the chance to go online. I went on the BBC news website. 'Brexit referendum: might the unthinkable happen?' read the headline. The UK's future hung in the balance. Most polls had Remain on 52% and Leave on 48%, but a recent YouGov survey put Leave ahead.

There was a discussion about whether the polls were reliable, but after months of taking it for granted that the electorate would opt for the status quo, there was now a real possibility the UK would vote to leave the European Union. Analysts stressed there were still six months before the vote – ample time for either side to sway voters.

The article featured a lot of interviews, but one caught my eye. John Goodman MP, Cabinet Minister for Business and Chairman of the Britain Stronger in Europe Campaign, was quoted as saying he was optimistic that 'voters would consider the implications of leaving the EU and decide it was in the national interest to remain.'

'For pity's sake!' I said loudly.

I tried to log in to my Facebook and email accounts but it said the passwords were wrong. The second and third attempts also failed. I racked my brain trying to remember if I had changed them, but the receptionist came over and told me I could only use the computer if I was a guest at the hotel. That was it then.

It occurred to me that it meant nothing that I had survived my first few weeks at Lutetia. As Roper said, I had 'behaved badly.' They could see I didn't give a damn. They clearly had an ulterior motive for keeping me on. This copyright job was yet another sadistic attempt to babysit me until I could be useful. But for what? I would not allow a repeat of the Bigboy fiasco under any circumstances.

I woke up on Saturday after four in the afternoon, drank stone-cold coffee on the balcony and stared into space. I didn't leave my flat until gone nine and didn't get to the bar until ten-thirty. It was a boozy joint with a DJ and packed with expats. I figured she had already come and gone. So be it.

But she was there – drink in hand at the bar, chatting to a muscular guy with a rainbow tee-shirt. She pointed to the empty barstool by her side without looking at me.

'What are you drinking?'

'Scotch – neat.'

'Trouble at work?'

'Yeah. Colleagues…'

Madeleine leaned into me and placed her hand on my knee. I breathed in her light scent.

'Ellis. I have one thing to say to you. Don't mess with anyone here. Don't mess with Roper, don't mess with hierarchy and don't mess with me. Don't think, just do. I am watching out for you. You won't believe me, but I like you. I am on your side.'

I raised an eyebrow.

'It's the truth,' she said looking into my eyes. 'No man's an island. You can't take them on alone and win. Plans are afoot that…'

Neon disco lights began flashing and the DJ ramped up the volume. I leaned over the counter to get another drink. When I turned around, she was gone.

I didn't know what to make of any of this – it was baffling. She looked and sounded sincere, but I couldn't bring myself to believe her. After three pints I had trouble remembering what she had said, and after five I didn't give a damn. I walked home, cursing and mumbling to myself.

On Sunday there were some changes in my cage. Blue pills mysteriously appeared by my bedside with instructions to take one with each meal. I immediately took three. They made me feel giddy and sleepy. The flat was a mess too. I had got used to my basic cleaning needs being taken care of. Now, abruptly, there was no clean linen and the rubbish was piling up. Was this a punishment?

I woke up late on Monday and slurped coffee out of a jug. My hands were shaking and I wanted to call in sick, but instead, put on the same crumpled trousers and shirt I had worn all weekend and left for work. Security was more of a nightmare than usual as I needed new clearance to access the fourth-floor offices.

By the time I arrived – fifty minutes late – Mickie and Roper were engaged in an intense a tête-à-tête. They were so close it looked like they were kissing. Roper frowned on seeing me in such a state and told me I'd missed important details, not to mention tea and croissants. I would have to wait until two o'clock for lunch. Madeleine would be joining us later.

I slipped into a daze as Roper droned on. I tried to act blasé though I felt like crap. My stomach was in serious trouble by ten, and I had to go to the toilet twice in half an hour. Roper insisted on interrupting the discussion until I returned, even if it meant lunch was delayed until two-thirty.

They gave up waiting for me in the end and made me read through some papers in the room next door.

I imagined what they were saying about me.

'Bad form! What a disgrace! Hardly an asset, I apologise…'

'Watashite! Feckin' pox is off 'is rocka.'

I sank into the chair, barely stirring when Madeleine came in.

'Coffee?'

'Uh-huh.'

She took off her jacket, revealing a low-cut blouse that showed off her cleavage and a miniskirt that did the same for her legs. She left the room to consult with Roper, coming back ten minutes later.

'Let's go for a walk,' she said.

We strolled along Boulevard Saint-Germain, across the Seine towards the Place de la Concorde.

We had a good chat – about our childhoods, travels, world-views and politics. On the bench beside her namesake, La Madeleine, she asked me what I liked in a woman and I told her a mistress and a mother. She said she wanted a lover and a little boy. We kissed and held each other for a long time.

Back at Hotel Lutetia, she locked the door to our office, shut the blinds and sat on my desk. She undid the buttons on her miniskirt, then pulled down her tights until they were just two bands of nylon on each knee. I took off her top and bra, slid off her panties and told her to straddle me.

I was woken up by a security guard, alarmed at finding an employee slouched over his desk in a dark office. He shone a flashlight that revealed the stains on my clothes.

'*Il est vingt heures, Monsieur. Rentrez chez vous!*'

I hastily gathered the papers scattered around my desk. It took me about a minute to see the message stuck to my computer screen – 'Why bother? M.'

That evening, there were new pills on my bedside table – red ones with instructions to take two at bedtime. They gave me violent, erotic dreams and I woke up covered in sticky wetness. I went out on the balcony and yelled like a madman, then sunk onto the floor and sobbed. The drizzle washed over my face.

I've no idea how long I stayed outside. I must have gone back in, taken off my clothes and warmed myself with a towel. I'm ill, a voice told me, and sick boys need their mothers. I wasn't close to mother, but she would be there for me at a time of crisis. My hands reached for the telephone and dialled home.

This would be a good point to talk about hitting bottom.

EIGHTEEN

I woke up with a jolt at 6 a.m. The night had left me feeling drained.

I was alarmed to see a new bottle on my bedside table – pink tablets to be taken twice every morning. I hadn't seen them the night before. This meant someone had entered the flat while I was on the balcony or asleep. How could they do this? I pondered this weirdness on my way to Lutetia.

I thought back to my meeting with Madeleine. I'd figured out why I couldn't trust her – because she was lying about the simple fact of who she was. At the pub, why not explain the Judy-Madeleine ruse? It was a noisy public space, nobody could have overheard. But no, she didn't even mention it. Or tell me anything of any importance. If she was on my side, that's what she would have done.

I was on my own. I had to start gathering a dossier of facts about ESIS and Camp Lutetia for the UK press. If the public got wind of what was going on, it could sway the Brexit referendum. This would be my big break into journalism. I should be careful not to be labelled a whistle-blower as I didn't want to end up like Julian Assange or Edward Snowdon.

There was much to be done. A meeting was scheduled on Monday to present the press release to senior ESIS figures. I was intrigued at this prospect and planned to take detailed notes about who they were for my undercover report. My aim was for the meeting to go well enough for me to be allowed to carry on my work.

I witnessed a change in myself. I was thinking about my situation and looking for a way out. This was a positive step and I resolved to do more thinking and less drinking. Should I even take the pills? They seemed to be a stimulant of some kind, but God knows what they were feeding me.

I arrived at the office before Roper, Mickie and Madeleine. By the time Madeleine got there at 8.35 a.m., I'd read all the papers relating to the job at hand.

'Someone's on form?'

'Uh-huh.'

'Need me to go over the task with you?'

'No.'

The job was to draft a press release that would inform the public about the existence of ESIS. A lot of factual info was to be included verbatim, which made the job somewhat easier. The main task was to find a tone that did not make it sound toxic.

Given the rise of Euroscepticism across the EU, there was a danger that politicians, particularly in the UK, would latch onto ESIS as proof of 'out-of-control Europe.' A British tabloid had already petitioned Downing Street demanding to know if rumours about a European secret service were true.

The statement had to succinctly make the case for a European supranational intelligence agency, while at the same time reassuring the Americans that ESIS did not pose a threat to them. 'Reassure' did not mean that the service was not intended to rival the CIA – it was. It didn't help that the acronym was only one letter different from ISIS, their most feared nemesis.

The statement should include a few sentences about Camp Lutetia's role in training ESIS agents. The Directors were still choosing between logos – one that had a small letter 'e' ('eSIS'), which made it look like an e-banking service, the other that hid the 'E' and 'I' behind 'SS' – in short, a PR nightmare.

Wednesday came and went. The woman calling herself Madeleine was busy and I hardly saw her. I left the office at eight, bought dinner at Bon Marché and went home to sleep. The cleaning service had resumed and the soma pills had gone, although I had put a few to one side. I arrived early on Thursday morning, still feeling energetic and brimming with ideas.

By 11 a.m., I had five pages of scrawl. I came up with some good lines and crossed out the bad ones. I wrote about the 'new age of cooperation ensuing from the tragic events of 9/11' and how the 'terrorists' core values are opposed to ours.' The next paragraph began: 'Who are we? We are Europeans.' This needed more development.

This hive of activity warranted a raised eyebrow and sigh from my writing partner. She walked up to my desk and looked at my notes like a teacher inspecting a pupil's work.

'It's time we confer,' she said.

'Yes, soon.'

'Huh.'

She ordered a lunch of chicken Caesar salad with extra fresh parmesan and no caesar dressing, then disappeared into Roper and Mickie's office for over two hours.

She was angry when she came back, thumping her feet and slamming her filing cabinet shut. She didn't say a word to me, and the silence was only punctuated by long calls to PR outfits.

I begrudged her cleverness and the way she would start to flirt if she wasn't getting her way.

I tried acting as if she wasn't in the room. I mumbled to myself and played soft jazz. I put my feet up on the desk, ate a sandwich noisily and read sentences out loud in French, Italian and German accents. By the end of the afternoon, a stubbornness pervaded the air.

I threw down the gauntlet.

'Judy – it is Judy, isn't it? Just cut the bullshit and tell me what is going on.'

'You just don't get it, do you Ellis?'

She kicked her chair away from her desk and stormed out of the office. I had expected more of a reaction – this didn't get me any further in my quest for answers.

I went home and planned my next move. I was sure my press release was fine, but Judy was required to give some input and to sign off on it. Our lack of collaboration meant we had little hope of being ready unless we buried the hatchet on Friday – tomorrow. If we turned up to the meeting without an agreed text, I was sure to get the blame. It was a lose-lose situation.

She didn't come back to the office the next morning. I pottered around, trying to connect to the internet, without any luck. There was still no sign of her by early afternoon, which made me anxious. I even knocked on Roper's door to ask if he knew where she was. He shrugged and said she was due in later.

She eventually turned up at 4.45 p.m., but she didn't say 'hello' and simply sat at her desk. She was on edge, pale and appeared to be holding back tears. An hour went by like this without her saying a word. I knew what I should do – get her feedback, then clear off. But I couldn't help picking up where we had left off.

'I'm ready to share.'

'Okay.'

'But first I want answers. What's the deal with the masquerade, Judy? We worked together a few weeks ago in Brighton, in case you'd forgotten. But you haven't forgotten. We had sex, then you framed me for murder.'

I scrutinised her reaction.

'Murder, Judy, murder!'

'Shh, not so loud!'

'And now you turn up here, as a different person, claiming to be my ally. Do you think I'm a goddamn idiot? It's bullshit, Judy. Bullshit. Tell me who you really are!'

She clasped her hands to her face, on the verge of tears.

'*I'm so-rri, Elise, for what 'as 'appened,*' she said in a strong French accent.

The storm cloud had broken. A result.

'I am Madeleine.'

I sighed. She was falling apart at the seams, so why continue to deny she was Judy?

Roper appeared at the door.

'An urgent word, Madeleine.'

The week was beginning to mirror the one working for Bigboy. I had a flashback to how that ended and left Hotel Lutetia as fast as possible.

NINETEEN

I REPLAYED THE CONVERSATION IN my mind. Did she mean Madeleine was her real name and Judy never existed? I figured she must have multiple identities, like an actress or a prostitute.

I tried to convince myself that I was like any other stressed professional before an important work deadline, but the anxiety was eating me up. New soma pills arrived – grey ones to be taken three a day. They made me even more nervous and gave me insomnia. I sat on the balcony for hours on end, unsure if I was awake or asleep.

I got up on Monday feeling drained of confidence. My hands were trembling. I had a premonition that it was going to be a fateful day and thought about staying at home and not going in, but I knew that wasn't an option. I had been awake since five o'clock drinking coffee, going over the press statement and rehearsing my presentation.

On the street, I was alarmed to realise I had left my notes on the table. As I fumbled for my keys, I caught sight of two suits standing across the road in front of a garage. I had never seen them before but suspected they were ESIS security agents. They looked me up and down, and one made his way over to me. I hurried inside and ran up the stairs.

I stood behind the door and counted to thirty, wishing them away. I couldn't see the agent through the peephole, but I saw him on the landing as soon as I exited. He didn't say a word but radioed into a mouthpiece and watched me go down the stairs. The other suit at the top of Sèvres-Babylone metro station also radioed as I walked by.

I arrived at Lutetia a little before nine, my heart beating fast and sweat trickling down my face. I cursed ESIS for orchestrating today's dose of hokum. Security did its usual checks, this time with extra zeal, and allowed me to proceed unescorted to the A. Toepfer boardroom on the seventh floor.

In the lift, I thought about making a run for it. I knew it was madness, but they had put the frighteners onto me and I had good reason to be worried about what lay ahead. I was spooked. The lift was already at the third, fourth, now the fifth floor. I pressed six and it ground to a jerky halt.

I stepped out onto a dusty corridor under renovation and spotted a CCTV camera concealed inside a ceiling light – I had a fifty-fifty chance of escape at best. I told myself I was about to meet the most senior members of ESIS and this information would be invaluable when things hit the fan.

I got back inside the lift and proceeded to the seventh floor. The boardroom was directly in front of the lift, but the door was locked. I could tell the conference was in session and strained to hear the voices. I knocked timidly and waited. No reply. I knocked again, and the voices went quiet. Two long minutes later I was invited in.

They had done level best to intimidate me, and I stumbled as I made my way to the only free seat at the table. The room had a long maple desk, oak parquet flooring and a metal railing that skirted the walls like on a ship's bridge. The circular windows had been covered with thick curtains which made it hard to see and silhouetted the men at the top of the table.

When my eyes adapted to the light, I beheld four men with a kind of presence and masculinity that made Roper and Mickie look like teenagers. Next to Dr Europa was a man whose height and build alone conveyed importance. The third man was overweight and wore a tweed jacket with a bowtie. The fourth was stout and bald with sinister eyes, like Hannibal Lecter.

They were like characters from a reoccurring nightmare. Roper, who had donned his most austere charcoal suit, sat at the bottom of the table with Mickie faithfully by his side. Hans and Athena were there too, crouched in a corner. Madeleine was also there, but she gave the strong impression of wishing she was not.

Hans and Athena had finished a talk and were fielding questions from the board.

'Which extremist group would make the most plausible culprit, Pegida or Alternative für Deutschland?'

'Pegida is yesterday's thing, so AfD for sure. We must also taint the National Democratic Party.'

'And which security service should we implicate?'

'The BND has a good reputation so it will be harder to make corruption allegations stick, whereas MAD – the Military Counterintelligence Service – has a rogue element with extremist sympathies. My recommendation is to implicate both, with a focus on MAD.'

'Athena – the MeRA25 leader is a high-profile guy. Will people buy it?'

'He's a figurehead for some very angry people. And the National Intelligence Service in Greece, NIS, is a shady enterprise.'

'What if the Russians get wind of the scheme? Could it inadvertently work?'

'No, it wouldn't have popular support in Greece. We invented democracy – we're still attached to it.'

The tall man spoke with an American accent, and the fat man with the bowtie spoke in a French accent.

'Thank you for that excellent report,' Roper sniffled. 'Mr Ellis, we will now hear from you. Are we to understand you were not able to complete the task?'

All eyes were fixed on me.

'We… I… have encountered some… issues in…'

I heard myself failing badly and understood that I had to do something radical.

'The press statement is ready.'

I started to read.

EUROPEAN UNION PRESS RELEASE:
ESIS & CAMP LUTETIA

After the terrorist attacks in the United States on 11 September 2001, counterterrorism and intelligence agencies across the globe began working with one another on an unprecedented scale. A new age of cooperation ensued from these tragic events resulting in thousands of security threats being prevented. Some of these are reported in the media, but many are not.

Who are we fighting? The enemy is not always a known quantity. He does not wear a uniform, hold giant rallies or greet us with strange salutes. But like the Nazi foe, he threatens the institutions that uphold our way of life. His values are fundamentally opposed to ours and he has no respect for the lives and freedoms of others.

Who are we? We are Europeans. We are diverse and cosmopolitan peoples but bound by a shared history, territory, ideology and economy. We are peace-loving peoples, but also realists who believe in the right to self-preservation. To this end, we are committed to taking all necessary measures to ensure peace and security on our continent.

The European Secret Service's (ESIS) mission is to centralise security and intelligence gathering services to make sure that Europe is in the very best position to counter threats made against her member states and to position herself at the forefront of the intelligence-gathering community.

The United States remains our most important ally in the fight against terrorism. Europe has a historic and close partnership with the United States in the field of intelligence and this is not about to…

'Is that so?' said the big man in a loud American accent. The others shook their heads solemnly. Objections came in thick and fast from every corner of the room.

'Too vague but too specific,' began Roper. 'A bizarre mix of historicisms and vernacular. You have not done what was asked of you.'

'Phff! Huh?' added Mickie.

'What does Nazi Germany have to do with ESIS, or anything at all? That was a long time ago, the civilised world has moved on. Only *arschlöcher* mention the war,' said Hans.

'He is taking the piss,' agreed Athena, shooting me a vile look.

The sinister bald man stayed conspicuously silent during this discussion – the charade seemed to be for his benefit. The only other person not to participate in the foray was Madeleine, who was staring forlornly at papers in front of her. She was a doll-like gouache of vulnerability, and I had difficulty reconciling the person I knew her to be with what I saw.

There was a lull. Not knowing what else to do, I continued reading.

ESIS will supersede the European Network and Information Security Agency (ENISA). The Lutetia Training Initiative has been instigated by the Council of the European Union to recruit the next generation of operatives to undertake key leadership roles within ESIS. We have anticipated substantial media interest in ESIS and the Lutetia Training Programme and will shortly be releasing more information on social media in addition to issuing a full press kit.

ESIS is regulated by directives 1049/2001 and 2009/101/EC of the European Parliament. Please email recruitment@esis.eu with queries relating to employment opportunities. European Union Equal Opportunities Policy applies.

My adversaries looked at me as if I were insane. I could no longer hold back the anger that surged in my veins.

'Yes, sign up! Or else you will be drugged, threatened and framed for murder! You too can have your civil liberties violated. Sign up! I may not know who all of you are. But I have seen your faces.'

The group gave nothing away of what they were thinking – they sat in silence, observing me like a lab rat, waiting to see what I would do or say next.

I got up to leave of my own accord, but the door was locked. I stood there with my back to them for what seemed like a thousand years. It opened at last and agents led me away.

TWENTY

'YOU WEASEL!' HE FUMED. 'WE PLAYED nice with you, Ellis, we played fair.'

Roper's voice was warbling and his accent – British, American – was skating all over the place.

'You broke my confidence and trust. You let me down, and you let yourself down. Mickie had been right all along. If only, if only, I had listened.'

Mickie had seen me for what I was – 'a lye-in bastard.' Why had he given me another chance? Mickie was very upset with Roper, and it was all my doing. It sounded like they were having a lovers' tiff.

'Believe it or not, I thought you would see reason. But evidently not.'

Roper was on the verge of tears. He passed me a telephone log showing more intercepted calls to mother. I didn't remember making them, but there was no point denying it. As absurd as it was, I was glad not to be talking about the boardroom.

'You have let me down good and proper. This time you're not going to get away with it.'

It was a strange turn of phrase. Father used to say that, verbatim.

The security agents returned, and I was placed in a holding cell in the hotel basement. It had probably served as an interrogation room during the war as it had an old wooden bench, large urinal and nothing else. It was freezing and I had to turn up my jacket collar to keep warm.

I was angry but rational. I cursed myself for announcing my plan to tell the world about ESIS – it was supremely stupid. It was going to be harder now to uncover the proofs needed to expose them. I vowed to redouble my efforts to make sure my threat was not an empty one. Never again would I be careless.

I also regretted my fateful hesitation in the lift. If in doubt, I must act boldly. They had upped the ante by imprisoning me. I had seen what they were capable of and it was sobering. But if they intended to make me 'disappear' – my intuition said they would have done so already.

I racked my brain for reasons to back this up. It came down to father, as always. As an ESIS insider, he would have a hand in my fate. It was no doubt his doing that I was here. I *had* to find out what his exact role was in the organisation. I imagined a scenario where he promised to save me so long as I expressed my undying gratitude, and I told him to go to hell.

The agents had confiscated my attaché case, but not my jacket which had a pen, paper and the Lutetia-issue phone in the inner pocket. Was this carelessness on their part? If so, I had to exploit this it. I set to work, noting down the people I'd just seen and a list of all those who I knew or suspected of being connected to ESIS, starting with the bigwigs.

I paused to put the names in some kind of order.

```
1. Father (John R. Goodman MP)

2. Sinister Bald Man
```

3. Bowtie & Tweed Man

4. American Big Man

5. Dr Europa

6. Roper

7. Mickie

8. Athena, Hans and the 27 Bastards

9. Scarlet and Black

10. Williams and Edwards

11. Bigboy

12. Gaz and Shaz

13. JUDY/MADELEINE

I wrote down as much as what I could remember from the boardroom meeting and did a rough sketch of the three bigwigs. I pondered why it was they seemed so familiar but drew a blank. My mind kept wondering to the thirteenth entry on my list – to *her*. I was certain now that Madeleine was Judy. So why did I write both names?

I also hesitated to brand her ESIS mafia. All the evidence pointed to her being one of their star agents, operating at the heart of ESIS. She had lied to me time and again, and I cursed myself once again for almost being taken in by the 'I'm on your side' baloney. It was also her doing that I found myself in this situation.

I took two photos of the list using the Samsung, one of the prison cell and a selfie to prove I was here, making sure they saved to the phone's micro SD card. I then ripped the paper into tiny scraps and dropped them into the urinal – pissing on them for good measure. I took out the phone's memory card and hid it in a fold in my boxer shorts.

They came for me in the evening. I was famished and thirsty but given nothing, not even water. I was led to a basement car park, handcuffed and bundled into the back of a windowless van. My inner compass told me that we were heading north, but in reality, I had no idea. About two hours later the van ground to a halt and the doors flung open.

I was standing in an empty field. The stars were shining, and my breath froze and ascended to the heavens. Still cuffed, I was frog-marched by two agents along a muddy path. It was so surreal I could hardly believe it was happening. I tussled with the men, but they pushed harder and I was too weak from hunger to fight back.

I knew these could be my final moments of life. But in the face of calamity, I was calm. I didn't know if this was bravery or not – I went on because I had no choice. I thought about the Jews and resistance fighters sent by the Nazis from Lutetia to their deaths. Was this my fate too?

I didn't confess or pray. I recited lines from Shakespeare under my breath.

'For who would bear the whips and scorns of time... but that the dread of something after death, the undiscovered country...'

I recalled the murder of Angie Hammond. I didn't want to be tortured. Please spare me that.

'A pair of star-crossed lovers take their life...'

I tried to picture my life before Camp Lutetia, but it was

blank. I managed to conjure hazy memories of my real father taking me down to Brighton seafront to see old cars. Madeleine came back to my thoughts. There was something I wasn't seeing – but what? Why was I under her spell?

We arrived at a derelict farmhouse, as desolate as in any film noir, and I was strong-armed into a black space. The stench of manure and chemicals made me gag – it must have been an abattoir. I was strapped to an iron chair. I struggled to free my hands, but it was futile.

My captors left me alone. It was deadly quiet, yet I felt myself in the presence of evil. A flame from a cigarette lighter lit up a man's face only a few feet away. The contours of his face and shiny scalp sent shivers down my spine. I knew this man from somewhere.

He was going to make me watch a recording before killing me. I was relieved when the blows finally landed thick and fast.

TWENTY-ONE

I AM AT HER PLACE in the XVI arrondissement of Paris. We are more excited than tired, despite the long day at HQ.

I've been fantasying about what we would do to each other since lunch when my libido recovered from its exorcising the night before. The spring warmth has invaded every nook and cranny of the flat, and the sultry air makes it easy to get in the mood. It feels like we are already in the South of France and I joke that we should just stay here.

I pour a scotch and a *kir royale*. She comes out of the bathroom wrapped in a towel and I turn off the TV so that I see her reflection in the glass. She notices this and lets the towel slip so that I see her breasts, then throws a cushion at me in mock protest. I stand in front of her and the towel drops effortlessly to the floor.

We kiss. My fingers work their way down her spine towards her bottom. She pushes us closer together and reaches inside of my jeans. I rip them off and push her gently towards the sofa. She makes herself comfortable as I kiss my way from her feet upwards and go down on her tenderly.

She leads me into the bedroom. She kisses me all over then takes me in her mouth with gusto. I am trying hard not to let go but can't hold on much longer and I come with abandon. She goes to the bathroom and I look out the window the

Eiffel Tower, that giant phallus in the sky. I wonder if this is happiness.

Dried blood clung to my lips and my body was badly bruised. I had no memory of who had hit me.

I rolled off a dirty mattress. I was in a small wooden cabin that was barely big enough to contain me. The air was stale and stuffy – beads of sweat were dripping from my forehead. A window looking onto a tree trunk a few inches away allowed only a few meagre rays of light into the room.

Apart from the bed, there were a few empty shelves and a chemical toilet – it was a far cry from the apartment on the Rue de Sèvres. I was only wearing my Calvin Kleins – none of my other belongings had made it with me. My stomach was swollen and I feared my ribs were fractured or broken.

I still had no idea what had happened. The last thing I remembered was being in the Lutetia basement cell, making the list of culprits and saving it to my phone. I reached for the micro SD card inside the lining of my boxers. Shit, it wasn't there. I took them off and tore them along the seams. The card fell onto the floor.

It was getting darker and hotter – a pool of sweat had gathered by my feet. Is this where I had been sent to disappear? They would make it look like an accident, if ever I were found at all. I combed the wall with my hands but there didn't appear to be an exit. I beat the wall with my fists, to no avail.

Out of breath, I collapsed on the mattress and calmed myself. If these were my last hours, I must get my story straight and leave evidence to help investigators. The SD card contained only names, but none of the trials and tribulations of the past months, so I set to work listing events.

I was stumped by not having a pen or paper. I wasn't going to write in blood or faeces. There was a loose nail on one of the shelves and I began scratching letters on the wood panelling by the window. It took a lot of effort, so I kept it as short as possible.

```
1.  Cell - end?

2.  Job @ ESIS - promo 4 press

3.  Madeleine @ bar - lies

4.  Night @ Pigalle?

5.  Training @ Camp Lutetia

6.  Arrest 4 murder - deported

7.  Angie H.

8.  Party @ Bigboy's, drugs

9.  BB grotto fire

10. Sex with 'Judy'

11. BB/Def. Tour Press & Promo

12. Letter ESIS/CL

13. Interview @ Leconfield House
```

I was tempted to add the death of the tramp at Victoria underground station but felt it best not to speculate. When this list was found, it mustn't seem like the ravings of a lunatic.

Thirteen events. Thirteen nightmares. ESIS was the brain-child of dangerous minds. It struck me that they had outwitted me at every turn by anticipating how I would react. They knew full well I would respond badly to seeing *her* again, fail at the camp and the task. I had been doomed to failure.

Their plots now seemed obvious to me, though several mysteries remained unsolved, notably Pigalle. My wallet and keys had been retrieved from the brothel, so it was safe to assume ESIS agents knew where I was. Could I have been lured there? That seemed farfetched. It was odd, all the same. Was I even sure it happened at all?

Angie's murder was the single most disturbing incident. It meant ESIS was capable of murder. A beautiful young woman with a promising life ahead had been savagely murdered. Was it *really* her corpse in Bigboy's bathroom? Did ESIS agents carry out this heinous crime? If so, I was dealing with forces beyond evil and I would probably die here.

I tried to pinpoint the moment I crossed paths with ESIS for the first time. Certainly before my arrest and the threat of charges. Before working for Bigboy – before even the interview in London? The first mention of 'ESIS' was in the letter signed for by Debs just before the restaurant dinner with father and mother.

Father. What was his role within ESIS? And how long had he been planning to be rid of me? He knew about the job with Bigboy, and my departure coincided with his political power grab – this was no accident. The evidence pointed to him being at the top of the ESIS hierarchy.

Father was an experienced plotter, but he could not have done this to me alone. His senior political advisor was a shadowy figure. As a child, he stood out from the other suits lurking in the shadows as being especially sinister. I racked my brain for names but drew a blank. Back then he had a full head of hair, but he must look much older now.

My thoughts returned to the now. The list made sense to me, but to outsiders? I scoured the walls again, removing the shelves, but didn't find anything other than a loose nail. It was odd that they had gone to such lengths to murder me. Why not shoot me and dump the body in the woods?

But the facts spoke for themselves – there was no exit and I was dying of thirst. I vowed not to drink the bleach in the toilet, which was sure to cause a slow and painful death. I ran the nail across my wrists. I did it again, harder, until a droplet of blood fell to the floor. I bent down to examine it and saw a square crevice in the floor – a trapdoor.

I didn't manage to lift it with my fingernails, so bashed it hard along the edge. It gave way. I descended a ladder into a dark space.

A motion sensor light revealed a small office with a desk, iMac, telephone and large TV screen, as well as a shower and kitchenette. I gulped down a litre bottle of water and inspected the jeans and t-shirts that had been left for me. I didn't care that they were horrid – I wasn't going to die today.

I sat in the office chair and took in my surroundings. A bolted steel door barred my exit, so it was still a prison. A folder on the desk contained a catalogue of 'house rules.' I must not leave the residency, I must not try to open the doors or window, I must not contact anyone without permission. It had Roper's paws all over it.

The iMac booted up without a password but showed 'no connection' to the only available network – ESIS1000. I tried a few passwords and looked for clues at the back of the machine.

A card adaptor sat conveniently in one of the ports. I went to get my card and began typing up the list of events.

I stopped in my tracks. In my excitement, I had been rash. The computer was surely relaying everything back to *them* and the office must be under camera surveillance. I removed the memory card. SD stood for secure digital – secure, my arse! I had to figure out a way to secure and encrypt it before I could work on it further.

I roamed the office. The door had a steel hatch built into it and was bolted from the outside. I kicked it, two, three, four times, but it didn't budge. I clawed at the walls until my fingers ached.

I had to get out of here.

I tipped the contents of Roper's dossier onto the floor. A USB thumb drive fell out. I inserted it into the iMac and QuickTime loaded. I began to revisit the horrors of the night before.

TWENTY-TWO

'Europe is the future! My future, your future, our future! Europe is great! I am great, you are great, we are great!'

I hit the stop button frantically, to no avail. Seeing father give the special lecture '21st Century Europe: In Varietate Concordia' at Camp Lutetia to the chosen twenty-seven was like undergoing open-heart surgery.

'We may not all believe in the religious sense, but we know deep down that Europe is our one true salvation. My salvation, your salvation, our salvation!'

Like a preacher at the pulpit, he worked his audience into a rapture. The clip was styled like party political propaganda – every thirty seconds or so cutting to the clapping audience. This alone was disturbing. The populism made me sick to the core.

The Conservative party had a Europhile wing, but nothing this extreme, this radical. I stared at the blank screen and wondered what the hell he was up to. If it leaked, it would be political suicide.

I was back in the deserted farmhouse, strapped to the chair. At first, I was relieved my ordeal was not physical, but watching father gave me a feeling of nausea in the pit of my stomach.

'For Christ's sake…'

My torturer stood behind the screen, watching me in silence. I still couldn't place him.

He played the video over and over again.

'Gonna give us more trouble, sonny boy?'

He spoke in an Estuary accent, with real venom. I recognised the voice.

'Fuck you.'

'Fuck me? That what they learn ya at Oxford?'

The first blow was to my stomach, the second to my upper back. He threw a nasty punch for an old man. I doubled up in pain, unable to breathe.

The next blows were to my head. Blood was streaming down my face.

'Fuck you,' I repeated.

He picked up a plank of wood with a nail in it. He was going to strike me when his phone rang. He grunted and left the room, returning some moments later.

'I will crush you!'

More blows to the face. I blacked out.

A loud ringing sound woke me up. It was the telephone in the office. I scrambled down the ladder in a panic.

'Good morning, Ellis.'

'You sick, twisted son-of-a-bitch. You will rue the day…'

An automated voice told me it was time to begin the day's activities. Meanwhile, a second alarm sounded and the hatch swung open.

It locked before I had time to react. I had barely slept, so I went back upstairs and curled up on the bunk. But curiosity got the better of me and I went back down to investigate.

The first package was microwave meals, bread, pastries, tins of tuna and pâté, cans of vegetables, coffee and bottled water.

I arranged the items in the kitchen space, brewed a big pot of coffee and ate an entire pack of brioches. So they weren't going to starve me to death, that was a relief of kinds.

The second package was bulky and difficult to open. It was newspaper clippings tied into bundles. I feared another insane task, but no – a typed note instructed me to simply read and study the materials. I picked out an edition of *Libération* for Saturday 1st April. Even in my comatose state, I knew it was still March.

Translations had been appended to the main articles, but I put these to one side and flicked through the originals. Key points of interest had been underlined. The headline was long-winded – 'Assault on a young man leads to a murderous brawl' – but the article made for lively reading.

An attack on a young Frenchman had taken place in an empty train in the Northern suburb. The assailants, three Arab youths, had chosen an easy target, twenty-five-year-old bank trainee named Jacques. Or so they thought. They couldn't have imagined in a million years that Jacques would put up a fight, let alone be carrying a gun.

They were even more astonished, the journalist speculated, that Jacques was a skilled marksman. He shot to kill – three bullets were recovered from each of the dead youths' bodies and two were shot in the head at point-blank range. The police said that three bodies had been taken to the hospital morgue in the suburban town of Argenteuil and declined to say whether Jacques was in custody.

The article speculated that the youths were radicalised Islamists, embarking on a campaign of terror against lone commuters, or about to carry out a terrorist attack. Investigators had yet to identify the men but expected to find ISIS connections. No explanation was given for why Jacques had a gun.

The article was written by L. Bertrand. I was friends with a Luc Bertrand at Oxford, although it was a common name. I stared at the date – 1st April. Was I absolutely sure it was still March? I checked the system date on the iMac – 29th November 2001. Great. I had no way to verify.

The next file in the dossier was a lengthy report by the General Directorate for Internal Security, the French equivalent of MI5. It was difficult to read due to the formal and pedantic language, so I picked up the translation, 'Report on Far-Right National Front Clandestine Activity.'

It related to a plot uncovered by French secret service agents who had infiltrated National Front gangs. The plan had been simple – to bait Arab youths and provoke them into conflict. White youths would take a beating, then play the victim and spread the word about Arab brutality.

The victims could be chosen at random – so long as they were of North African descent and Muslim. After the attacks, the National Front would provide 'proof' they had been radicalised by fundamentalists, at home or abroad, and were about to participate in ISIS terror campaigns. These news stories would boost National Front popularity.

There were photos of National Front skinheads taken at gyms and housing estates. They were a bunch of thugs with long criminal records – all downright dangerous. The plan had failed spectacularly. This was because the National Front youths could not bring themselves to 'lie down and take it' and had thrashed the Arab youths within inches of their lives.

More than few reporters had jumped on the bandwagon and

brazenly declared these incidents proof of home-grown Islamic terrorism. But others had smelt a rat. They had not believed the Arab youths were jihadists and rightly suspected the National Front thugs of provoking the unrest.

The end of the report made for especially disturbing reading. The French Ministry of the Interior had got wind of the scheme and initiated a highly classified study to see if the National Front could be aided and abetted in their scheme. *In black and white, the French government was considering assisting the National Front to provoke France's volatile immigrant population into acts of violence.*

The report gave a succinct rationale for the Ministry's dark chicanery. First, the media outrage at this latest spate of violence would help to pass new legislation clamping down on Islamic religious freedoms. It could also be used to justify deporting juvenile delinquents to Algeria, Tunisia or Morocco – even those born in France.

After this was accomplished and the storm had died, the DGSI would judiciously turn the tables on the National Front, exposing their nasty plan by leaking evidence to the media. They would be shown up to be the thugs and racists that they are – a threat to France – and their perpetual climb in the polls would be stopped.

The plan thus killed two birds with one stone – inciting anti-Islamic sentiment and discrediting the National Front. Its genius and its madness lay therein. The report acknowledged that the European Union was likely to accuse France of mistreating its Islamic population, but it conceded this would only result in empty rhetoric and toothless censure.

The main risk of the plan was that the conflict could create a volatile situation that spiralled out of control. If the secret service's hand in the situation was discovered by the media, it would lead to international condemnation as well as to mass protests, instability and bloodshed. It could topple the government, lead to civil war and the collapse of the French Republic.

This was heavy stuff. I went upstairs to digest the information. Why the hell were they feeding me such sensitive material?

TWENTY-THREE

THE DELIVERY CAME AT SEVEN the next morning. The first box contained food and water, the second a hefty stack of newspapers.

I set to work on the new materials. *Libération* for Monday 3rd April reported that Saturday's killings had led to a National Front 'mobilisation' with demonstrations and protests up and down the country. It added that the police were under pressure to reveal the whereabouts and full identity of Jacques.

The conservative press was less hostile towards the National Front. *Le Figaro* thought it credible that the deceased youths were radicalised and involved in a terror plot. It revealed that one of the teenagers came from the same estate as the Bataclan concert attackers and surmised they knew each other from the local mosque.

The paper featured interviews with the National Front rank and file. Each one said that an innocent Frenchman had been targeted by immigrant scum and the attack was the vindication of all their prophecies of doom. The party spokesman lambasted the Socialist government for failing to act on its rhetoric in the wake of recent Islamic terrorist attacks.

On Tuesday, it was reported that the National Front was planning a major protest rally in Paris. Their parliamentary *députés* would be sponsoring a bill to strip terror suspects of

French citizenship and to give the public the right to bear arms and to use them in case of terrorist attacks. It was expected to pass with government support.

Le Monde stated this would be the first time a French government had colluded with the far-right. France would have the world's most stringent anti-terror laws and be the only Western country aside from the United States to allow the public to carry weapons. It noted that the National Front leadership had turned their back on recent efforts to 'soften' its image.

Tuesday's edition of *Libération* reported that the morgue in Argenteuil had become a 'site of conflict.' Locals had gathered to demand the bodies so they could be buried according to Islamic tradition. French Muslims and civil rights activists stood opposite National Front skinheads hell-bent on violence.

Wednesday's papers all carried the same story – National Front brutality. The standoff had rapidly descended into a bloodbath. The mob's first victim was a young Muslim woman. A group of hooded white youths ripped off her hijab and bra and took selfies with her in lewd positions in front of the morgue.

Like hyenas in heat, the mob moved on to its next victim – an elderly Imam, who they stripped naked and doused in petrol. Meanwhile, a biker gang rounded on a group of Arab teens, pounding them with baseball bats. Two thirteen-year-olds had their skulls broken and had to be induced into comas.

A thug shouted that he recognised the uncle of one of the train attackers. The crowd seized the man, punching and kicking him until he lay unconscious on the ground in a pool of blood –a hooded teen then slashed him across the neck with a knuckleduster. He was taken to hospital but declared dead on arrival.

Libération had an exclusive on Thursday. It had uncovered the identities of the three dead youths. Mohammed Bin Mohid, Ahmed Hakim and Mourad El-Gamal were exemplary high school students with no history of trouble. The police had disclosed that no weapons were found with the bodies, or any evidence they were radicalised.

Facebook photos showed healthy, well-rounded teens. Mourad, who was only fifteen, had an angelic smile. They shared a passion for football and their grieving families and friends swore that on the day of the killings they were en route to the Stade de France to watch their beloved Paris Saint-Germain play Olympique de Marseille.

There was another scoop on the next page. An anonymous source at the Ministry of the Interior claimed Jacques was a National Front Youth activist. He or she also revealed that the Ministry was privy to intelligence that the political party was planning to stir racial tensions in the wake of forthcoming elections.

Libération had previously accused the National Front of stoking racial tensions, but this was the first time they had material proof. The source had leaked a report by the National Front Executive Council listing the kind of provocations the Arab community would respond to and stating what the French public would willingly believe.

This was enough for *Libération* to accuse the National Front of hatching a malicious plot to foment anti-Islamic feeling. The editorial said that the party had shown itself beyond doubt to be 'morally abhorrent,' and demanded that the government break off talks with France's 'home-grown extremists.'

More revelations surfaced on Thursday. WikiLeaks posted a

data dump from the National Front's main server. It included a modus operandi for recruiting thugs to provoke violent conflicts with Arab youths and tips on how to pass the victims off as the bad guys. It also listed the editors and journalists who were 'sympathetic to the cause.'

The National Front's spokesman denied its authenticity, but by Friday morning it was considered an accepted truth that the political party had murdered the three young Arabs. The French nationalists found themselves at the centre of a maelstrom as politicians from all sides piled in to condemn the 'evil of fascism.'

Thursday night had seen massive suburban unrest, with cars up and down the land torched and the police attacked. The government had imposed a curfew in 'hotspot' estates and was rumoured to be on the verge of deploying troops. It was a dangerous, volatile situation, the likes of which had not been seen in years.

Le Figaro and *Libération* reported on the stand-off situation at the morgue in Argenteuil. An army of National Front skinheads was facing off against thousands of French Arabs across makeshift barricades. Riot police made up a third camp, but admitted they were powerless to intervene. It was no longer a question of if the situation would explode, but when.

I drew a deep breath. This nightmare scenario had given me a migraine. I badly needed to step outside, have a drink and turn on a TV to reassure myself that none of this was really happening. The newspapers seemed one hundred per cent authentic – and this was starting to screw with my head.

I had to find a way to escape. The cabin had only two openings – the upstairs window and the door. The window was sealed and only a few inches from a tree. The door was sturdy but had a weak point – the hatch. I could try to stop it from bolting shut after it opened. But it was not large enough to climb through.

I rummaged through the delivery box and came across sheets of paper lying at the bottom.

```
From:       CC Roper
To:         Little Boots, Foxtrot,
            Capitaine, Eagle, Dr E.
Subject:    ESIS Op. 'DOUBLE BLOW'
            < 24.06.2016 >


FRANCE:
Phase #1:   Arab Spring, FN
            Brutality - FN blamed
Phase #2:   INT & DGSI implicated,
            'drip drip' media
Phase #3:   Neg. with INT. DGSI →
            ESIS; else -
Phase #4:   DGSI & INT destroyed,
            ESIS to power


GERMANY:
Phase #1:   AfD/NDP syn. attack
Phase #2:   BND/MAD implicated,
            'drip drip' media
Phase #3:   Neg. with BMI. BND/MAD →
            ESIS; else -
Phase #4:   BND/MAD/BMI destroyed,
            ESIS to power


GREECE:
Phase #1:   YV/MeRA25 + NIS + RF
Phase #2:   Coup exposed
Phase #3:   ND → Order restored,
            ESIS to power
```

There were notes for each member of the European Union. I skipped to the last entry:

```
UNITED KINGDOM:
Phase #1:    ESIS for REMAIN
             (cash, media, trolls)
Phase #2:    ESIS against LEAVE
             (media, trolls)
Phase #3:    REMAIN Victory, LB → PM,
             ESIS to power
```

I read it back several times. Other than 'ESIS to power,' it made almost no sense. I started with the codenames. 'Dr E.' was Europa. 'Capitaine' might be the Frenchman of the Lutetia boardroom. 'Eagle' could be the American. That meant the sinister bald man was 'Foxtrot' or 'Little Boots.'

The UK was the easiest to decode. ESIS planned to illegally aid the Remain campaign to manipulate the election and ensure victory. With the UK committed to staying in the European Union, there would be little scope for resisting ESIS. I pondered 'LB → PM.' Why was father's name not here? Was he LB Little Boots?

I focussed on France. FN was the National Front, PN the National Police and INT the French Ministry of the Interior. I deduced that ESIS was going to carry out their own version of the National Front's plan – staging a terror incident to inflame anti-Arab sentiment and provoke large-scale violence. At the height of the tensions, the National Front would be revealed as the perpetrator. 'Arab Spring' referred to riots among the French Arab population.

So far, the plan was the same as the Ministry of the Interior's. But ESIS would again turn the tables, spreading rumours about a collusion between the National Front and the French security services. Fake news and leaked documents would 'prove' the political party had not acted alone. The mysterious disappearance of Jacques would add fuel to the fire.

'DGSI → ESIS.' ESIS intended to use the crisis as leverage to establish itself as the main intelligence service of France. ESIS would hold back from utterly discrediting the DGSI, so long as they acquiesced. If they refused, ESIS would take down – 'destroy' – its rival, taking France to the brink of civil war in the process.

Operation 'Double Blow' entailed similar plots in every EU country. Germany would be conned into believing its security services had conspired with extremist parties in some dastardly attack. In Greece, a fake revolution would pose a threat to the country's survival. Each situation would justify an ESIS intervention. The operation was timestamped 24th June 2016 – one day after the UK referendum.

The fallout from this memo was terrifying. It was odd that they had included it in the bundle – was it an accident? I set about memorising it word for word. The more details I could give, the more powerful my testimony would be. *The world must know, the world will know, and this plan must be stopped.*

I held it up to the light to see if it yielded any further clues and saw a note pencilled on the back.

> Times are tough but so are you. Do what you have to do. All will be clear.
>
> ~ M ~

TWENTY-FOUR

No delivery came the next morning, disappointingly. I wanted to know what would happen in Argenteuil.

I brewed coffee. There wasn't much food left – did they plan to starve me after all? Like so much else, it made no sense at all. I paced up and down, ranting at ESIS and lashing out at the sparse furnishings. I flung yesterday's newspapers onto the floor and hunted for things to destroy.

The iMac came to life. The dock loaded and a webpage in Safari. I stared at the screen incredulously.

Cabin fever (also known as House Syndrome) is an idiomatic term for a claustrophobic reaction that takes place when a person or group is isolated and/or shut-in, in a small space, with nothing to do, for an extended period. Symptoms include restlessness, irritability, irrational frustration, forgetfulness, laughter and excessive sleeping, distrust of anyone they are with, and an urge to go outside even if this is not advisable or possible. Cabin fever also denotes a lack of sexual intercourse.

They knew I had it bad, the bastards. I tried my luck and typed in the address to my email login page. It loaded. I could send emails! I entered a state of blind panic about who to contact. A newspaper? WikiLeaks? Mother? All I knew was that it had to be done at the speed of light.

As I went to retrieve the SD card to upload my lists, the

hatch opened. Caught off guard, I darted towards the door to attempt to stop it from shutting. By the time I realised it was impossible, the internet had gone offline. I cursed myself violently for letting anger and insomnia blunt my ability to think.

I hurled the packages against the wall. I took deep breaths to calm myself, then went over to inspect. One of the deliveries was food. So I wouldn't starve. The other was so heavy it had made a dent in the wall. I ripped it open to find an automatic pistol in a leather holster.

The hairs on the back of my neck stood up. If it was loaded, it was my ticket out of here. It took me a few minutes to understand that it was a replica.

'Welcome to weapons training module 1A – handling your firearm. Unpack and install your gun.'

The loud American voice boomed out of the television, which had been activated remotely. It was a firearms training programme. I tried to turn it off, but the only way forwards was to comply.

I plugged a Bluetooth transceiver from the gun into the back of the television and followed instructions for calibrating and handling the weapon. The virtual instructor was not impressed with my skills, telling me sternly that my 'hands were unsteady' and I was holding it 'like it was a bar of soap.'

The first two hours were spent learning how to load and look after the weapon. I was finally allowed to start target practice by firing at a target board on the screen. I had to aim at the bull's eye, shoot and reload. I was reprimanded for hitting wide of the board.

'You failed. Try again.'

Another pot of coffee. I had always been against guns and never been to a shooting range, but I was starting to get psyched. The programme was like a sophisticated computer game and I enjoyed decimating the virtual targets with a few flicks of my finger. The instructor never gave praise, but I was allowed to go on to the next level if my scores were good enough.

In the next module, I had to shoot enemy combatants in an Afghan desert. I liked this one even more. The system shut itself down around midnight. I reacted by trying to pelt the screen with virtual gunfire. I had just taken down five Taliban fighters, shooting three of them in the head. I packed the gun back into its case and pottered around the cabin, unable to sleep.

The alarm sounded at 6.35 a.m. I got up mechanically, like a soldier, and made coffee. I hadn't slept enough and was angry – even more so than the day before. I had dreamt about shooting all night – I kept missing the targets and being insulted sarcastically. Awake I was keen to improve my accuracy and to get on to the higher levels.

The session was arduous and mind-numbing – hours of non-stop shooting from different angles, ranges and requiring faster and faster response times. The new simulations were more like *Grand Theft Auto* than military exercises, although the virtual instructor was as exacting as ever.

In one scenario I had to take out an armed robber by shooting him in the knees and stomach. The violence was gratifying. I was expecting a break when the system announced hand-to-hand combat training. I attached sensors to my arms and legs and learned some basics. I then had to disable an armed guard and fend off three muggers, one armed with a knife.

My head was aching and my hands were shaking with

adrenaline. I was half-aware, in the back of my mind, that this training must serve a dark purpose, but I was so engrossed I didn't take a moment to reflect. I barely even noticed the day's delivery drop-off. I made a pot of coffee, went up to the mezzanine level and opened the package.

It contained legal documents about French police procedures for tackling armed criminals and guidelines on how to respond to terrorist attacks. I couldn't imagine what it had to do with me, and in any case, I was too buzzed to read a word. I crumpled it into a ball and threw it down the trapdoor.

At the bottom of the box, there was an old-style Polaroid. I was naked on a massage bed. The girl next to me had long dark hair that obscured most of her face. The eye was drawn to her near-flawless breasts, marred only by a dark spot. It was Madeleine all right. A shadowy female figure was lurking at the door.

So Pigalle happened. Why were they showing me this? I curled up in a yoga position and vowed to escape tomorrow. Or else.

I went over the options again – the window or the door. The door was hopeless. Even if I stood by the hatch as the delivery arrived, it was unlikely I'd be able to prise it open so that I could unbolt the door. The window upstairs would be hard to smash, but not impossible. I would ram it with the kitchen microwave or the wooden shelf.

Once outside I would climb down the tree to the ground. I was sure to be a bloody mess and God knew what lay beyond – a security fence, a sentry post? I had some vague idea about making it to a port with ferries going to England. Having no ID, money or credit cards would be obstacles to overcome.

I would make the breakout at 7.45 a.m. – rush hour if I was anywhere near a town or city. That would increase my chances of finding a bus or a train. I also figured it would be harder for them to arrest me in broad daylight. Maybe, just maybe, they weren't counting on this rashness.

I would only have one shot at this, and it would almost certainly end in failure – capture, torture or the 'end' – whatever that was. But my decision was final.

I lay meditating on the bunk for hours. The feeling took me back to my early teen years and the last day of the summer holidays. I was ecstatic to escape father's clutches but terrified about what lay ahead.

TWENTY-FIVE

I was woken by a loud thud at 5.47 a.m. The delivery was early. I pretended to sleep for five more minutes, then got up, made coffee and picked up the package.

They mustn't suspect a thing.

There were several layers of plastic and bubble wrap that were hard to remove. I got to the last one and uncovered a metal box with red warning labels on it. I fumbled with the latches and removed a handgun and two ammo clips. It was like the one used in the simulator, a Beretta M9 9mm, but this one was the real thing.

Oh my god.

I retrieved the holster that had come with the virtual gun and fastened it around my waist. It fitted. I loaded a clip into the Beretta and removed the safety. It was going to be messy, but if I shot ten rounds at the edges of the window it would weaken it enough for me to break it with a few kicks.

I gulped down some water, gathered a few items from the kitchen and put on fresh clothes. I slipped the SD card into the back pocket of my jeans – hardly a secure place, but it was as good as useless anyway. I had memorised the lists, memo and newspaper articles as best I could. The only truly safe place was my head.

I hadn't noticed that the door was ajar. I stared at the crack, not believing my eyes. A mistake or a trap – both were possible.

All I knew was that I was leaving. My heart was beating at a hundred miles an hour. I flung the door wide open and waited. Nothing. I crouched down and rolled across the threshold.

I was in a small garden enclosed with tall hedges. I filled my lungs with fresh air. The exterior of the treehouse prison looked like a garden shed. Twenty feet away stood a wooden gate barely wide enough to let a car through. There was no way to know what lay behind, but there was no barbed wire or security fence.

I crept up to the end of the garden as quietly as possible and looked out for signs of life. Nothing. I gave myself the all-clear.

'*Alerte orange!*'

The gate was opening. There was no time to weigh up the options – I dealt a sharp blow to a security guard's stomach and neck. He collapsed with a groan. I expected him to get up and reach for his gun, but he didn't. The training made me stop and check. Man down, affirmative.

I ran out onto the street, looking in every direction for more guards. A quick reconnoitre revealed a country lane with new houses, private driveways and empty plots of land. It was the suburbs of a town or city, so buses and trains could not be too far away. The priority was to get out of the obvious search perimeter as fast as possible.

Sirens. I stopped in my tracks, hoping that they would go away, but they got louder. I quickened my pace, adrenaline surging through my body. I was rewarded with a stairway leading to a cramped alleyway. I dived into it as two police motorbikes and an ambulance sped by.

The alley led to a main road running parallel to the country lane. A man in a suit brushed past without looking at me. He looked like he was late for a train. A train. I strained my ears and heard a familiar mechanical drone. The station could not be more than a couple of hundred yards away.

I flew down another flight of stairs leading to the platform and a waiting train. I didn't have time to read the station name or see where the train was heading, but a blue Transilien sign told me I was in the greater Paris region. This was good news. I would travel to the capital and work out my options from there.

I could not miss that train.

I leapt into the air and thrust a hand into the closing doors. My arm was guillotined and I stood in limbo – my elbow inside the carriage, my body outside – while a teenage hoodie yanked the doors open and pulled me in. I fell to the floor, panting like a madman.

The hoodie took a step back on seeing the Beretta, which was dangling out of the holster. I untied the strap and tucked it into the back of my trousers. From the training, I knew I must act like a normal commuter – not one that had broken out of a secure detention centre. Easier said than done.

I located a map of the route. I was in the northern suburbs on a train heading to Paris via Argenteuil. I managed to find a window seat on the upper level so that I could see around me. The carriage was full of businessmen, workers and students, mothers and children. The normality did little to calm my nerves.

There were four stops to Argenteuil and another six to Paris – each one was a potential danger spot. The first was Chanteloup-les-Vignes, a sprawling wasteland of grim housing estates. A gang of loud teens boarded and loitered at the doors. A Rastafarian with face piercings and tattoos sat next to me.

I saw the inspectors from afar as the train approached the next station. I knew they would board my carriage, and they did. Four of them stood a few feet from me, ready to check tickets and passes. I was paralysed. Should I get off or stay put? By the grace of some unknown power, they turned around and stepped off the train before the doors closed.

The train departed from the next station without incident. It was one more stop to Argenteuil, where I could change there for the fast RER train to Paris. Moments into the journey, the train halted abruptly. There was a muffled announcement in French, but the train stayed put. Five long minutes later, we were on our way again.

At Argenteuil, armed police lined the platform. My heart froze. Were they lying in wait for me? All the other passengers left the train. I slumped down into my seat in a state of panic and tried to figure out what to do. The police were certainly going to board any moment. The game was up.

I hid in the aisle and looked for escape routes, but there were none. Staying put was my only option. I counted to ten to delay the inevitable. Looking around, I saw there were other people in the carriage – a suited businessman slumped in a corner, fast asleep, and three youths loitering at the end of the carriage.

Did the train go to Paris after all?

The door-closing noise sounded. The suit woke up and darted out of the carriage, but the youths stayed put. Okay. Perhaps they spent their days riding up and down the line. The train began moving in the direction we had come from. It didn't matter – I had escaped the clutches of disaster. I would get off at the next station and make my way on foot.

I consulted the map above the door as soon as we had safely cleared Argenteuil. The next stop was Conflans-Sainte-Honorine. One of the youths sidled up to me. He was dark-skinned with stubble, about sixteen years old. It was odd he hadn't got off with the other passengers, but he looked harmless enough.

After a minute of slow-crawl, the train ground to a halt mid-station. I didn't sense trouble until he followed me back to my seat.

'*Téléphone, mec! Téléphone!*'

There was no point telling him I didn't have one – it was a robbery. The Beretta was more trouble than it was worth. I struck him in the face with my right elbow and punched him in the stomach. Winded, he gasped for breath and doubled up in pain. I shoved him into the aisle and told him to stay down, kicking him to make sure he understood.

His friends were at the end of the carriage, watching the scene unfold. They were taller and stronger than the kid. Bearded and dressed in black, they bore a resemblance to jihadists. As the pair closed in on me, I realised this could not be resolved without violence and reached for the Beretta.

'I'm warning you…'

The kid grabbed my foot and yanked. I tripped and fell onto the seat, dropping the gun. It sat on the floor for a few seconds, two feet away from me and him. The boy was fast and our hands reached the gun together.

If it were just me and him, I would have prevailed. But his friends came to his defence and battered me with blows until I lost my grip.

'*Couteau! Le couteau!*'

If it was do or die, I was not going to die – not there and then. I leapt towards the gun with a superhuman effort and got it back. I slid my fingers behind the trigger and pulled.

It wasn't like in the simulator. The empty shells came out with such force I thought my assailants were firing back. A deafening noise raged in my ears. I couldn't breathe. I fired twelve rounds in six seconds. I fired three more at the train window, shattering the glass.

I reloaded but there was nothing left to shoot. Nothing living at any rate. The carriage was a slaughterhouse – the seats and windows were splattered with blood. The scrawny kid lay dead at my feet, his baggy trousers halfway down his legs. Blood trickled from the back of his head. The bodies lay on top of each other like wax sculptures, eyes glazed over.

I jumped out of the shattered window, slicing my hand on a shard of glass, and crawled through the rough grass by the tracks. I vomited. The voice from the simulator spoke to me. *You must not enter a state of shock. This is how soldiers get killed. You must keep moving, look out for danger and get to safety.*

I staggered to my feet. I could hardly see at all and the noise still raged in my ears. I had no idea if there were other passengers on board the train or if the driver knew about the shooting and dead bodies. It didn't matter. No one would risk crossing paths with a madman wielding a gun.

I stumbled over a short fence and made towards a car park about a hundred yards away. Car parks lead to roads. There was only one car in the lot – a black BMW with tinted windows. The training had taught me that this was suspicious and to approach with caution. I reached for the Beretta.

A tall man in a dark suit stepped out of the car. He smiled broadly and pointed to the sky. I looked up – it was clear and blue – and received a blow to the back of my neck.

'Easy-peasy,' he said.

I had a vague sensation of being bundled into the boot of the car.

PART THREE

TWENTY-SIX

SHE WAS THE FIRST THING I saw when I opened my eyes.

Sitting on an antique chair in the middle of the room, she was reading. She was a work of exquisite beauty, an angel. A sculpture framed by ornate mouldings and lavish drapes. My own Florence Nightingale was caring for me. I looked on from a poster bed where I was wrapped in fine sheets and dressed in silk pyjamas.

It was a pleasant dream for a sick man. I tried to get up and look around but couldn't so much as lift my head. I could only see her – my angel of mercy. I held out a hand to touch her, but as I did so she rose into the air and faded from view. I also ascended into the clouds and set off for the lost hinterlands of eternity.

I slept for a very long time. A bedside clock said 11:03 – I assumed it was night as the room was pitch black. I felt awful, like I had the flu or worse. I remembered that I had been imprisoned and in serious trouble, but not much else. Amnesia was a familiar friend – almost a comfort. I knew it was only a matter of time before the trauma surfaced.

I hauled myself up, turned on a bedside lamp and stared into space. It had not all been a fantasy – this was real. The room was like a nineteenth-century museum, with mouldings, parquet floor and fireplace. I stepped into a dimly lit corridor decorated with Dutch paintings and antiques.

I was drawn like a moth towards flickering lights. Someone was watching television. I opened the door. It was Madeleine. She was curled up in a nightgown on a luxury leather divan. Antonioni's *La Notte* was ending.

'Hi.'

'Hi.'

She was alluring in her nightgown. We stood there, like boarders with senior privileges.

'Welcome to your new home. We'll be sharing for a time, if that's alright.'

'That's alright,' I muttered.

'I told you to hang in there. I'm proud of you.'

She led me back to the bedroom.

'Rest,' she said. 'I'll be in the living room if you need me.'

I still couldn't remember what I had escaped from, other than that it was terrible and best forgotten.

In the morning, I climbed out of bed and pulled back the curtains. The Eiffel Tower's lofty legs loomed at me from across the Seine – it was less than half a mile away. The room had a sink, so I splashed water on my face then dressed in the shirt and jeans neatly arranged on the dresser.

I was lured down the hallway by the smell of fresh coffee. The dining room and kitchen were basking in a white light that made me squint. A breakfast of toast, croissants and marmalade awaited me on the kitchen table.

'I thought you might be hungry. Coffee?'

Madeleine was cooking scrambled eggs. Dressed in a large tee-shirt, loose bottoms and no makeup she still looked the picture of elegance.

We said very little to each other over breakfast. That was fine by me as my head was still sore. After eating she told me that we wouldn't be alone again until later that day. ESIS hierarchy would be paying me a visit. But I wasn't to worry, there was *nothing to worry about anymore.*

'Everyone is very pleased with you. Relax and enjoy.'

The new home, judging by the comings and goings, was a Lutetia safe house. I was back with them. With her. I had a feeling of déjà vu. I had been ensnared in a trap, given a reprieve, saved from disaster, and now had yet another chance to get real answers from Madeleine and to expose Lutetia. The only problem was that my resolve was wearing thin.

I lay on my bed, mulling things over. I feared the visit from hierarchy meant Roper and Mickie. My suspicions were confirmed around lunchtime.

'You are here,' Roper said neutrally.

He looked like John Steed from the old Avengers, with briefcase and umbrella in hand. Mickie stood by his side, like an obedient dog. I supposed they had made up since our last meeting, though I sensed some tension.

Mickie was holding a plastic bag with a half-eaten baguette inside.

'Brought ya some grub,' he blustered.

Roper gave me a large folder and told me to study its contents. His eyes showed a cool hatred for me. Either he didn't dare be civil with me in front of his beloved Mickie – or he truly blamed me for jeopardising their relationship. I didn't care for this circus act and had to repress the impulse to seize his umbrella and choke him.

I was escorted back to my room. Michael and Roper gave

instructions to Madeleine and left without further ado. I lay on the bed, weighing up my options. As I wasn't shackled, I could follow them. I fully expected the trail to lead to Lutetia headquarters and to get caught, but so be it.

I listened for the clank of the elevator then slipped onto the landing and followed the spiral staircase down five flights to the ground level. I took note of the street address – 22 Avenue du Président Kennedy – then hid behind a bus stop. I didn't see them at first but figured they couldn't have gone far in just a few minutes.

The duo was heading northwards. I tailed them at a distance of about fifty yards but had to keep stopping to find new places to hide as they were walking at such a slow pace. They eventually arrived at the iron bridge, the Pont de Bir-Hakeim. Roper gave a fistful of coins to Michael, who went inside.

Two armoured police vans passed by, obscuring my view. Mickie came back with a bunch of newspapers and they hung about on the street reading them. Roper neatly folded the papers into his briefcase and climbed the steps leading to the bridge. He had a spring in his step – they were overjoyed about something and were chatting excitedly.

More emergency vehicles passed by. I had to see what they had seen. I counted to thirty and went inside the bar.

Saturday's coffee-stained *Libération* was lying on a bar stool. The front-page headline read, 'Assault on a young man leads to a murderous brawl.' I couldn't say at first what was strange about it. A chill went down my spine. I realised it was word-for-word the article I had been fed in captivity.

The paper had been lying around all weekend, which meant it was old news. Monday's *Libération* led with the story about

149

the National Front 'mobilisation' – the largest ever seen in France. A second front-page article was critical of the police for not revealing the identity of the assailant, Jacques.

Le Figaro's coverage was even more forthright than the issue I had read in captivity.

'Are they right?' asked the article on the mass rallies organised by the National Front. The paper's editorial attacked the sitting Socialist government's 'history of failure' when it came tackling the extremist threat.

Le Parisian, *France Soir* and *Metro* headlines were more sensational. 'Is this a point of no-return for France?' 'Arab violence at all-time high.' 'Mohammed, Ahmed and Mourad: where were you going?' 'Who and where is Jacques?' I didn't want to believe what I was seeing.

Nobody minded that I was reading the papers without buying one. Everyone was glued to *France24 news*. A waiter turned up the volume so that it could be heard above the sirens. The anchor talked solemnly about 'la situation' unfolding *en direct*. The National Front had just announced they would be holding their largest rally yet to try to force the government to take a more hard-line stance against criminals of immigrant origins.

A journalist came on air from Argenteuil. She reported that the youths' bodies were being held at the local morgue, but that the families were demanding they be released so they could be buried according to Islamic tradition. Skinheads with National Front banners could be seen screaming obscenities.

Analysts in the studio expressed fears that this could trigger a crisis of historic proportions. If the National Front hooligans clashed with the capital's suburban immigrants, it would result in bloodshed. The government had the power to impose a curfew in towns like Argenteuil, but the police would be powerless to enforce it.

The studio chat was interrupted by the news that the President would address the nation on the evening news after meeting with the Conseil d'État. The sound faded out until I couldn't hear anything at all. I closed my eyes. This was my doing.

I was Jacques. I had killed three men.

TWENTY-SEVEN

'Ain't alri't t'be out o' ye' box, son.'

Mickie's ugly mug was staring at me from behind a rack of papers.

'Should'o learn b'now no' to feck aboot,' he grunted. 'A'm packin' so dun ev'n fink aboot it.'

I didn't see the gun but believed he had one. The stakes had been upped – this much was clear. I was frogmarched back to the safe house and locked in my room. Sensing things were amiss, Madeleine broke off a phone call – but she was brushed off.

'Read ye feckin' brif, or a'll be readin' it to ya and it'll no be a feckin' lull'by. Step out'a 'ere agin, 'm feckin' goin' kill ya.'

He punched the door for good measure. I collapsed onto the bed, exhausted. I was trapped in a perpetual hell. In less than a week I had been groomed to be a Lutetia assassin. I had done exactly as they'd wanted. I had been their bitch. They had made me into a killer.

It was unbearably painful to accept that the escape had backfired so cataclysmically. A priori, they could rely on me to do their bidding and resistance was futile. The consequences of this misdeed that went far beyond my personal dilemmas. A nation's future hung in the balance.

I was in urgent need of relief. I lay on the bed and touched myself, but nothing happened. I felt something under the pillow – it was a plastic bag containing the bloodied t-shirt and jeans I'd worn the day of the breakout. I dug out the SD card from the back pocket. ESIS might as well have labelled it as 'read and copied.'

I picked up the dossier Roper had handed me. I didn't have to look through it to know it was a bloody protocol manual. I was not to breathe a word about my training, internment or the 'clandestine operation detailed herein.' The consequences of breaching the rules would be severe, etc.

It came with a Lutetia-issue Samsung Galaxy and SIM. It went without saying that making calls, using it to make notes or trying to access the internet was futile. It was nothing more than a spying device to feed them information about me. I pulled a book – Camus' *L'Étranger* – from off a shelf, ripped out some pages and got to work.

I began by adding the codenames from the memo to the list of ESIS hierarchy. I wrote 'Capitaine' next to 'Bowtie & Tweed Man' – the Frenchman who appeared like a dowdy professor – and 'Eagle' after 'Big American Man.' I felt sure about being on the money with these two.

I next wrote 'Foxtrot' next to 'Sinister Bald Man.' The silent man at the Lutetia boardroom meeting was also the man who beat me up in the farmhouse before I was sent to the treehouse prison. I had finally placed that Estuary accent – the man was a long-time associate of father. I racked my brain for a name but drew a blank.

I wrote 'Little Boots' next to John Goodman. Father. I had no proof, but it was more than intuition – I was certain of it. Father was one of a quartet behind ESIS, the fourth man. He was the British Prime Minister-in-waiting once the

EU referendum was won. ESIS was funnelling cash into the Remain campaign to manipulate the election result.

I described the treehouse prison and weapons training. I was able to recopy a lot of the secret memo about operation 'Double Blow,' the plot to stir up turmoil across the European Union by provoking extremist elements, framing security services for corruption and ushering in ESIS as their replacement. Events were coordinated to coincide with the UK referendum in June.

I gave a detailed account of the French plot, including how at the height of the turmoil, *Libération* would reveal that the French police and DGSI secret service carried out the attacks on the Arab youths, pointing to shadowy figures in the government. The calculation was that the crisis would bring France to its knees with bloodshed and anarchy.

I explained how I had seen pre-drafted proofs of the newspaper articles in captivity. It dawned on me that this would be hard to prove now they had been published. I left out an account of that fateful day when I acted as the catalyst for this calamity and turned my attention back to the new dossier.

First-class rail tickets and a hotel reservation fell on the floor. I was about to pick them up when the door unlocked. Madeleine cast a claire-obscure silhouette in the doorway.

'The coast is clear,' she said.

'It's time to talk.'

She led me to the living room without saying a word and gestured for me to sit down. I remained standing. On television, the French President was addressing the nation. He looked more anxious than in his previous interview when he'd stood accused of fathering a minister's child.

'*Français, Françaises!* I declare that my government will restore law and order. The filth responsible for this unrest… ungrateful children of immigration… will be washed from the streets into the gutters!'

A socialist President was using rhetoric that hardcore nationalists avoided under normal circumstances. I roamed around the living room looking for the remote control. I couldn't find it, so I turned off the power.

'They're listening to us, huh?'

'Did you get my note? You did, didn't you? That's why you are sitting here, I was looking out for you.'

'It was a setup. Like in Brighton, like during the Lutetia training. Like now…'

'I'm on your side.'

'Uh-huh.'

'You've been used, Ellis, but…'

'I've been *screwed*.'

'I can help you.'

Madeleine's eyes were wide open and sincere. It felt uncool being rude to her. I sighed. The moment had passed.

Staring at the girl whose long flowing hair now lay in my lap and whose body said it wanted me as much as I wanted her, I faced the fact that I was a fool or an incurable optimist. She led me back to my room and I didn't protest. What did they expect me to do? It was too late for scheming – there could be no resisting.

She parted her lips as if to say something but didn't. I felt her warm sultry breath on the back of my neck. A moment later our bodies were interlocked. We embraced passionately – like lovers who have been apart for too long. She steadied my shaky hands as I pulled down her dress, and I sucked on her breasts like an infant in its mother's bosom.

I felt relief as I entered her, but also shame at losing control. I tried to hold off coming for as long as possible. One, two, three… Three dead men. A robotic killer had become an automatic lover.

I lay on my back with a heavy expression on my face.

TWENTY-EIGHT

'WE'RE OFF TO CANNES!'

'Uh?'

Madeleine got up around eight to make breakfast. I could have sworn I had been awake all night, mulling over my quandaries, but the clock said otherwise – I was sound asleep at 9 a.m. when she brought me scrambled eggs, bacon and coffee in bed.

She was wearing one of her silk nighties. As she bent over the bed with the tray, a nipple slid out from her top. I pulled her towards me, turned on by her firm breasts and the smell of unwashed sex from the night before. We made love missionary style, with Madeleine moaning sweetly as we came.

Afterwards, I played with her pear-shaped breasts – perfect apart from the cross-shaped mole on the right breast. I drifted off and she sat up, covered herself in a bedsheet and tucked into the breakfast she had brought me, dangling bacon under my nose.

'*C'est bon!*'

We met again in the living room at ten to get to work on the new assignment. I arrived showered and relaxed. Part of me was glad to have something to put my mind to. A routine implied the semblance of normality.

'Our task is to write a marketing pitch for a feature film produced by ESIS.'

'It's a joke, right?'

It wasn't a joke. *Birth of a Continent* was an epic history of Europe and anthology film made up of segments directed by twenty-eight directors, each from a different European country. Some big names caught my eye – veteran directors with long careers. The film would be premiered at the Cannes film festival, where it was officially in competition.

A media event to launch the film was planned in Paris in one week's time, but no one had put together a press kit. That was the official line, at least.

'The imbeciles,' she said. 'Still, I know you have expertise in this sort of debacle.'

She smiled ironically. I didn't like this nod to our prior work – it spoiled my fantasy that we were starting from scratch.

If it all went well, Madeleine and I would go to Cannes to promote the film. Hotel reservations at the Majestic Hotel had already been made for the ten days of the festival.

'You might even enjoy it.'

She was talking about the festival, not the film. I couldn't imagine why ESIS had produced a movie. I went to lectures at university on propaganda films like Sergei Eisenstein's *Battleship Potemkin* and Leni Riefenstahl's *Triumph of the Will*. State-sponsored films were often artful anomalies but rarely box office hits.

We spread out the contents of the pack. There was a hard drive with the film's script, behind-the-scenes photos and all kinds of technical details, shooting schedules and so forth. The film had been made into a Blu-ray disc marked 'classified' and stamped with the ESIS logo.

Almost everything in the materials defied belief. The

twenty-eight segments were meant to have been capped at five minutes, but as the film ran to a phenomenal three and a half hours it was clear that directors had exceeded their quota. The length would be a major obstacle in getting people to watch it.

The film's musical score was on a separate CD. The sleeve promised a 'rousing rendition' of Beethoven's ninth symphony. This was followed by Debussy's *Ode à la France*, the overture to Mozart's *Le Nozze di Figaro* and Vivaldi's *Four Seasons*. The pieces were all performed by famous European orchestras.

I slugged through the script, thankful that it ran to a mere eighty pages. Birth of a Continent was the story of Europe, circa AD 500 to the present day. It was ludicrous from start to finish. The screenplay was authored by 'E.U.', which I took to be a joke. If it was the work of a single writer, he was a madman.

The plot was divided into three parts. Act I took place in the middle ages. The scenes read like a 'horrible histories' of early modern Europe – the barbarians against the Romans, the pillaging Norse men, the Huns and Saxons, the Vandals, Angles and Celts. The Islamic Moors were cast as Europe's most dangerous foe.

Act II was about the unifiers, heroes and visionaries who restored order to the chaos and starved off evil. The 'great men and women' were an eclectic bunch – Boadicea, Charlemagne, Hannibal, Christopher Columbus, William the Conqueror, Joan of Arc, Leonardo da Vinci, Shakespeare and Napoleon. Scant attention was paid to chronology or historical accuracy.

Act III was a 'vertiginous kaleidoscope of twentieth-century imagery showing the horrors and high points of this tumultuous era.' The grand finale depicted the founding of the European Union – its 'awe-inspiring accomplishments' and its 'destiny-fulfilling duty to prepare Europe for its finest hour, the European millennium.'

A wacky subplot told the apocryphal story of Jesus' visit to the British Isles. A Galilean fishing vessel carrying the Lord and a few chosen disciples steered itself towards England. On arrival, they were greeted by flocks of peasants from the cliffs of Dover to the Cornish Coves, and Jesus preached to thousands in an amphitheatre in Londinium.

'Go forth, conquer and unite in my name. Build cathedrals and bridges, rid the world of evil and spread the good word. Unite as one people, and you will bring glory to me and to yourselves.'

Elgar's *Jerusalem* played throughout. The film ended in a 'dizzying montage of modern Europe's most celebrated monuments and landmarks' – the Eiffel Tower and Arc de Triomphe, Mont Saint-Michel, the Leaning Tower of Pisa, the Trevi Fountain, the Coliseum, the Parthenon, the Sagrada Família, the Brandenburg Gate, Stonehenge, Big Ben and the Tower of London.

I tried to envisage it with my eyes closed. All I could see was a TV schedule filler for students and stoners. After hours of sifting through the materials and making wry comments, we decided to watch it. Beethoven's ninth boomed from the speakers, accompanied by Victor Hugo's 'Opening Speech of the Peace Congress of 1849.'

'A day will come when you, France – you Russia – you Italy – you England – you, Germany – all of you, nations of the Continent, will, without losing your distinctive qualities and your glorious individuality, be blended into a superior unity, and constitute a European fraternity…'

We watched the epic unfold before our eyes. It was as compelling as it was absurd. For three and a half hours, we didn't hear or see anything other than the sounds and images of *Birth of a Continent*. Even the police sirens and ambulances outside faded into the background as we were shocked and cajoled by this work of historical fantasy and political propaganda.

'What… the hell.'

'Uh-uh. Mhm.'

Madeleine was the first to get a handle on it. For a collaborative work with sequences from twenty-eight directors each known for his or her unique style, it was strange that the transitions were seamless. More than half the film was CGI – so done in a computer lab. So, was this film really made by the people in the billing?

We started talking about the historical inaccuracies and made a list of twenty facts to check. If our doubts were confirmed, we would have to explain why it played fast and loose with the truth.

The first job was to craft a summary of the film. Our draft was as stilted as our discussion. How could we condense this sprawling mess into something coherent? After a great deal of labouring, we conjured up as factual a retelling as possible, omitting the Jesus subplot.

The next task was to write a logline – a single sentence that conveyed the essence of the film. We settled on 'an epic journey through the ages full of discovery and surprise, by Europeans for Europeans – a film about who we are and who we used to be.' We weren't satisfied, but then we were utterly unconvinced by the film.

We were at a complete loss for the poster's tagline too. We

tried an old copy-writing technique of writing a letter to a friend to sell a product. It was 'a romp through history' – too sexy – 'a cinematic odyssey' – too much like 'oddity' – 'unadulterated genius' – too enthusiastic – and 'an original work of art' – too sceptical.

I couldn't work any longer. I hadn't been outside for two days, and I felt an urgent need to leave the confines of the flat.

'Can we go over to the Champs de Mars? I need air,' I pleaded.

'Patience, *mon amour*.'

She lowered the blinds, took off her top and lay on my lap. Breaks meant sex, it seemed. As we lay side by side post-coitus, I thought that despite recent traumas, it was nice spending time with Madeleine. It was not just a silver lining to a bad situation. If this bond was true, we could yet find our way out of here together.

We worked some more and called it a day around eight. There was still only a hint of dusk on the horizon. Madeleine led me by the hand onto the balcony and brought wine and cheese. In the far distance, I made out sirens and screams. I inhaled sharply – the air was heavy and laden with the whiff of sulphur. Something was amiss.

Madeleine said a volcano had erupted in the Arctic Circle, spewing ash across Europe. I wondered if it was an omen for some future tragedy.

TWENTY-NINE

IT WAS A HUGE RELIEF to be on the street after a week holed up inside. I filled my lungs with air and enveloped myself in spring sunshine.

I was in a better place than a week ago, mentally. The television had stayed unplugged and without the internet, I was more or less oblivious to the world's woes. I ate and slept well. We got up after ten, had breakfast and worked until we had an appetite for lunch and the energy for sex.

In the afternoon I read short stories by Balzac, Flaubert and Maupassant and excerpts from Sartre's essays. Towards evening I felt a twinge of guilt about being so inactive. I poured myself an aperitif, ate some nuts and cooked dinner with Madeleine. This made me feel better.

It was impossible, of course, to entirely escape the outside world. The sirens were audible even when the balcony doors were shut. I turned on an old radio in the kitchen and tuned into *France Info*. The presenters spoke too quickly for me to understand, but I gathered the situation was grim.

Madeleine appeared at the door.

'Looking for music?'

'Sure.'

I turned the dial and Jacques Brel's 'Madeleine' began to play. *'Ce soir j'attends Madeleine, j'ai apporté du lilas, Madeleine elle aime bien ça.*'

We danced a Viennese waltz around the flat, getting faster as the song's rhythm accelerated.

'*Madeleine, c'est mon horizon, c'est mon Amérique à moi... elle est toute ma vie, Madeleine que j'attends là...*'

We fell onto the sofa at the end and kissed.

I had acute cabin fever on the sixth day of confinement. Our work was nearly done, and I feared this temporary reprieve from reality was over. Madeleine reassured me that everything would be fine and that after the launch party for *Birth of a Continent*, we could take a stroll along the Parisian quays and cobbled streets.

I smiled. I had resolved not to give away my plan under any circumstances – the unexpected must truly be unexpected. I had only learned the night before that the film's launch event would be at the British Embassy. This didn't make things easier, but it didn't change things majorly. I would just have to be even more cautious.

We hardly encountered a soul as we made the brisk walk to Passy metro station, which was oddly deserted for morning rush hour. The train carriage was also empty. We finally met other commuters at Charles de Gaulle–Étoile metro station, but as we made our way to the RER fast train, it was announced that the service was down due to an 'incident' at Châtelet.

The station turned into Hades as hundreds of suits tussled and tugged for a place on the trains that were running. We eventually made it to metro line one. The *20 minutes* free newspaper was shoved in my face by a young guy. I didn't dare look at it until we got to the next station.

Madeleine, who had been on edge since we set out, now

looked pale. I worried that she was suffering from having been cooped inside. It was my turn to comfort her – she'd helped me a lot. As I lifted the newspaper to my face, she tried to turn her back to me but was wedged in by four commuters and the door. She coughed and gazed at the floor, avoiding eye contact.

I opened the paper in the middle. The day before, fourteen civilians and twenty riot policemen had lost their lives in what had been the bloodiest suburban conflict since the Algerian war. Hundreds of others were injured. Most of the victims were innocent bystanders with no direct role in *la crise*.

It was already a few days since *Libération* had revealed that the National Front had framed the three innocent youths. The story was met with scepticism at first, but it had gained traction and caused a meteoric storm. A judge had issued an arrest warrant for the party's leadership and their politicians had been ejected from parliament.

The reaction on the street was even more violent. An angry mob stormed and trashed a police station in Saint Denis. In the evening, thousands of cars were torched. A teen found with National Front pamphlets was locked inside a van and burned alive. A racist old man was thrown from the top of a five-storey car park, causing a traffic accident.

Libération had since published new evidence that pointed to a police cover-up. Journalists were now openly speculating that the killer on the train was an undercover agent. No one considered it necessary to withdraw accusations against the National Front, but the focus of France's fury had shifted to its security services.

I turned to the front page. The headline read: 'Qui êtes vous?' The accompanying picture was from CCTV footage, grainy, dark and blurry. It was taken inside a train and showed a light-haired male next to three lifeless bodies. The grainy image had not been kind to my features.

'That's me,' I said.

I turned back to my photo. It was a massive shock to see my face in print. As we exited the carriage I caught sight of *Le Figaro*, which carried the same picture. My legs gave way and I fell onto the floor, buffeted and trampled on by the hordes.

I had been led to my execution like a lamb to the slaughter and was about to be delivered to a lynch mob. I felt a surge of anger against Madeleine. She knew my face was all over the paper, that venturing outside was dangerous. Why else would she bring me here? She wanted me gone.

A squeeze of my right arm. Madeleine had fought the crowds to find me. Her grip said 'don't jump to conclusions' and 'I am here with you, it's going to be okay.' I got up and followed her. But as we exited the metro station, I was again seized with the condemned man's fear – of open spaces, crowds and the police, who were out in force on the Rue de Rivoli.

Getting safely off the street was a priority. We walked down the Rue du Faubourg Saint-Honoré towards the Embassy. Madeleine assured me I couldn't be recognised from the photo. You are a media executive in a smart outfit. No one knows the culprit is not French.

'Who leaked the photo?'

'Not us. I swear.'

By 'us' she meant ESIS. I must not forget that she was with *them*, after all.

I stopped every five steps to fight off nausea, to take stock of my surroundings and to make sure that we weren't being followed. I was certain everyone was looking at me and that at least one policeman eyed me with suspicion. It took ten minutes to walk five hundred metres.

At the Embassy I was screened and security cleared. The atmosphere was tense inside. We were led into the courtyard and directed to the Grand Entrance Foyer, where we were met by *Canal Plus* employees and Sir John Pembleton, Minister for the Department of UK Culture, Media and Sport (DCMS).

They all knew Madeleine and ignored me. We were escorted through the luminous Glazed Gallery where Damien Hirst's *The Physical Impossibility of Death in the Mind of Someone Living* was the room's central exhibit. 'New acquisition by GAC – Government Art Collection,' said Sir Pembleton. It looked out of place, sitting on an antique French carpet and below an ornate chandelier.

The Media Tent was in the embassy's garden, where fifty or so journalists were milling around, eating Embassy croissants. I reflected that this was as far removed from *la crise* as was possible. Madeleine and I were told to sit on the media panel, next to Sir Pembleton and the TV people, and to wait for the keynote speaker.

The culture crowd were probably the least political people in France – they were too self-absorbed to actually read the news and so more or less oblivious to the current turmoil. The irony of being France's most wanted man in plain sight of the French media elite made me want to laugh out loud.

Roper and Mickie were on the front row. So *they* were out in force today. Roper was smiling like a maniac and chatting with a handsome journalist next to him while Michael was shooting the man filthy looks. Oh boy, trouble was brewing. Not for the first time did I wish I still had the Beretta.

It was time to ready myself to put the plan into action. I surveyed the crowd, looking for someone who fitted the bill. I had a basic mental image of what the person should look like. On first glance, I saw no one. I worried that I hadn't thought the plan through well enough, but it was too late for getting cold feet.

A few moments later, the guest speaker was ushered through the Grand Entrance by the Ambassador himself. I glimpsed Dr Europa's silvery mane from above the heads.

The reporters broke off their phone calls as Sir Pembleton started speaking.

'Ladies and Gentleman, Mes*sieurs, Mesdames, bienvenue à l'Ambassade Britannique pour ce film extraordinaire…*'

His accent was excruciating.

'*Ici pour vous parler du film…*'

I looked up and down the aisles with urgency. I still hadn't found anyone who fitted the bill and was fast running out of time. There were only a handful of empty seats – I would have to take a chance. I braced myself for action, adrenaline surging through my veins.

I stood up. Sir Pembleton glared at me and lost his place. There was a murmur in the crowd. Madeleine's hand shot out from under the table. Somebody took a photo. Roper's jaw dropped and Mickie mouthed 'you're dead' and shot me with an imaginary gun.

I lingered for ten seconds, as if I was going to interrupt Dr Europa's talk, then deliberately walked away from the panel and took a seat on the back row between two reporters. There was nothing they could do to stop me without causing a scandal.

I'd bought myself at least a few minutes.

Sir Pembleton resumed his talk. To my left was an attractive middle-aged lady engrossed in her phone. To my right was a bespectacled man in his late thirties. He was conspicuous by his red trousers and unkempt hair. His press badge said *Libération*.

'Ellis?'

The person wasn't meant to know who I was. I turned to face my accuser. He took off his glasses and my heart sank to the floor.

THIRTY

'ELLIS? WHAT THE 'ELL...'

'Luc? It's you?'

It clicked straight away. Luc Bertrand was a doctoral student while I was in my final year at Oxford. We belonged to a club called 'Eternal Scholars' – a rare group of freethinkers who enjoyed philosophy and spent inebriated soirées debating Nietzsche and Foucault. It was a welcome change from the toffs.

Luc stood out as being different at Oxford, not just because he was French. He was a genuine outsider who despised politics and was against all bourgeois institutions and government in general. He had a bad relationship with his father, who was a high-ranking civil servant.

I only had fond memories of Luc, he was one of the best. For a time, I counted him as a close friend. He could have no connection with them.

'Are you alright?' he asked.

Madeleine was introducing Dr Europa as 'a world-renowned cultural historian and enthusiastic cinephile' (I heard 'paedophile') who had come to 'shed scholarly light on the singularity of this fantastical enterprise.'

I was no doubt drawn to Luc because he was a familiar face. But his sudden appearance was odd and threw me off guard. I had been dealt a curveball and needed time to figure things out.

'I'm surprised to see you!'

It hit me in waves. Luc's surname was Bertrand. I had seen the name L. Bertrand recently – in print. The *Libération* articles fed to me in captivity. This was no coincidence. Luc had authored the article that broke the story about the attack on the train. He had also written the article revealing that the Arab youths were not radicalised and that exposed the National Front's malicious plan.

What's more, his father wasn't any old civil servant, but an officer in *Les Renseignements Généraux* – the French secret service. He had to be working for ESIS. For all I knew, he could be high up in the hierarchy – maybe at the very top. Shit. That was not good – not good at all.

A million thoughts raced through my mind as I tried to process this latest twist. Could ESIS have used his name without his permission? Could it be a coincidence? No. Luc was an ESIS insider. I had *once again* walked into a trap and my plans had been thrown into disarray. I had to abort.

Yet I hesitated. If they had drafted him against his will, as they had done with me, then we were in the same boat. Luc was a journalist at one of France's most respected newspapers. Even if his hands were tied by the ESIS-Lutetia mafia, he must have access to resources and people who could help.

Madeleine was eyeing me furiously from the panel. Roper was frantically looking in all directions and Mickie got up to leave. I could delay no more.

'Luc. Give me your card.'

'*Quoi?*'

'Listen carefully to what I have to say. I'm in trouble. You might be the only one who can help me, no joke. Take this, examine it thoroughly.'

I thrust the scrap of paper into Luc's hand containing my notes and a letter scrawled in pencil.

'Camus?'

'Take a photo with your phone then destroy. I'll be in touch.'

It was always going to sound absurd, but this was the least of my worries. If ESIS owned him, I had given them an excuse to get rid of me once and for all. I could only hope that he sensed my urgency and that against all the odds, he was not tainted goods.

I got up without waiting for a reply, lingering in the Glazed Gallery to listen to part of Europa's lecture. He was talking about how European directors, from Bergman to Buñuel, Renoir to Rossellini had tried and failed to make *Birth of a Continent*. It was fascinating gibberish, as ever.

I circled Hirst's shark in the impressive three-cubed tank. I understood something about it now. The shark wasn't a reflection on human mortality, in spite of its pretentious title. It was the embodiment of an empty and wicked soul. How suitable that the British Government had brought it here.

Europa's talk had reached its end and the journalists began flocking to the media tent to pick up the press pack. Madeleine was busy in conversation with reporters. Yes, it was a revolutionary work of cinema. Yes, it would win the *Palme d'Or*. In spite of everything, I wanted to be by her side.

It was high time I left. I searched for the exit down an imperial corridor, taking a wrong turn and finding myself in the Throne Room. No tacky modern art here – only a giant portrait of King James II. His arrogant stare reminded me of father. A few more wrong turns and I exited onto the Faubourg Saint-Honoré.

I was surprised security did not stop me, as they were surely monitoring me. I pulled out the Samsung from my pocket. Why not throw the damn thing away? I walked across the Place de la Concorde, towards the bridge. I wanted a soundtrack for my walk and opened the phone's Radio App.

'Take the Long Way Home' crackled out of the speaker.

'So you think you're a Romeo, playing a part in a picture show.'

I cursed my bad luck. Luc's father was in the French Secret Service. Luc had authored the articles planted by ESIS. These facts spoke for themselves. I was deeply angry at my old friend for having abandoned his principles – I'd been sure that if anyone would see out his days as an *incorruptible*, it would be Luc.

I walked along the Quay d'Orsay towards the Esplanade des Invalides.

'Lonely days turn to lonely nights, you take a trip to the city lights.'

Luc was a good person, but they had got to him just as they had got to me. I tried to imagine the horrors ESIS had inflicted on him.

'You never see what you want to see, forever playing to the gallery.'

How could they have been sure I would leave the panel and sit next to Luc, of all people? This was truly baffling.

I turned left towards the Esplanade des Invalides. It was as hot and humid as a summer day and I longed for the grey and drizzle.

'I was a fool to cry and I knew it.'

I was alone. I could walk into any consulate or newspaper, tell my story and ask for protection. Someone would listen – I had nothing to lose. This was probably my last chance.

'Does it feel that your life's become a catastrophe, oh it has to be.'

I headed down the Rue St. Dominique towards Les Champs de Mars and the Eiffel Tower. I was upset, but it wasn't Luc's doing. It was over her, of course.

She had told me time and time again that she was on my side. So why did I still not believe her? I pictured her in my mind's eye and saw Milady bewitching the Duke of Buckingham on the orders of Richelieu. She was hiding something from me – something of major importance.

I was in love with her.

I sat on a bench in the Champs du Mars, my face clasped in my hands. School children skipped by, paying no attention to the desperado. They saw it all the time. There was a dark enigma surrounding Madeleine that I had to fathom. I headed back to the apartment to try to figure it out.

THIRTY-ONE

'Where were you? I was worried.'

'Nowhere.'

'I waited for you. I'm glad you're back.'

The tension went away as soon as we were alone. She was sorry about the 'sheety' (her French accent was stronger when she was upset) press conference, but she would make it up to me. We would spend more time together, just me and her. We were going to Cannes in only three days.

We let our bodies do the rest of the talking. We made love – in between, reading poetry, sipping wine and eating foie gras. Some days ago, I had casually told Madeleine that body hair was a turn-on. She stopped shaving that day and was already sporting a lush growth of bush that glistened in the shower and left a sexy damp spot on her silk nightie.

Our bodies carried on their communion into the next day. We had a lie-in until eleven-thirty before enjoying brunch on the balcony. The warm weather showed no sign of abating and we basked in crisp sunshine. Madeleine mentioned that she had a Citroën on loan for the weekend. We didn't even talk about where to go until we were in the car.

On a whim, we went to Versailles and spent a leisurely hour walking hand-in-hand around its picturesque centre. In a boutique, we tried on some overpriced hats and handbags. I picked out a blue and yellow silk scarf.

'It's perfect – the EU colours.'

'And of Sweden and Ukraine!'

'I'm buying it. Give me your card.'

'Huh, *quelle galanterie!*'

Afterwards, I suggested we go to the Château Petit Trianon at the edge of Versailles' gardens. It was used by Marie Antoinette to entertain her lovers and nowadays had a terrace wine bar to die for. Madeleine was suitably impressed. We spent an afternoon drinking Sancerre and frolicking in the gardens.

We got home late that night, drunk and happy. She made coffee and served madeleine cakes.

'I get to taste what you're made of!'

'Ah-huh. I'm the best French sweet.'

We took a long shower together and snuggled up in bed. It had been a beautiful couple of days. But lying next to her, I understood things had changed. The trust we had built had taken a knock, it was dishonest to pretend otherwise.

When I was sure she was sound asleep, I picked up the iPhone by her bedside table and went to the toilet. She didn't stir. I had seen her enter the pin a few times that day but there was still a risk I had got it wrong and the phone would lock. I typed '#1981' – it didn't work. I tried '#1984.' I was in.

I did what I needed to do, then opened her private emails. I'll admit it, it felt wrong – but I couldn't stop myself. There was one unopened message in her inbox with no subject heading. It read:

Transfer tomorrow.

J.

There was a photo of Madeleine next to the sender's email

address, js@esis.org. That was odd. But there was no time to probe further – I could hear Madeleine stirring. I marked the email as 'unread,' put the phone back on the table and climbed into bed.

'Merde! Merde, merde, merde!'

'I told you to set the alarm!'

'Hurry!'

It was 9.15 a.m. The train left at 10.14 a.m. from the Gare du Lyon – twenty minutes away by taxi. I began to pack while Madeleine showered.

I folded the tailored tuxedos that had appeared in my closet as tidily as possible into a suitcase. Madeleine was taking her time in the shower. She finally came out, naked except for a towel wrapped around her waist – she breezed past me seductively, touting for a kiss. I obliged and she flung her arms around me, letting the towel slip to the ground.

I wanted her, but I also wanted to get that train.

'The taxi comes in ten minutes,' I said, pushing her back.

'Why the rush? Let's take the next one,' she groaned.

I pulled out her suitcase and started taking random items from her wardrobe – panties and blouses, until she understood that I meant business. After ten minutes of frantic packing, I hauled our bags onto the street and into the waiting taxi.

She still hadn't come down two minutes later, so I dashed back up to the apartment. She was in the bathroom doing her makeup. I dragged her into the lift, not giving her time to put on her shoes. Halfway down the stairs, she said she'd forgotten the train tickets.

The taxi left at 9.55 a.m. Five minutes later we hit a traffic jam at the Quai des Tuileries forcing the driver to take a detour to Opéra, where we hit more traffic. She stared out the window in silence.

'*Merde!*' I said loudly.

At 10.13 a.m., I was carting a furious Madeleine and two suitcases across the station floor. I didn't like being so physical with her, but what choice did I have? We were ten feet away when the door-closing signal sounded. I ran towards the train and prised the doors open with the heaviest case.

She sauntered towards me – it was as if she was *trying* to miss the train. The doors slammed shut, catching the scarf I'd brought her in Versailles. I tugged at it and it tore in half.

'It's bad luck to miss a train,' I said lamely.

Madeleine shot me a murderous look. She was a mess – her hair was ruffled, makeup smudged and dress crumpled. There were tears in her eyes. She was not wearing a bra and she looked unsteady on her feet, like she had been at a rave all night.

We made our way to our seats in first class, Madeleine cursing all the way. She knocked into an old lady without apologising and kicked a bag out of her way. Our carriage was practically empty, and she chose to sit across the aisle and turned her head away from me. I put our cases in the racks and let her be.

I took a snapshot with my phone and showed it to her. The frown softened and folded into a smile. Then she gave a little laugh.

'Who says it's bad luck to miss a train?'

'I made that up.'

'Dumbass!' she said, poking me.

Madeleine's eyes lit up – there was a kind of wild excitement in her gaze. She led me by the hand to the toilet, locked the door and plastered me with kisses. I was startled by the change in mood. She lifted up her skirt and we made love. I came as the train cleared the Parisian suburbs. A ray of sunshine lit up her face, and she looked tender and nubile.

We stumbled back to the carriage, breathless and light-headed, and she fell asleep with her head against my chest. I laid my head against hers and stroked her hair. The road ahead was not clear – our path would be rocky. But I had never known anyone like her. *Madeleine, mon Amérique à moi*. She was the one for me. This was true love.

I got up in search of the buffet car and was surprised to see Luc drinking coffee, even though I'd asked him to be there.

'Hello old friend.'

I had sent a message to Luc from Madeleine's phone that night. It was risky, but I had to be sure he had read the materials and to give him instructions for our next meeting. I made it clear that it was imperative that he took this seriously and that he was not to reply. I deleted the chat and emptied the phone's cache.

'I have some information for you,' he said, gesturing for me to sit down.

'Your story checks out, at least the bits I've looked into. Europa is an interesting guy. Real name Eugene De Villiers – father French, mother English, he comes from old money. He was destined to be part of the establishment, but he developed psychotic tendencies as a child. He tried to murder his father, aged nine.

'He was sent overseas, in aristocratic tradition, to the best boarding schools in Britain – Fettes and Harrow. But he was never far from trouble – his teachers said he was as dangerous as he was brilliant. Mad, bad and dangerous to know, etc. He read History at Cambridge but was sent down for a racist attack on a Black professor.

'In the early 1980s, he got into bed with extreme English nationalism before joining an underground network of intellectual fascists. The police infiltrated the group and he was busted for a plot to kill the Labour Leadership. He did time in maximum security prisons – then went off the radar.

'What the hell he was doing as a guest speaker at the British Embassy is anyone's guess.'

This was the first time I had proof from an outsider that ESIS was rotten. It should have felt like a triumph.

'This story could be promising,' said Luc drily. 'But I doubt *Libé* would run it. We don't just print what we like – these days stories come from our paymasters rather than from editors.'

'Is that so?'

My doubts about Luc resurfaced. I studied his face, but it didn't give anything away. Our history of friendship and his offhand, matter-of-fact delivery had made me forget that his integrity had almost certainly been bought and that he was a plant and an informer. I almost asked him outright how they had got to him.

'What about the others? Roper, Michael O'Reilly, the Lutetia training camp... my story? My role in...'

I couldn't bring myself to say it.

'In the Argenteuil... business?'

There were a thousand other things I wanted to ask, but I left off there for fear of sounding like a madman. Even if he was on the ESIS payroll, he was still a valuable – and my only – source of information.

'I need more time, *mon ami*. A lot is going down in

intelligence circles right now. Rumours abound of plots in every European country, similar to what is happening in France…'

'Tell me more.'

'I can't do that yet. Let's meet in a few days.'

He told me that he had scanned my notes, encrypted the file and shredded the paper. We discussed places in Cannes to meet.

'Just one thing. Did you think it odd I asked you to meet me on this train?'

'*Pas du tout*. I was already booked on it. I'm covering the festival.'

I've never believed in coincidences. I made my way back to a sleeping Madeleine.

THIRTY-TWO

'I WANT TO SLEEP MORE.'

'Then sleep, *bébé*.'

'You'll be here when I wake up?'

'Of course.'

She spoke in a little girl's voice and her eyes were bloodshot. I wondered if she was ill and touched her forehead – warm, but not feverish. An hour later I tapped her gently on the shoulder and asked her if she would like to eat.

'I love you,' she replied.

She wasn't acting like herself.

'Don't go,' she pleaded.

'I'll be right back.'

She tried to grab my leg, but I was already standing. A voice told me not to leave, that something was wrong.

'I'll be right back,' I repeated to myself.

The train entered a long, dark tunnel and swayed from side to side. Screeching sounds filled the darkness and I had a strong sense of trouble ahead.

I came back and she wasn't there. I was immediately worried. I went to the toilets at either end of our carriage and called her name, but there was no reply. Was she too sick to answer? A darker thought occurred to me. Had she too gone to see Luc? I paced up and down the carriages but didn't see either of them.

A quarter of an hour later I was anxious – we would soon be in Cannes. I asked some passengers if they'd seen her leave. They hadn't.

There was still no sign of her by the time the train pulled into Cannes. I went to pick up the bags and noticed that hers was missing. This was most odd. I got off the train, not knowing what else to do.

I was blinded by the fierce Provencal sun. She was standing there as if we had been together all along.

'Bloody hell! I lost you…'

'Follow me and take the bags.'

I was relieved she was okay. Madeleine led the way without saying a word and I trailed at a distance, admiring her classy gait.

At the taxi rank, she made small talk with the driver while I loaded the bags into the back. They carried on talking – gossip about celebrities and hot events in town this year – as we sped down the chic Rue d'Antibes, turned onto the Croisette and pulled up at the Majestic Barrière Hotel.

Paparazzi snapped us as we got out of the taxi. Madeleine didn't flinch as she strode towards into the lobby, cameras tracking her every movement. I looked at them in annoyance. Did they know who we were, or did they simply take pictures of everyone coming into the hotel?

A porter took our luggage while Madeleine checked in at the reception desk. *Oui*, she had a reservation for the two-bedroom penthouse. *Oui*, we would like to use the club lounge and executive rooms during the festival.

'Two bedrooms?' I asked in the lift.

She ignored me, continuing to check messages on her phone.

I noticed she had been rude to the receptionist and hadn't said a single word to me since our arrival in Cannes.

Suite 701 had a spacious master bedroom and luxurious second bedroom, both with emperor beds, and a breezy living room that led onto a balcony. The décor was white and airy, and a red armchair and sofa lent a touch of kitsch. A Piet Mondrian hung on the wall. The view from the seventh floor – palms, pools and sea – was suitably majestic.

It was certainly big enough for us not to be in the same room at the same time, which is what she wanted. She had shut the door to the second bedroom and was talking on the phone. Were we not sharing a room? I was feeling piqued by this point. It seemed Cannes had brought out her inner diva.

By far the most exciting feature of the suite was the fully stocked cocktail bar. I set to work on a large Vodka Martini. I took a swig from the shaker – it needed more vermouth. She was probably overwhelmed by the duties awaiting her and I should try to be patient.

She emerged from the bedroom half an hour later.

'Settling in?'

'Admirably. Your drink is ready.'

She had changed into a sexy black dress and had fixed her makeup. She looked ready for the red carpet. She took her place at the bar. I was unsure if she was playing some kind of a game, where I was the barman and she the starlet, like in the movies.

I tried to think of something suave to say while I made another Vodka Martini. She carried on reading messages on her iPhone.

'Don't you hate that?' I said at last.

'Hate what?' she mumbled.

'Uncomfortable silences. Isn't that when you've found somebody really special? When you can just shut the f…'

She wasn't listening. In the alcoholic haze induced by two cocktails, her behaviour had become extremely irritating. If this was a game, I wasn't enjoying it.

I poured myself another Martini. Ten minutes went by before she put down her phone. Her eyes met with mine and gave the impression that she was about to start a fight.

'You have trust issues,' she said flatly.

'Why should I trust you?'

'I've told you a thousand times, I'm on your side. Do as I do, stick with me, partner, you'll be good. We'll expose these sons of bitches for what they are.'

We'd had this conversation countless times before. It was what I wanted to hear and what she was supposed to say. But this time she said it in such a way, with so many Americanisms, that I didn't believe a word.

I stared at her from across the bar.

'Madeleine – what the hell's got into you?'

No response.

'Fine – I'm out of here. There are a thousand journalists in this town – one will do.'

I walked over to her and laid my hand on her phone. She grabbed it back forcefully.

'I thought you already took what you needed? A few nights ago?'

I took stock of this earth-shattering revelation. Acting on impulse, I prised the phone out of her hands, pushing her off the stool.

'Wanna play rough, huh, Ellis?'

Our eyes met – hers furious, mine hurt. I held her at bay while she tried to claw at my wrists and hit me, and when this didn't work, she lunged at me with her teeth. We glared at each other fiercely. The anger suddenly went away and gave way to desire. Our mouths locked, our tongues touched, and we kissed savagely.

She knocked over the cocktail mixer as she jumped on the bar, then lapped up the spilt liquid with wild lashes of her tongue. The spectacle was vulgar and exciting. The animal in me was awoken too. I poured vodka over the bar and joined her in lapping it up – my tongue brushing against hers.

Her dress was soaked and her eyes were delirious with lust. I tore off her panties and she groaned with pleasure as my fingers touched her clit and reached inside her. I lifted her splayed legs onto my neck and guided my cock between her legs. She thrashed around on the bar, her hands reaching for mine but finding only vodka.

I pulled her up towards me and she slapped me across the face. I responded by lifting her dress over her head and holding it there with one hand until she gagged and choked, then spinning her round and entering her from behind. She was now grunting feverishly, in a state of ecstasy.

We fell onto the floor and she straddled me from on top. Her thrusts were harder than mine. In the raptures of orgasm, she pushed her face against my chest, biting hard and sinking her nails into my thigh. This hurt and I pushed her away with some force. We came together, deliriously.

I stared at the drenched body before me. Her eyes were shut tight and her breathing was steady – the anger had subsided and a degree of peace had returned to her face. Her body had got its satisfaction. I saw a cut on her breast, then remembered about the birthmark under her left nipple.

I pottered about, looking for my clothes. I couldn't say what exactly, but something was irking me. Then I realised – the iPhone was gone. She had taken it back during the tryst. I may just have had the most amazing sex of my life, but once again, the evidence said she was a fraud.

I hurled myself onto the sofa and contemplated this latest episode.

THIRTY-THREE

THE SUN WAS ALREADY RISING, its rays fiercer than in Paris. A Mediterranean breeze entered the suite from the open balcony.

I sensed the day was going to be tough. I couldn't remember exactly how the evening had ended. The door to the other bedroom was shut and the lights were off, so I assumed she was fast asleep. It was upsetting that we hadn't slept in the same bed. I was half-minded to join her but thought better of it.

Traces of our sex bout lay around me – spilt vodka and bite marks on my chest. For a moment it struck me that whatever was going on between us was fixable, then I scolded myself for thinking this. Her behaviour was so absurd and off the wall, I was better off alone. I needed out.

I was hungry and set out in search of a hotel breakfast. The restaurant was almost empty – a couple of film production people and hired hands stocking up for the day. I filled my plate from the buffet but found that I didn't have such a big appetite after all. I stared absent-mindedly into a black coffee.

Why was she so angry? If it was a masquerade to convince our minders that she had me under her thumb, why carry it on into the bedroom? And how the hell did she know about her phone? Was there surveillance absolutely everywhere, or had she been spying on me even then?

A man sitting at a table a few metres away took a picture of me. I stood up briskly.

'That's enough, dammit!'

'Woah, calm bro. Dude can't test a new camera?'

I was about to go back to the suite when a group of revellers stormed into the hall. They had clearly been drinking all night and were loudly hushing each other. A lady bearing a striking resemblance to Madeleine caught my eye.

It was Madeleine. She was earnestly whispering into the ear of a young man in a tuxedo. I walked towards her.

'That him?' the man asked.

'Yeah,' she replied as she picked up a knife and fork.

'Meeting at 10 a.m. in the suite,' she said to me without turning around.

Back in the hotel room, I tried to figure out how Madeleine had managed to go out all night. She returned around nine o'clock, disappeared into the bedroom and came out again at ten, fresh and alert.

'There's a photocall for *Birth of a Continent* this afternoon. You're manning the booth. Do not screw up.'

She flung me an ID card. So the press could know my name? That was sensible.

It was all business from there on. Our mission brief came in a box stacked with bulky folders. All the information required for a 'successful outcome' of our task was contained in these files. She added that I would be tested on the materials later, and she meant it.

As with the other Lutetia operations, I almost admired the audacity and rigour of the planning. The dossiers profiled four members of the Cannes festival jury. Their real names were concealed as a 'security precaution' and they had been given the pseudonyms – 'French Fatty,' 'Holly Hotshot,' 'Silver Stranger' and 'Chica Loca.'

They read like detailed fanpedias with biographies, future projects and relationship gossip. They also had tons of random stuff such as their personal finances trainers, workout regime, and tastes in food, clothes and leisure. There were at least a dozen long-lens photographs of them going about their everyday lives.

A file marked 'highly confidential' said that our job was to approach the jurors on each of the next four evenings, pass them in a sealed envelope and to make sure they opened it. *They had to open it*. It gave the time and place of the 'drop' and the people likely to be with them.

'You get to do celebrity spotting after all,' she said coldly.

Madeleine and I were to approach the jurors in tandem – she would deliver the envelope to the male juror and I would deliver to the women. We were to rehearse before each drop. The jurors would likely be upset by our visit, but we were to avoid causing a scene at all costs.

I asked about the purpose of these envelopes and she told me it was on a need-to-know basis. It was blackmail, of course, but I wanted her to say it. Jurors would be spared personal embarrassment if they made sure *Birth of a Continent* swept the floor at the awards ceremony and won the Palme d'Or.

'Just read the files.'

I was feeling depressed. It was hard to believe the decadence of the night before took place. Our love story too seemed a distant memory. All that drivel about 'being on my side' was utterly untrue. She had always been one of *them*.

I had to leave for the photo event – it so happened it was also time to meet Luc. Madeleine blocked the door.

'It got cancelled.'

'Really?'

'Turn on the T.V.'

BBC World News was running live coverage of a breaking story. The anchor was saying that the last few days had seen the first lull in violence since the riots in Argenteuil. Fewer than a dozen deaths a night – compared to fifty at the height of *la crise*. But a new scandal threatened to reignite the conflict.

Libération had published an explosive article claiming that Jacques was not a National Front member, but a police agent. The source was rumoured to be a high-ranking official in French security services. He had leaked classified documents that were being examined by experts.

There was a close-up of the newspaper article. I thought I glimpsed the initials LB at the bottom of the page, although the print was small. The reporter was about to interview one of the journalists behind the scoop when the bulletin cut to the Hôtel Matignon where the Prime Minister was giving an emergency press conference.

The opposition had already called a vote of no confidence in the government. A commentator said that if the allegations were proven true, the government may not survive. Another argued that it was irresponsible to print the story unless it was cast iron, as it would plunge France back into bloodshed and anarchy.

Libération was holding its own press conference to confirm the source's credibility and to defend their right to print. The editor-in-chief and a panel of intellectuals argued that citizens had a right to know if something was rotten in France, even if it led to mass violence. An angry mob was gathering outside of the Police Headquarters at 36 Quai des Orfèvres.

A round-up of other news was under the banner 'crises in Europe.' In Germany, far-right and anti-fascist groups had clashed following an attack on a synagogue that had killed ten children. In Greece, mass demonstrations led by the MeRA25 movement had caused the government to go into lockdown. In Spain…

'It's good news, things are going our way,' she said, turning off the television.

I asked myself what kind of person found bloodshed good news. I was relieved they didn't show my picture on the news report, but it was still all too much for me to bear. I shuffled around noisily.

I was late for my meeting with Luc and I searched for a good reason to leave.

'We're out of vodka.'

'Call room service.'

'I'll head down to the bar.'

'No drinking until after the drop.'

Madeleine's phone rang. I took my chance and left the room. I had no trouble finding Luc – he was circling a luggage trolley, looking in every direction but mine.

'You came.'

'Hurry, there is a lot we have to discuss.'

THIRTY-FOUR

I HAD NO DOUBT THAT LUC was bent – the facts were clear enough.

Madeleine had also shown herself beyond all doubt to be a double-dealing fraud. But there were limits to what she could have reported back on me. It was highly unlikely she had seen me take her phone in the dark that night. Luc was far more likely to be the culprit. He had, after all, penned the *Libération* articles igniting the conflict.

The news and deterioration in relations with *her* made me on edge. I was inclined to out Luc in public as the traitor who was to blame for the current mayhem. But what was the point? I counted to ten and collected myself. Luc was still my only chance of getting the information I needed so badly.

To hell with being secretive, I thought – our meeting was surely being relayed to an army of snoops. I gave the receptionist our suite number and asked to use a conference room.

'I'm sorry Sir. Only J. Schneider from your suite is registered to use the festival conference rooms.'

'Who, what?'

I wrangled a swipe card, but it didn't work. A hotel cleaner reluctantly let us in. Luc looked shifty under the fluorescent lights.

'I don't know if you are aware?' he began gravely. 'I have

some connections in the intelligence community.'

I could no longer hold back.

'Cut the crap, Luc. Please.'

He looked slighted, but I caught my breath and carried on the offensive.

'Three questions for you, Luc – when, how and why?'

He shifted about in his seat.

'What?'

'Let me help you out. When – a few months ago I was living a normal life. How – I was framed for murder – murder! Then I was blackmailed and pressganged into joining Camp Lutetia. Why? I can't answer that.'

'Ellis, I've been a journalist for *Libé* since Oxford.'

'Oh come on! You're up to your eyes in this, as plain as day…'

'I'm sorry about your problems. I have information that can help you.'

Silence. I didn't understand why Luc was holding out in the face of all the facts. I suspected it was because he was feeding our conversation directly to ESIS.

'For the love of God, let's have it.'

'Let me first tell you a story, *mon ami*.'

I sighed loudly.

'A year ago, Mossad – which keeps tabs on the world's security services – was alerted to a spate of resignations among junior agents in almost every European secret service – the Spanish CNI, the Italian AISI, the German BND, the Belgian SE, etc.

'Just as they were scrambling to understand why so many agents had flown the coop, three high-ranking intelligence bosses from the world's biggest agencies – the CIA, MI5 and DGSI went AWOL. It caused a storm of epic proportions.'

He paused for effect.

'This was the intelligence equivalent of a nuclear meltdown. The US Secretary of State and the British and French Foreign Ministers met over fears that they had defected to God-knows-where – Russia, China or North Korea for all they knew.

'There was palpable relief when they turned up in Paris. Politicians were desperate to bring them in – but the intelligence community urged caution. They wanted to know what the hell was going on before nabbing them.'

'Details, Luc. What is known about these bosses and their role in ESIS?'

'About them, absurdly little. Capitaine, Foxtrot and Eagle are French, British and American. They rose to the top by the usual means – ambition and double-dealing. Each has multiple aliases to hide their real identities. We weren't even sure about their ESIS codenames until we read your notes.'

I asked myself if Luc's use of 'we' was an admission he worked for intelligence? I bit my tongue.

'But we know far more about the people they recruited. Each brought their own into the field, you see.'

'Roper and Mickie?'

'They belong to Eagle. The man you know as Roper was formerly a middle-ranking nobody at the CIA. He was a handler for agents in Ireland at the end of the Troubles – mostly republican volunteers willing to divulge paramilitary secrets at a price.

'That's how he met Michael O'Reilly. His shady dealings came to light after the Good Friday Agreement and he was exiled from the Republic. He was working as a mercenary in Afghanistan when Roper brought him into the ESIS fold.'

'Europa?'

'Eugene de Villiers belongs to Capitaine – it seems they have some family tie. Their families go back a long way, as European aristocrats tend to. De Villiers is a powerful man, who moves in high and low circles. He supplied Lutetia with its army of thugs.'

'What about Bigboy?'

'I have no idea.'

Luc had cleverly steered the conversation away from the ESIS intelligence bosses.

'Tell me what you know about Foxtrot.'

'Honestly not much. Foxtrot began his career as a military man – a colonel, although he spent most of the past two decades in the secret service. He was number four at MI5 when he went missing. Officially, the Brits refuse to believe he has defected and insist that he is being held against his will.'

Luc glanced at his watch.

'You haven't mentioned Little Boots. What do you know about him?'

'He is also from your country, old boy. He's rumoured to be the biggest fish of them all, and also the most elusive. He goes by another alias too – 'the man from Brixton.' He is not from intelligence circles, like Foxtrot, Le Capitaine and Eagle. He is a public figure – and a big one at that.'

The answers were getting closer to home.

'Go on.'

The air conditioning was on full blast, but beads of sweat were dropping on Luc's temple.

'Your information is a godsend to the intelligence community. Thanks to you, we have a direct link to Little Boots.'

'Oh, how so?' I cut in rapidly.

'You belong to Little Boots – you *know* that, right?'

An alarm sounded from inside his jacket pocket.

'*Merde!*' he gasped.

'Tell me about *her*.'

He was about to say something when the lights cut out in
the room.

'I can't do this!' he whispered, rattling the doors.

A suited security agent, who looked just like the cleaner,
appeared at the window and let him out. Luc darted down the
corridor, the agent in pursuit.

I tried to make sense of this. I had either asked a forbidden
question, or Luc had given away more than was allowed and
his ESIS minders had pulled the plug. I had to find him and
hear what he had to say about Madeleine.

There was no sign of him in the lift lobby. He wasn't in the
reception area either. I had a pang of guilt, fearing that I had
put him in mortal danger by being reckless. Then my phone
rang – it was him. Christ! Luc was *never* to call that number.

'The hotel driveway. *Now!*'

Luc cut a pathetic figure at the hotel driveway, cowering
behind a marquee for limousines.

'It's not safe here,' he muttered. 'We're in danger.'

'I know.'

'You want more answers, don't you?'

I saw genuine fear in his eyes. I took a deep breath, grabbed
hold of his shirt with both hands and asked the only question
that mattered to me.

'Who is Madeleine?'

Luc reached over as if he were about to kiss me. Instead, he whispered a coded message into my ear. I repeated it back to him and he nodded. A black BMW pulled over and a voice spoke from behind dark glass.

'*Luc Bertrand, montez s'il vous plaît.*'

It was an order, not a request. Luc got into the car and it drove off.

THIRTY-FIVE

I LOOKED FOR SURVEILLANCE TEAMS in the Majestic lobby. The receptionists, porters and rich kids slouched on the sofas all seemed normal enough.

I was losing my grip. A black car was coming for me too – of this I was sure. I roamed the hotel corridors in search of a drink, eventually stumbling into *Le Bar Galerie*. Newspapermen and film critics were mulling over their schedules.

'Double scotch.'

'*On ze rox?*'

'Neat.'

'*You 'ave ze face of wor-ie young man. Work? A lay-dee?*'

'Lady.'

The face of worry. Yes, that was me. I downed another whisky and gathered my thoughts. Why had I pushed Luc for answers about ESIS and not Madeleine? Was I frightened of the answer? It was odd that the car had picked up Luc and not me. Was the whole episode a stunt to put the frighteners on me? If so, it suggested that they still needed me for their goddamn mission.

Time passed quickly between the second and fourth whiskies.

'Go to Lukotokía, the white place. 45's the number. Once you know where, you'll know when,' Luc had said. Luko-where?

What the hell did that mean? I wrote it down on a coaster to be sure to remember it.

I ordered a fifth whisky and found myself in a heightened state of paranoia. Which of the hacks were undercover agents? They all seemed perfectly normal, with their crumpled shirts and middle-aged spread. All the more reason to be suspicious. What about the barman?

'*Toujours les troubles, mon ami?*'

'She's not who she says she is.'

'*Je sais,*' he replied.

My thoughts went back to Madeleine. Why did I continue to obsess about her? She had shown kindness to me, she had a softer side, fragile even. At times she was good – but darkness lurked inside her soul. She was harbouring a secret that I had yet to fathom.

I must crack the mystery. She was in trouble. I had to help her. She appeared at the door and stormed towards the barman.

'*Tu lui as donné à boire?*'

'You're with them?'

'*Hélas oui et non, mon bonhomme.*'

'How will you do your job tonight?' she screamed.

'I will… save you,' I said drunkenly.

I tripped as she frog-marched me out of the bar. Ten paces later it was clear this wasn't working, so she made a phone call. The agent who had pursued Luc came to assist, shoving and pushing me along. I was in no condition to fight back. Madeleine ordered him to 'deliver me' to the suite and went on ahead.

I was made to sit down and told not to move. The agent told two men on the sofa to 'look after me.' The first was the young man in the tuxedo at the breakfast buffet. He looked leaner and meaner, dressed in a wife beater, silver chain and ripped jeans. The man who had taken a picture of me sat next to him.

'Bring on the goons.'

'Shut it mate!' the thug said in an east London accent.

'Shall we do it?' said the fake cameraman.

A hand wrapped itself around my neck and another muzzled me. I feared they were going to suffocate me or break my neck, but instead pills were forced into the back of my throat and I was forced to swallow. If I was going to die, I hoped the end would come swiftly.

After the deed was done, the hands let off. I stood up to take a swing at my assailants. I missed. The room spun and I tottered. Seconds later I was thrashing around on the floor like a man on fire. The door opened and a pair of heels entered the room.

'How many did you give him? Two? You goddamn idiots!'

I was taken to the bathroom while she made phone calls to a doctor. I could barely see, my throat was burning and was gasping for air. I collapsed onto the floor and passed out.

The next thing I remember is my head being lifted, a belt tied around my arm and a needle being prepared. A potent force surged through my blood and into my brain. I faintly recognised a familiar silvery mane of hair at the door.

'He should be okay for the next five or six hours. Test his cognitive faculties and if he fails, give him the other dose.'

I had a shower and got changed, feeling oddly sober. Madeleine ordered everybody else out, made me drink black coffee and a litre of water and interrogated me about our mission. I did my best to answer her questions.

The new plan was so simple, even a 'screw up' like me could pull it off. We would both go to tonight's party as planned. I would be 'tipsy' but not so out of it that I wouldn't get in. *I would not be refused entry*. Once inside, she would approach the target, codenamed French Fatty, while I stood by at a distance.

She needed a minute. That was sixty seconds, count them. As soon as she had handed him the envelope, I was to move closer, place a firm hand on the target's shoulder and escort her away. She made me act out the scene three times in front of an empty chair before letting me rest.

I didn't understand why she insisted on me being the minder, it was a huge risk.

'Take one of the goons, I don't…'

'Shut it.'

It was my responsibility to show that we meant business. The party was in the Majestic hotel's private club. This was fucking fortunate, she kept saying. I was in deep shit and would pay the price for my actions – but for now, I should focus and not screw up.

I had a bastard of a headache. I could no longer stand being hounded like this – whatever they had in store for me, it couldn't get worse. I vowed to do the job to the best of my ability in the hope that she would leave me alone to sleep.

It was time to go. Halfway down the corridor, my vision clouded over and I was unsteady on my feet again. I hid it as best I could but seconds later had to bury my head in an icebox to be sick. She kicked my calf with her high heel shoe and told me to get a move on. It was malicious.

At the door, our IDs were checked and we were allowed in. That was half the job done. It was pitch-black inside – until a white strobe struck me deep in the retina lighting up a topless blonde waitress with a tray of champagne and a waiter with a six-pack wearing only a G-string.

French Fatty was alone in a private booth cordoned off by a fluorescent VIP ribbon. The name did him justice – he was obese. He was talking into an earpiece and pouring himself champagne from an ice bucket. The strobe light hit me in the eye again, knocking out my vision, this time for longer.

The waitresses were now naked and touching each other on a podium. I was utterly transfixed by the spectacle. Madeleine beckoned me angrily to follow her before striding towards our target. She whispered into his ear, her hair dangling over his face, and I counted to sixty.

Another attack of blindness. She was sitting on his knee like a schoolgirl with her legs wide open so that her panties were lit fluorescent in the club light. French Fatty took the envelope with one hand and appeared to fondle her crotch with the other. The strobe hit me again and the image was burnt onto my retina.

I acted on impulse, marching towards them and yanking Madeleine's hair backwards. She resisted and when I let go, her head sprang onto his lap, knocking the envelope out of his hands and scattering its contents on the floor. French Fatty didn't see me at first and cradled her head as if he was expecting a blow job.

The strobe struck again, shedding light on photos of Fatboy taking part in an orgy with very young children – boys as well as girls. It took a moment for him to react, then he let out a howl of rage, picked up the bottle of champagne and smashed it on the table. Shards of glass flew in every direction.

Another wave of blindness and I came face to face with a wild animal. Madeleine's hair was a mess and her bloodied lips were quivering. Agents came out of the shadows and I was roughed up and taken back to the suite.

I was in a bad way by the time she came in – on the verge of being sick. She stood over me and bombarded me with insults. I had failed and was now going to be punished. A belt was strapped to my right arm and the goons prepared another injection.

'One dose or two, boss?'

'Three!' she ordered.

I slumped down in the chair, no longer in control of my body. A device was strapped to my head.

'Adieu,' she said.

THIRTY-SIX

THERE WAS NO LIGHT BUT there was space.

I took a nervous step forwards, then another, and brushed against a surface. I probed it with my hands – it was firm but flexible. I traced its contours until I found an opening and entered another dark space. I pushed hard against another weak point and this time landed headfirst in the open.

I was at the top of a stone turret with a stairwell inside. I tottered on my feet, tripped on a ledge and came within an inch of falling into the void. It was night. Faint stars shone above and below was an expanse of blackness. I sat on the ground in a yoga position for what seemed like an eternity.

In front of me was a black tent in the style of a camp from the olden days. I went into the turret and down the stairs, which opened onto a lower terrace with a broad ledge and railings on either side. The view to the north was of land and city lights, and beach and ocean to the south. I was on the roof of the Majestic Hotel.

A gush of warm air ran across my face and the clatter of music and people filled the air. I walked in the direction of the noise. It wasn't long before I ran into three young men in tuxedos drinking wine from bottles. The relief at meeting other people was short-lived as they paid me no attention at all.

I trailed a second group heading towards the party. A courtyard was lavishly decked with a marble statue of David, Moët champagne fountain and banquet table. The guests were served by an army of waiters like those in the Majestic – all toned hard bodies, naked from the waist up.

There were hookers too, scores of them, in skirts barely thicker than belts and tops that showed off cosmic cleavages. The revellers were moving in rhythm to a cool beat that oozed sexuality. The dancers were professionals and models, their rolled-back eyes a sure sign they were high.

The owner of the biggest reality television and talent show franchise in Europe was being mobbed by nubile girls. One of them bent over his lap while he signed his name on her buttocks and another pulled up her top while a friend took a group selfie. But this was only a burlesque sideshow in the celebrity carnival of horrors.

At the rear of the terrace, bodyguards were preparing the arrival of A-list stars. People were trying hard not to look or to speculate about whether it was Christian, Hugh, George, Leo, Matt, Cate, Nathalie, Jennifer or Scarlett. Just as it seemed like it was a false alarm, George swept by with a woman who was not his wife.

The Hollywood brat pack formed a circle around the champagne fountain. Ben was talking to his agent. Quentin was dressed in a scruffy T-shirt and jeans and was telling a long anecdote to a young hotshot director who had just signed Alec for an indie. The hotshot waved to George hoping for an exit, but he pretended not to see him.

Joel and Ethan sat back-to-back on a bench and were having their photo taken ironically with two hookers. In the darkest part of the terrace, a revered French film director had his hands all over a girl who was not yet sixteen. A rude boy nearby in ripped jeans and vest had his hands down an older, fat man's pants, while another man took pictures.

The scene made me feel ill and I shifted to another spot, but I couldn't shake the feeling of déjà vu. It were as if everyone had been displaced from real life into a dream. The DJ for instance. He wore a Hawaiian shirt and was leaning over his mixing reel with a glass of champagne in hand.

I saw to my horror that it was Bigboy. He raised his glass in my direction and winked. Next to him were Gaz and Shaz, jumping up and down, blowing me kisses and waving at me like court jesters. I was the only one upset by this sight. No one else paid them any attention, as if they were invisible.

I downed a strong vodka tonic served by one of the impossibly handsome studs and looked for obvious signs that I was tripping but could find none. It was all so very, very real. This began to get distressing. What if I was trapped inside a perpetual illusion and could never come back to reality?

A portly man in a beret strode towards me. From his tweed jacket and bowtie, I recognised him as Capitaine. He looked uncannily like the pimp who had lured me into the brothel in Pigalle.

'Do you remember my face?' he said, saluting me.

The A-list celebrities had gone and the chatter died down, leaving Bigboy's vinyl scratching to fill the air.

The man codenamed Eagle was the next bigwig to come out of hiding. He had been posing as one of the A-list star's security team, looking every bit the part.

'You blew it, Ellis,' he said gruffly. 'You screwed up.'

More ESIS figures emerged from shadowy recesses. Europa strode by, wagging his finger at me.

'I prescribe a little less indulgence, young man.'

It was Roper and Mickie's turn to take to the stage. They were not holding hands but looked every bit an item. Bigboy spun a remix of the YMCA, but the joke fell flat and two security agents, who looked like Scarlet and Black, or Williams and Edwards, cut off the sound.

'We had high hopes for you,' Roper said in his fake British accent. 'I tried to help you, but you let me down, badly.'

They lingered, not ready to give up their moment in the limelight.

'You behaved… quite badly, you know. Bad form, old boy.'

'Yer camin with me, int ya!' Mickie said.

His hand made contact with my shoulder. It felt far too real to be a trip. I acted on impulse, punching him in the stomach and wrestling with him on the terrace. Roper looked on anxiously, worried I'd go after him too. Mickie was strong and got the upper hand, forcing me into a headlock.

The lights around us gradually got brighter and the people less visible. Mickie's grip weakened, then relaxed altogether – a moment later he shrank away, and the others too. The fountain, statute and DJ deck were gone too. I stood in awe of the desolate space and misty vacuum.

A fierce gust of wind blew across my face, making me shut my eyes. I opened them again and found myself back on the turret looking down into the black sea. There seemed to be something going on inside the tent. I heard muffled screams, then a woman emerged from the hidden door.

She wore a latex bodysuit that showed off a winged demon.

'*You giva this to mia?*'

She made the come-hither sign and pointed to an envelope on the floor marked 'Silver Stranger.'

I took a closer look. It was a package for one of the jury members. Dozens of sadomasochistic images spilt onto the ground, of a woman abusing hooded prisoners and goading preteen boys and girls to perform sex acts on dogs. The woman in the pictures was younger than the one before me, but it was her.

I got down on my knees and scrambled to pick them up.

'*You taka these picture?*'

I looked at her in a way that did nothing to calm her rage.

'*Talka to mia, you basta'd!*'

She lashed out violently, kicking and spitting at me. I curled up into a ball to protect myself.

'*I no hear you begga fora mercy.*'

She was panting heavily, her voice raw with emotion. I wished that she would vanish but to no avail.

I felt soft hands on my legs and arms. I had not seen the little women emerge from the tent. They gently rubbed and kissed my bruises, spread my arms and legs and lifted me away from the wild woman and into the tent. My guardian angels had come to rescue me, I had no more cause to worry.

I was lowered onto a bed like an infant taken to his cot. It took a few moments for my eyes to adjust the candlelight. Six hideous freaks – barely female, such were their deformities. I was not in a bed but a large coffin. I struggled to lift myself up, but abnormally strong hands forbade it.

My head was turned to one side. I beheld a beautiful dark-haired woman next to me. She was smiling at me, but her cold eyes said something was not right. I tried to free myself from the hands and pushed backwards violently.

Her head was severed from her body.

My scream was muffled by the slab being lowered over my head. I lay in total darkness as the lid was fastened, not daring to move. The devil women were singing and performing a ritual that spoke of untold horrors and the coffin was lifted as we journeyed to some unknown place.

As it moved from side to side, the corpse's head rolled against me, its lips kissing my neck. I broke out of my torpor, yelling and screaming at the top of my voice. I pounded the lid and threw myself against one side with all my strength. The coffin swayed and fell to the ground.

I kicked at the lid and clambered out like Dracula from the tomb. The devil women scurried away and left me convulsing on the floor.

'Enough,' I pleaded. 'Enough!'

I was in a chamber decorated with gothic candelabras, statues and thick velvet drapes. Black candles illuminated carvings of satyrs and apes in obscene sex acts. I sensed a presence nearby – one yet more sinister than the devil women.

A statuesque female figure emerged from behind the drapes. She was naked except for an occult pendant and black swan mask. Her hair was as wild as Medusa's and her breasts were smeared with blood. She ran a finger up her long legs and slid it deep between her thighs.

'You failed,' she cackled. 'And now you're fucked.'

THIRTY-SEVEN

SUNLIGHT STREAMED THROUGH THE WINDOW onto the vomit on my face and chest. I was on the sofa in the hotel suite.

The devil women and the headless corpse were etched onto my retina. I didn't move my head for fear of being violently sick. I knew I'd been fed a near-lethal cocktail of drugs and feared my brain would never recover. But I also sensed that drugs alone couldn't explain these horrors.

It was a colossal effort to put on a t-shirt and shorts. I sunk into one of the armchairs and observed the suite. It had been arranged *too* carefully – my clothes neatly folded on the sofa, a glass of water and pills on a coffee table with instructions to take two. Like good old times. My wallet was there but the Samsung was missing.

Madeleine's clothes – a skirt, bra and her yellow and blue scarf – were scattered around the suite. I thought fondly of our day in Versailles. Then I remembered her nasty ways of late, our weird sex tryst and the tirades of abuse. It made the pain from the drugs comedown much worse.

Flashbacks to the trip. The turret, the celebrity party on the rooftop of the Majestic, the DJ deck. The memories were a blur, but they were more real than any trip – drugs alone could not have done that. I decided to go to the roof terrace in search of evidence, but en route I was seized with ravenous hunger so exited the hotel in search of food.

The sun on la Croisette was overwhelming. I cowered in the sun like a man blinded. I looked like a lunatic, stumbling around and muttering to myself. People stepped out of my way, unsure if I was putting on an act. An elderly man asked if I needed a doctor. I told him I had been drugged and tortured but was okay now and just needed to eat.

I stuffed down a panini. Couples walking hand in hand and families with laughing children passed me by. Pretty girls in white blouses and floaty skirts rubbed sun cream into their necks.

'Can't you hear this beauty in life?' played from a speaker.

The food made me feel almost human again. I slapped my cheeks and set off towards the beach to revitalise my senses. A young lady drove past in a vintage convertible Mercedes wearing dark sunglasses and a light blue scarf. She was the spitting image of Grace Kelly. She blew me a kiss.

A thunderbolt. The yellow and blue scarf. It had got torn in the train doors in Paris. There was no way it could have found its way into the hotel suite. It couldn't be one just like it – it was too unusual. Here was proof that the hotel room had been tampered with. But why? I had to return to the scene to find out.

Back in the room, it struck me that other things were out of place, but I couldn't say what. The bar was running low on alcohol, more or less as I had left it, and Madeleine's clothes were strewn around the living room, as they had been. The scarf was the only item that didn't fit. I held it up to my nose – it was unworn.

The door to Madeleine's room was closed. I knocked but got no answer. I knocked again and went in. It was empty and clean – untouched. She had never been here. But I had seen her come in and out of this door with my own eyes. I was on the verge of tears. It made no sense whatsoever.

I stepped into the corridor. Nothing was amiss. I had exited suite 701 – our suite. I paced up and down the corridor aimlessly. The suite opposite was 700, followed by 703, 705 and 707. 701 was followed by 702, 704, and 706. I stared at the numbers for a good long time before it clicked. Suites 700 and 701 had been switched.

I swiped my room key in the door to suite 700 and the light flashed green. I knew straight away that *this* was the room we had checked into. The air was stale, the shutters half-closed and puddles of vodka and stacks of unwashed glasses lined the bar. Shredded papers from our mission littered the floor.

The Samsung was on the chair that I had been forced to sit in, next to a gadget that looked like a pair of hi-tech binoculars with bulky headphones. I adjusted the focus wheel and took them to the window. Black. I found an 'on' button and the device sprang to life.

'Oculus Rift SX-10 system loading…'

It was a virtual reality headset that worked with a smartphone. I slid the Samsung into the slot, strapped on the headset and after some fiddling began the experience.

Blackness – only the sound of footsteps and soft rustling. This time I escaped with ease from the tent and navigated the turret onto the walkway leading to the terrace. The music got louder as I approached the main terrace. I looked past the hookers and spotted Bigboy and Eagle.

I threw the device on the floor. So that's how they did it – a virtual reality film enhanced with psychedelic drugs. ESIS had upped its game since the crude edits to the CCTV footage in the grotto. I had been pumped with drugs and handled liked a lab rat. I vowed that it was the last time ever.

I stomped around the suite, kicking at furniture. Was my mind so fragile that I could be duped so easily? Part of me persisted in believing that some of what had happened to me at night was real, in spite of the evidence to the contrary. The trip was so visceral, so repugnant – and the madness felt coherent…

I detected a dim light and soft chanting emanated from the bedroom. I marched towards the door, ready to take them on. But I held back. My gut told me that evil lurked within. I tried to turn the door handle, but my hand froze. This was one last chance to get away. I braced myself for the worst kind of shock.

Smoke and incense wafted into my face. Large black candles in a gothic candelabrum flickered by a mirror. Scarlet drapes and carvings of satyrs engaged in sex acts stood next to Tiki figures with giant phalluses. It was the room of my trip. This part had been real.

I was enveloped in darkness as I moved further inside. The stench of acrid aromas told me that evil was close. I sensed suffering all around me. In this sordid den, age-old mysteries would soon be unravelled. But the truth would not help. It would make the pain worse. Irrevocably worse.

I turned around to leave but tripped. The terror was slow to unfold. At my feet, there was a coffin with ropes attached to it. Inside was a female body. She was naked, and her hands and legs were spread cruelly apart. A large dildo and jagged metal tools lay by her side. But she was alive.

It was Madeleine.

'*Je suis désolé Ellis, je suis désolé.*'

I went to free her, but a cackle from behind the drapes made me freeze. The sadist monster of my trip emerged adorned in a black eye mask, stilettos and gloves. She held a leather whip in one hand and a pistol in the other.

'You failed. And now you're fucked,' she hissed.

She made her way towards us, cracking the whip.

'Mirror, mirror on the wall, who's the fairest of them all?'

'Madeleine!' I cried.

She struck Madeleine, drawing blood from her left breast.

'Here ends our ruse. Now you must choose!' she snarled.

The monster hid in darkness then surfaced beside her victim, holding a large candle to her face. Madeleine murmured in pain as the flame touched her skin. The monster brought the flame to her face and allowed it to burn her lips, then took it back to Madeleine's. One contorted in agony – the other in ecstasy. But the faces were the same – a female Janus.

I had seen what I had not wanted to see. I knew what I had not wanted to know. What I had seen once before. What I had known all along. The beast was the beauty. They were identical. One was Judy and the other was Madeleine.

'We are two! What a coup!'

Blood had trickled down from Madeleine's upper body and formed a pool around her vagina.

There was no time to process the horror of the revelation. The sadist's whip tore into my arm. I ducked to ward off a second blow, hit my head and collapsed to the floor. I was half-aware of having my clothes taken off and being dragged across the floor. Judy was unnaturally strong for a woman of her size. I came to as she was binding my hands and feet to the coffin.

'It's time to say adieu!'

Madeleine turned towards me. Her eyes gleamed in the dark. There was despair but also strength. She moved her lips though no words came out. It didn't matter. She had been on my side. She was not a liar. She loved me. I loved her.

I was filled with a new resolve. It had been a terrifying spectacle, but I had learned the dark secret and was still standing. It was a trick – the décor, costume and even the gun were fake, a masquerade. It was time to turn the tables. She might be through with me, but I was not done with her. I would not take this secret to the grave.

Our enemy doubled her efforts to tie me up, but I managed to free an arm from the ropes. I lunged at the wicked twin, knocking her off balance. Madeleine had also managed to loosen her hand, enough to pick up one of the torture instruments and to strike the monster below the knee. As she fell backwards, the whip wrapped around her body and dug into her thigh. The pistol fell to the ground two feet away.

I reached it first. It was real enough. Her hands reached it seconds later, her nails digging deep into my flesh. She sprang to her feet and aimed at her twin. I had no doubt she was going to shoot and dived at her feet. The bullet tore into the drapes and shattered a glass window.

The monster was quick to get back on her feet. I faced my destiny on my knees. To die – to sleep, no more. The final point of no return.

She pointed the gun at Madeleine again. She fired. The bullet sped past me in slow motion. I went to take it. But it was too late. Madeleine let out a piercing scream.

She aimed the gun at me. She fired and I fell.

THIRTY-EIGHT

FALLING THROUGH A BROKEN GLASS window was a sobering experience.

I couldn't be sure the first bullet had weakened the window enough so that it would give way. It was blind chance. Jagged glass tore into my neck, back and arms. For a few long instants, I was Icarus flying into the sun. My wings melted, and I was Icarus falling from the sky.

I landed on a sixth-floor balcony, ripping through a cover that collapsed on top of me. I was still conscious but expected to black out – I had been shot, after all. I counted to ten to delay the inevitable and tried to see where I had been shot. I got to twenty before I dared believe that I had dodged the bullet.

In that instant, I became my animal-self. He was like me but stronger and more fearless. He didn't care that blood was streaming from his right arm and left knee, that his back was badly bruised, his head concussed or that he was naked. He cared only about survival.

He walked into the hotel suite and picked up a bathrobe on his way out to the corridor. He was oblivious to the shrieks of the cleaning staff. He didn't cover himself until he got to the lift, leaving a trail of bloody footprints. On the ground floor, he toppled a baggage cart, injuring an elderly Asian couple.

On the hotel forecourt, he sighted a man running after him.

He darted into the road and was knocked down by a reversing limousine. The driver got out of the car then swiftly beat a retreat. The animal staggered up, limped onto a grassy terrace and pushed past palm trees before ditching the bathrobe and plunging into a pool.

Water splashed onto a posse of models and a dead ringer for Ryan Gosling.

'Oh my God, he's butt naked! *Il est nu! Lui è nudo!*' the women shrieked.

The animal wasn't embarrassed by his nakedness. He pulled himself out of the pool and made his way towards them.

The Gosling lookalike barely had time to put down his drink before he was thrown headfirst into the pool. The giggles turned into screams as the group fled like frightened hyenas, leaving the man to thrash about haplessly. The animal gathered up his Levi jeans, Armani shirt shoes and Ray-Bans, and fled the scene.

I ceased being my animal-self. I was about fifty yards from the Croisette and the beach. There were dark storm clouds on the horizon. I could hear police sirens. I knew that my chances of survival depended on acting quickly and avoiding detection by ESIS agents.

The clothes hid my injuries, but I was vulnerable in the open and so made my way towards the beach. The sea was a possible means of escape. There were half a dozen large luxury yachts moored near the shore, but how to reach them?

I was about to turn around when a motorboat rolled out a floating dock.

'*Les Hot d'Or or ov ze Continen?*' asked the skipper.

I sat next to two young men in tuxedos. It seemed like I had been mistaken for someone but figured the mix-up would buy me valuable time. We sped towards the yacht furthest from the beach. It was decked in a big red banner that read: 'Les Hot d'Or – fête du cinéma porno.'

I climbed up the mooring ladder. The bouncer was watching the X-rated movie playing on a large screen and didn't care who he let in. Rowdy men of all ages and porn stars were shuffling around, cocktails in hand. A sign pointed towards the 'Pornhub live gangbang' on the lower decks.

I stumbled into a group discussing the philosophical themes in an 'arthouse porno.' The lead actor complained the film hadn't done justice to his cock and whipped it out to prove the point.

'Show us yours!' they yelled.

I shrank back, colliding with a woman in black PVC bondage gear. A mistake. I had to get off this yacht.

The nearest boat was docked about a hundred yards away and hosting a far less raucous party. On one sail there was the word 'Birth.' The other sail bore the letters 'Conti–.' The hairs on the back of my neck stood up.

I found the motorboat operator and told him to take me back to shore.

'*Malade? Homosexuel?*' he slurred.

As I was waiting, a military helicopter loomed on the horizon with a searchlight directed onto the water. It passed by our yacht and hovered over the *Birth of a Continent* boat. A rope ladder was lowered onto the deck and a man climbed up it.

The captain fired up the engine and we sped towards the jetty, but a few hundred yards from the beach the motor faltered and cut out.

'*Merde!*' he yelled.

He yanked the cord – to no avail. The helicopter took off

in another direction, then did a three-sixty manoeuvre and flew towards the *Hot d'Or* yacht at a low altitude. It was stationary for a few moments before advancing on us, its searchlight scouring the ocean floor. I was soon blinded by its harsh beams.

The drunken skipper waved his fists at the aircraft, not understanding what was going on. He tried the motor one last time and we took off sharply, the helicopter in close pursuit. The boat slammed into a sandbank seconds later and I was catapulted from my seat. I sprinted towards the road, not daring to look up or behind me.

I clenched my teeth to fight the pain in my back and tried to compose myself. I set about merging with a group of boisterous actors, but they crossed over the road to avoid me.

'Get it together,' said a female voice in my head.

The American film pavilion was heaving with bodies. They had tight security in place, but it was possible to get in. There were people there who could tell my story to the wider world. But I decided it was too late for that now.

I walked on by. There was a hive of festival activity outside the casino. I thought about hiding out there until the night was over, before realising I was staring into a roaming surveillance camera. They were everywhere in a casino.

'Make a plan and fast,' said the voice. 'You are running out of time.'

I battled the crowds outside Caffé Roma. I hated their carefree ways. The fact that there was still no sign of my enemies was starting to make me extremely worried. I knew for sure they were lurking in the shadows, waiting to strike.

I walked towards the hotel. Why would they look for me in

the most obvious place?

'That's a bad idea,' said a voice in my head. 'If you remain in Cannes, you will die.'

The fastest way to get out of town was by train. It was getting late, but I had a fighting chance of making the last TGV to Paris. If I missed it, that was it.

I had lost all bearings and didn't know where the station was. My hand brushed against something heavy in Gosling's trouser pocket. It was an iPhone – with no security protection. I clicked on Maps and told the device to plot a route up the Rue du Maréchal Joffre to Place de la Gare.

Three tall security men wearing black suits and earpieces came out of the Olympia cinema. I picked up the pace, and so did they. I turned left onto Rue Venizelos, and so did they. The iPhone must be a tracking device.

I threw the phone into the gutter as one of the men laid a firm hand on my shoulder.

'*Monsieur, Monsieur!*'

I swung around, ready to fight.

'*Eh, oh. Du calme. Voulez-vous participer à…*'

'Back off!' I screamed.

The man obeyed. I ran up the street and took a right along an overpass. I caught a glimpse of a sign for the SNCF parking structure. The station was on the street below, but there was no access. I climbed over the barrier, dropped ten feet to the ground, then hauled myself over a railing into the station.

The departure board listed one train for Paris at 21:33. It was 21:32. I raced up the escalator nearest to me, not even checking the platform number. If it was the wrong one, I was a dead man. I threw myself between the closing doors.

The voice, *her* voice, told me to take a seat.

PART FOUR

THIRTY-NINE

A FLEETING GLIMPSE OF PALM TREES, the beach, the bright lights of Massalia, then tunnels and darkness. It was a stopping train that wouldn't get to Paris until the morning. I made a wish that the journey would last forever.

I took a seat in an empty carriage. Rocked by the gentle swaying of the train, I fell into a deep slumber. I was only slightly bothered by the rustling and flapping noises that got louder and louder. I thought it must be a child, but then concluded it must be an animal. It brushed against my leg like it was trying to get my attention.

I was amazed to see a three-foot-tall golden eagle.

'Beware 'em little boots,' it squawked. 'Beware the fox 'n all.'

It spoke like a parrot that didn't understand what it said. I was about to ask it a question, but it flapped its wings and stomped around the carriage.

The reason for the bird's agitation became clear. A bald man dressed like a maître d'hôtel had entered the carriage with a dwarf in a white vest and leather boots, holding a gun.

'Have the boys fixed it? Got the loot?' asked the eagle.

'Fuckin' betta 'ave,' said the waiter. 'Let 'em 'ave it!'

An unshaven man with a potbelly, dressed in a sailor's outfit, entered the carriage. I was fed up with all this nonsense and wanted them all to go to hell.

The giant, the dwarf, the sailor and the eagle stood in silence. The eagle broke the stand-off by flapping his wings and yanking the emergency brake cord with its beak, causing the train to come to an abrupt halt. I was thrown to the floor and two gunshots were fired, followed by grunts and groans.

The lights came on and I beheld a scene of carnage. The sailor was lying in a pool of blood, shot in the head. The giant and the dwarf were gone, presumably out of the broken window, leaving a trail of blood in their wake. The little man's boots lay on top of the dead sailor's chest.

'Go to Lukotokía, the white place. 45's the number. Once you know where, you'll know when,' said the eagle.

It was the message Luc had given me. At that, the bird flew out of the broken window and was gone.

A ticket inspector was tapping me on the shoulder.

'*Votre billet, Monsieur, s'il vous plaît.*'

He issued me with a fine and I handed him a credit card from my stolen wallet. By some miracle, the transaction went through. I held the card up to the light – it really did belong to R Gosling.

I stared vacantly out the window and repeated Luc's message back to myself. A hazy part of my brain told me that Lukotokía was Greek for Lutetia. Luc's 'white place' was at 45 Boulevard de Raspail – Hotel Lutetia. I had cracked the first part of the message and knew where to go.

The train was hurtling through suburban stations only a few miles from the Gare de Lyon. Even the ugly buildings looked nice in the golden dawn. I did not want to arrive. It seemed like an eternity ago that I had dragged Madeleine across that station floor to her fate. This was the last time we had been truly together.

'Don't go,' she'd said on the train.

But I had gone and evil had taken her place. She had suffered terribly. It was all my fault. I had not protected her. I hadn't seen the blindingly obvious. A week ago, there had been a chance of getting out of this alive. A glimmer of hope that was now extinguished.

I was buffeted by the hoards towards the metro. I looked over my shoulder and jumped over the turnstile. Having no ticket was the least of my problems. Half the world's intelligence agencies were no doubt tracking my movements and I expected to be arrested at any moment. The net was closing in.

The platform made me remember the tube station where the tramp had been killed. The horrors I had seen. If only I hadn't gone to London. If only I'd never opened that letter. If only I'd not gone to Bigboy's party. If only I hadn't laid eyes on her. If only, if only, if only. Glorious bloody hindsight.

I squeezed into a commuter train and picked up a free newspaper from the floor. 'Anarchy in Europe,' read the headline. Every EU country seemed to be undergoing large-scale turmoil.

Hundreds of thousands of protestors in Germany had descended on Alexanderplatz protesting against the far right and the security services. Greece teetered on the brink of civil war.

I turned to reports about the UK. Campaigning for the UK's referendum on Europe was suspended due to violent clashes between skinheads and pro-Europeans. A female MP with two small children had been stabbed to death outside her constituency office. The government had so far rejected calls to suspend the election.

'Le Brexit à 50/50,' read another article. Experts thought the British were still most likely to opt for the status quo, but they stressed the vote could go either way. One said that politicians had misjudged the extent of UK voters' anger with the EU and accused the Remain camp of being complacent.

I stepped out at Auber-Opéra. Why did a station need two names? My mind was working overtime. I was sweating and dehydrated, but this was no time to stop. I took metro line eight, alighting one stop later.

'*Allô Madeleine!*' said a young man on the phone. 'Madeleine' was embroidered on a woman's cotton bag. I was at Madeleine metro station. I could bear it no longer. Madeleine was dead.

An invisible hand squeezed mine. It said, 'it's not over till it's over.' Move on, move on, echoed the crowds. I headed towards line twelve. A train pulled up and I got in. Assemblé Nationale, Solférino, Rue du Bac, Sèvres-Babylone. The nerves in my body were at breaking point as I exited the metro.

Hotel Lutetia stood before me, resplendent in the morning sunshine.

FORTY

THE SCAFFOLDING AT 45 BOULEVARD Raspail had been taken down, revealing a fresh exterior. Lutetia's art nouveau façade was the epitome of class – grander than the Majestic's.

The hotel was calling me. It said 'take care of unfinished business.' It said 'come home and don't leave.' A man in a dark suit and earpiece was sitting at the reception desk.

'This way, Mr Ellis.'

I followed him down the black and white tiled corridor to the lift. The mouldings and floor were less dusty and the air less stale than on my last visit. In the lounge, a dozen suits with clipboards, men as well as women, were talking into earpieces. A sense of urgency hung in the air.

We walked down the long corridor where Lutetia seminars had been held. There was no sign of Lutetia mafia or the twenty-seven bastards. I was told to wait outside the wood-panelled bar. I imagined ESIS bigwigs gathered to pass their final verdict on me, or Lutetia heavies lying in wait.

The suit returned and escorted me to a large man sitting in the corner of the room.

'Paperboy has come,' he announced.

The large man was studying a wall collage of wartime newspaper clippings about General de Gaulle's triumphant return to Paris, the public head shavings and hangings, etc.

'The war didn't end in '45,' he boomed. 'Hitler got his come-uppance, but the Nazi foe morphed into more dangerous and powerful forms.'

Eagle offered his hand.

'Call me Frank. Frank Schneider.'

'Hello Frank,' I said.

He flashed me an American smile and poured bourbon into two whisky glasses. He looked more like a bear than an eagle with broad shoulders and a full head of hair. I wondered what his real name was.

'Don't try the windows, they're double-glazed,' he grinned.

'A history lesson, Ellis,' he went on. 'Looks like you need a rest, old boy, so kick back and relax.

'I am American of Polish-Jewish origin from my grandmother and German from my grandfather. A talented chap, Franz Schneider – Professor of Human Genetics at the University of Berlin at the age of twenty-five. He was one of the first to succeed in decoding human DNA.'

I took off my jacket and sat down on a barstool.

'Carl Schneider, his brother, is the famous one. Infamous. Look him up! The archetypal scientist turned Nazi madman. In the name of 'national therapy' – ridding the Aryan race of psychological and physical impurities – he set up training centres specialised in the mass murder of children. Ended up topping himself in prison.

'Look up Franz Schneider, you'll find diddly squat. Franz knew how to keep his nose clean. A born survivor. They were twins, curiously.'

The mention of twins piqued my interest.

'While Carl was all into killing kiddies – Franz was doing

serious science in the field of genetic engineering. His mentor was a certain Otmar von Verschuer, a Nazi 'racial hygienist' and eugenicist who developed the 'twin methodology' which was supposed to prove the supremacy of heredity over the environment, ergo the superiority of the Aryan race.

'Von Verschuer's most infamous student was a certain Josef Mengele, the *Weisse Engel*. The most ruthless and sadistic of the bunch, Uncle Mengele took the twins obsession to a new level, killing them by lethal injection, shootings, beatings and deadly experiments. On one night he massacred fourteen twins by injecting chloroform into their hearts. That dude was sick.'

Eagle told this story as if it was commonly known trivia.

'Franz did none of that. He was a theory guy, all about uncovering DNA. Which he would do – before the Americans! Sure, he may have published a paper or two about the ideal conditions for beautiful blondes to make twins. So what? He was a scientist, not a supremacist. These subtleties were lost on the powers-that-be. For them, he was a Nazi eugenicist.

'Franz Schneider was put in charge of a lab on the Swiss border and told to make Aryan children in a year. He took some big first steps, but the lab only churned out a few dead babies. The Nazis shut down the lab before the end of the war and sent Franz Schneider and his team to the Eastern front in Poland to fight against the Ruskies.

'It was a death sentence in all but name. Half of his colleagues died in transit before they saw action. The rest were easy pickings for Soviet snipers. In these appalling circumstances, Grandfather Schneider sought comfort in the bosom a local farm girl, Maria. They spent a tense night together, during which Maria confided her own terrible secret. She was Jewish and had escaped from Auschwitz.

'Facing certain death, Grandfather Schneider did the one truly good deed of his life. He hid Maria, in the sewers of his barracks and gave her food. Knocked her up, too – but he did *not* send her off to Auschwitz. He saved her bacon!'

He guffawed loudly. I looked at the floor, embarrassed.

'Jews can make Jew jokes,' he chided. 'Along came the Ivans and Franz Schneider was carted back to Berlin as a prisoner. They weren't too sympathetic towards Nazi eugenicists with Jewish mistresses and things looked grim for a spell. They shipped him off to Nuremberg to stand trial with Germany's other big brains and evil scientists. Do you know what their main line of defence was?'

He seemed to think I might know the answer.

'That the Americans were doing it too. Now... historians tell us they mightn't have been entirely wrong about that. In any case, it so happened that Uncle Sam needed chaps just like Grandpa Schneider, and the Russians couldn't afford to throw away bargaining chips for trifling matters of ideology. After some intense horse-trading, Grandpa was shipped off to the USA.

'In his first week in New York, he ran into Jewish Maria – future Grandma Schneider – fresh off a boat from Ellis Island.'

I raised an eyebrow.

'I don't give a damn if you believe it,' he snapped. 'Edgar Hoover wanted to make a movie about their life story.

'Gramps and Grandma were given US citizenship and settled in Washington DC. Franz was officially an employee at the Office of Scientific Research and Development. In fact, he headed a top-secret biogenetic research programme with an army of scientists working under him.'

'Doing what he did for the Nazis, but for the Americans?'

Eagle frowned. I wasn't meant to ask questions.

'Thanks to Grandpa, our scientists made rapid advances in reading genetic codes. The door was opened to modifying and improving human DNA. But all this science stuff is a story for another time. The next chapter is about the United States of America and its relationship with Europe.'

He swigged his bourbon.

'In the 1950s and 60s, life in the USA was hunky-dory. In the day we frolicked in the fields and at night we rolled in the mud. You guys on the Old Continent didn't have it so good – bomb damage, bankruptcy, millions dead, etc. We felt kinda bad about that, so we financed your recovery.'

'The Marshall Plan?'

'Yeah, that's public domain. What is not so widely known is what we were buying. Because there's no such thing as a free lunch, Ellis old boy – you remember that! Do you know what it was?'

I pondered the question.

'A new world order,' Eagle cut in. 'A world order where America ruled the roost and where Europe finally learned its goddamn place. A continent that bought our gizmos and where Uncle Bob and Aunt Sue spent their vacations. A large strategic area that hosted our nukes when the Ruskies got out of line.

'And do you know what the longest-running operation is in the history of the CIA?' Eagle asked abruptly. 'EUROFOE. Surveillance of our European partners. Running since 1945 and not yet shut down. We couldn't just allow you to squander those billions of greenbacks, could we? No way, Jose. The only way to guarantee a return on our dollar was to keep close tabs on you guys.

'As part of EUROFOE, we were also tasked with making sure that European nations loved each other enough to live side by side – but loved us a whole lot more. The plan worked a treat. We had a load of fun staking out your leaders and their mistresses in fancy apartments in Paris and Rome.

'Back then, nobody was really worried that a continent which had spent six years tearing the bejesus out of itself would ever again be a threat. By far the hardest part was getting the Brits to play ball. You clung to our American butts like a pervy uncle, banging on about some weird special relationship.'

Eagle was talking excitedly.

'Sure, our movies and magazines were propaganda to make you guys purr with envy. We had our problems too. The feel-good factor of the Kennedy years was steadily eroded by Nixon, Ford and Carter. Viet-Fucking-Nam. The Iranian hostage crisis, etc. By the end of 70s, our newfound supremacy was already on the wane.

'Fast-forward to the 1980s. Things were back on track. Greed is good, and all that jazz. New York traders were making more money than some country's GDPs. And the end of the cold war was in sight. The Ruskies had been a worthy opponent – the toughest, but they couldn't go the distance and were crumbling. We'd won, goddammit!

'But the big picture game plan hadn't quite materialised. European countries were starting to get pissy with each other, and bolshy with us. American support for the Israelis against the Arabs and our meddling in Latin America didn't help. The underlying problem was jealousy over our financial, military and cultural domination.

'Enter the fray the men you will come to know as Eagle, Capitaine and Foxtrot. This part of the story is about you and what we have to do to save your ass,' he said looking me squarely in the eyes.

The agent interrupted Eagle with a message.

'Intermission, old boy.'

FORTY-ONE

'He's been helping us with our enquiries,' Eagle said flatly.

Luc cowered in the corner, the picture of shame.

'It's not like it seems,' Luc spluttered. 'I'm a hostage... they got to me. *Crois-moi, mon ami*, I didn't have a choice. Don't trust the Ameri...'

Eagle made a sign for him to be taken away. Luc froze like a waxwork and the agent carted him off.

'What do *you* think, Ellis?' Eagle asked once he'd gone. 'If it looks, smells, feels like shit – likely is shit, huh? If you have friends like that, who needs enemies?!' he roared.

I sighed deeply and tried to make sense of things.

'Now, where were we? Let me tell you more about myself. Trust me, Ellis. Your life depends on it.'

Eagle cleared his throat.

'Yours truly was born in 1965,' he said proudly. 'Son of Franz Junior and Mary Lou. Boomers, bless their 'earts, not a care in the world. Simple people in simple times. The leafy suburb of DC where they grew up was about as far removed from the horrors of Nazi Germany as is possible.

'Franz Junior graduated high school, got a mediocre job in a bank, married Ma and moved to Queens, New York. He lost his job every time the economy dipped, which was often. Ma did okay as an Avon Lady, when she wasn't off the wagon. I came along and we moved to a rough neighbourhood in Newark.

'Little Frankie Schneider was a good kid but left too much to his own devices. Months went by without seeing, his hero, Gramps, who couldn't understand how he had begotten a feeble American son. But he saw himself in me – the brains had skipped a generation in our family.

'Me and Gramps, now there's a team. Cut from the same cloth. Franz Schneider taught me everything there is to know about the world and how to get on in it. He was a patriarch, a patriot and a leader.'

Eagle smiled proudly.

'Gramps tried to get me excited about science – gave me electronics kits and chemistry sets, but that didn't cut it for me. Teen years were tough – fights at school, petty vandalism, tagging, girls. I got kicked out of high school. Grandpa took me to DC and beat my ass. He was a hard taskmaster, brutal at times.

'I ran away – slept on the streets till I was picked up by the police. Gramps beat the living daylights out of me. I ran off again. Police picked me up. Another beating. This went on and on. But Gramps didn't want to lose me to the dark side, so in the end we came to an understanding. If I went straight, he promised to score me the prototype IBM PC.

'The day that bulky mother came through the door changed my life forever. I was the envy of the block – me and my buddies played Asteroids and Pac-Man for days. One rainy afternoon, I got a visit from a guy who said he was from IBM offering free BASIC computer programming classes. I'd found my calling, hallelujah!

'In the early 1980s, we were already using the internet, or ARPANET as it was called back then. Surfing and hacking. The network wasn't yet clogged with mountains of crap, and security protocols were easier to crack. IBM Man came once a week to teach me software development and advanced coding.

'Yours truly – part of the first generation of computer hackers! My alias was Hawk. I was soon operating in the same league as Black Bart, Tennessee Tuxedo, Mentor and Warlord. I hit Harvard and Yale, the New York City Department of Education, the Public Library, Mount Sinai Hospital and Chase Bank.

'There were two rules of hacking. First, once you'd gotten in, you got the hell out. The point was the hack, not the spoils. Second, every target had to be bigger than the last. Big hacks needed manpower and multiple computers, so I hooked up with a prototype hacking community called Flock.

'Flock was one hellova thing. It did things I had no idea were possible. We hacked NASA, the Federal Government and the FBI. Things started to get out of hand when the group set its sights on the CIA, the holy grail of hacks. The risks were enormous, but then so were the kicks.

'The hack worked. We got in, out and shook it all about – hiding our asses behind military-grade VPNs. But it took the spooks all of ten minutes to smash down my door and cart me away in cuffs. I saw IBM Man lurking in the jail corridors later that night, and it all clicked.'

'You were set up.'

Eagle scowled.

'I faced trumped-up charges – accused of being the mastermind behind Flock – and given a choice – face felony charges under the Computer Fraud and Abuse Act, about twenty years inside, or join the Company, no strings attached. Guess which I chose?'

'I was like a kid in a candy store for a while, testing and programming the latest software. But it turned out I had to do some hard graft after all – infiltrate hacker gangs, some of them my former heroes, and hand them over to the cops. No such thing as a free lunch, remember that Ellis, old boy!

'But I was damn good at this line of work. I busted a gang that was going to take the Bank of America for a hundred million. Those boys are still inside. That was not a fate shared by Frankie Schneider, oh no. Frankie rose in the ranks thanks to special skills and a knack for making people do what needed to be done.

'I graduated from the hacking scene in the mid-80s. Got some field experience, ran a few drugs busts in South America and monkeyed around in Africa. I went undercover in the blood diamonds market. The sellers were major league demons, but I held my own and even made some friends in high places.'

My brain was aching with all twists and turns of Eagle's story. I longed for him to tell me something relevant.

'Africa, 1989. The year I crossed paths with Foxtrot and Capitaine. Both bastards were raring to make a name for themselves, get a piece of the post-Soviet pie, take revenge on former foes and recruit new operatives. They played fast and loose with the rules to get what they wanted.

'Foxtrot went by the name of Tom Smith back then. Born in London in 1955 to a single mom and unknown father, he joined the army, reaching the rank of corporal major by the age of twenty-eight. He had a reputation for being a brutal thug, albeit more intelligent than the average hood.

'In the late 80s Smithy was headhunted by shadowy figures in Whitehall looking for henchmen to do Thatcher's dirty work in Northern Ireland and beyond. He acquitted himself admirably. Over the years he also gathered a long list of compromising materials on British civil servants and politicians. He's Smythe-Sinclair now, don't ya know.

'Capitaine is a different kettle of fish. Born in Neuilly-sur-Seine in 1959, François-Guillaume Bertrand hails from French aristocracy. He was destined for glory at the Foreign Ministry, following in the family tradition. But France's influence was disappearing faster than oil in Alaska, and Capitaine wanted to put that right.

'He lent his talents instead to France's secret services. He was behind the sinking of the Greenpeace boat *The Rainbow Warrior* – that's the kind of nice guy he is. He did France's dirty business in sub-Saharan and Northern Africa with zeal, crossing swords with more than one African warlord and living to tell the tale.

'In Africa, Foxtrot and Capitaine were buying diamonds to aid rebel militia in Ivory Coast. They put in a huge order for far more money than they had. Their governments didn't cough up and our duo was left up the creek without a paddle. Guess who whisked them out of the cauldron?

'They bled their pussy hearts out, about how their people had let them down, how their countries had gone to the dogs, etc. At the American Embassy in Morocco, they got drunk on vintage wines and agreed, absurdly, that the Yanks were to blame for everything. For stealing their colonies, for poking our bugles in where they didn't belong, for having money but no culture. Talk about ungrateful!

'They weren't in love with the idea of Europe – they were nationalists. Foxtrot didn't give a rat's ass about France and Capitaine held the UK in contempt. But they were both nostalgic for the time when Europe ruled the waves and Uncle Sam was just a sperm in Old Man Europe's schlong. If the EU was a means of restoring the old world order, they were in.

'They hated having their asses saved by a CIA agent but had to admit they owed me big time. We parted on good terms and agreed to stay in touch.'

Eagle chuckled loudly.

'After filing my report back at Langley, I was hauled in front of the Director of Special Ops. The big boss had a hunch Foxtrot and Capitaine were POPIs – People of Potential Interest. I was assigned to EUROFOE and told to infiltrate Foxtrot and Capitaine's inner circle.

'The rationale behind the mission wasn't what you might think. If Foxtrot and Capitaine were safe pairs of hands, the CIA intended to aid and abet their careers. Remember that the point of EUROFOE was to hold the EU together so it could be a useful subsidiary partner to the USA. Our lapdog. If they could make that happen, these were our guys.

'It took some convincing to be let into their little club. I'm an American, after all. I said I was more German than Yank and spun a yarn about Uncle Sam ruining my life and the world. The first time they heard me out was right here – at Hotel Lutetia. It was a fateful day. A bond was formed that two decades later gave birth to ESIS.

'By the time I made partner, we'd realised they were psychos and we'd made a huge goddamn mistake.'

FORTY-TWO

'And the third man of ESIS? How does he figure into things?'

'The Right Honourable John Goodman, UK Foreign Minister? Your pa.'

'He's not my father!'

Eagle ignored me.

'You're smart – you should've worked it out by now. But you want to hear it from the horse's mouth. Okay. Your pa and Smithers are cut from the same cloth. Grew up on the same projects – I mean 'estate' – in South London. Got done over by the same thugs, thrown in the same lockups, lost their virginity to the same hoes, etc. They were as thick as thieves.

'Smarter than your average hoods, they made a pact to help each other make good, whatever it took. Your pa sold fake Rolexes and gold chains and conned a few old ladies out of a few fancy pearls. Tommy Boy pushed dope till he stepped on gangland territory and had to skip town fast.

'He enlisted in the army and planned to do a bunk after a few weeks. Instead, he got a taste for military life. There were a few discipline issues – but he was damn good at being a soldier, he'd found his ticket outta dodge. He tried to recruit your pa, but he wasn't cut out for it. This led to some bad blood between 'em.

'More Rodney than Del Boy, your pa made a pile, then lost it several times over – he had the brains but not the brawn. He did better with the old ladies and became something of a gigolo. He found his ticket when met Lady S and became a 'respectable' businessman. Then he got into politics and his stock price soared.

'Smithy had risen through the ranks and gone over to MI5 by this time. Obvious outsiders, both he and your pa needed allies outside of their spheres. They buried the hatchet and traded military, business and government secrets to further each other's careers. The dirty duo was reunited.

'Fast-forward to end of the 1980s. Yours truly – I told you how – came into Smithy and Bertrand, aka Foxtrot and Capitaine's, murky worlds. It didn't take long to figure out the duo was a threesome. I fished for more, but they clammed up like old virgins. It was clear to me the third man was calling the shots – and was very, very protective about his privacy.

'It was several years before his identity was revealed to me, and then a few more before I had any direct contact with him. As a politician, he couldn't be seen with the likes of us, so meetings were brief encounters in backstreet hotels, dodgy bars, etc. And when he became a minister, the face-to-face contact stopped entirely.

'He was against my inclusion in the Lutetia inner circle. He didn't buy my backstory and suspected me from the start. And he was right, godammit. I was a mole! As shrewd as snakes, Goodman – that's how he's made it to the top of the greasy pole. Fortunately, the agency dug up some leverage to grease the wheels.

'You blackmailed him?'

'Whose side you on, Ellis?'

Eagle went to get a huge stack of newspapers from the bar. I was sick of Eagle's endless fictions and glad that it was at an end. But one glance at the papers and I was confronted with a nightmarish reality. I was suddenly sorry Eagle was no longer prevaricating. There was no going back.

The New York Times was top of the pile. The crisis in Europe had grown, with anger mounting at security services across the EU. Cracks had opened across the union, not just in vulnerable countries like Greece, Portugal and Ireland, but in the power-houses – France, Germany, Spain and Italy. Europe had not faced such an 'existential threat' since World War II.

The EU was under pressure to come up with rapid solutions. An emergency summit had been convened with European heads of state to discuss taking 'new security measures across the union' to tackle the unrest. Rumours of 'a unified security service' were rife. The EU Commissioner was due to announce proposals this evening.

British papers were alarmed about events at home. *The Times'* headline read: 'Brexit vote goes down to the wire.' The EU referendum was in two days, with opinion polls showing a dead heat. The turmoil in Europe had been eclipsed by violence in the Leave camp. The man who murdered the Labour MP had proven links to the British National Front and English Defence League.

The Telegraph focussed on the political angle. '3-to-1 odds on Goodman becoming next Prime Minister.' The major story was how the Prime Minister's lacklustre campaign had put the Remain victory in jeopardy. In a television interview, he had been unable to give two reasons why we should stay in and didn't seem to care how the vote went.

It was reported that the Prime Minister loathed his Business Secretary. *The Sun* quoted the PM as telling an aid that 'he didn't give a crap if Leave won, so long as it did for Goodman.' Downing Street denied it, but the damage was done. It was compared to John Major's 'bastards' gaff.

The Prime Minister had hunkered down in Downing Street, an aura of impending political death hanging in the air. The *Daily Mail* – formally his biggest ally – branded him a Judas and claimed ten frontbenchers and a hundred MPs would back Goodman if he were to challenge the Prime Minister for his job, 'so long as Remain carried the day.'

Goodman, in contrast, had hit the airwaves with slick interviews. His ardent defence of the EU infuriated his Eurosceptic colleagues, but his passion bordering on zeal made a huge impression on journalists, the public and most MPs. Several journalists compared him positively to Tony Blair.

'Leave,' said Eagle. 'The US government needs a Leave vote. It's the only legitimate way to be done with ESIS, Goodman and his men. We are pulling out all the stops – twitter trolls, fake news, the works. The Russians have been allies in this cause, albeit as part of their havoc-wreaking agenda.

'If Goodman moves into Number 10, ESIS has a clear path to power. Gone know-your-place Europe and the status quo maintained by MI5, DGSI and friends. In its place, nationalist madmen and ESIS *über alles*. Your Uncle Sam does not want that. You don't either. It's time to clear up the mess.'

'That you created.'

'You did their dirty work. You're one of them, as far as Interpol's concerned. Part of the Lutetia family.'

He paused for effect.

'You've been part of their plans since you were a kid.'

'And… is she…?'

The words failed me.

'Madeleine and Judy? Who, where, *what* are they?'

I pondered this strange turn of phrase.

'Look, I know you're smitten with one of 'em. If you do what I'm asking, I'll tell you everything about her. Everything.'

Eagle took a call and gestured for me to wait for him.

'She's alive,' he mouthed.

I gulped my bourbon with shaky hands. Eagle had made me privy to information that could expose ESIS to the world. But it was too late for that. If the UK voted to leave the European Union, ESIS's dreams would die – father's Machiavellian schemes alongside them. If the UK voted to remain…

'Listen up, Ellis. Things are moving fast. Capitaine, Foxtrot and their army of thugs are holed up in a new HQ. They are hurting by my defection – and the fact that we have surveillance ops right up their asses. But they are still in the game. If the UK votes Remain, they are poised to strike.

'We cannot and will not allow that to happen. The CIA has approval from the US Commander-in-Chief to launch a pre-emptive strike on foreign soil.'

I tried to fathom the meaning of this.

'We're taking ESIS out – militarily. Ready, soldier?'

I wasn't ready for this call to arms.

'I have a choice?'

'There's always a choice Ellis,' Eagle said gravely.

I could walk away. If ESIS failed, he would see to it that I probably wouldn't be prosecuted. I could have my old life back.

But I would never see Madeleine again.

'Or you can do as I ask. There's a new life waiting for you in the USA, with CIA protection. Same goes for her. You'll be together.'

He spelt out what was required of me.

'Aka, nada. It's a win-win situation.'

I had ten minutes to make a decision.

'There's no such thing as a free lunch,' Eagle had said on several occasions. He had boasted of a knack for making people do what needed to be done. The man was a born liar.

Nine minutes later, I still hadn't made up my mind. Eagle got up to leave the bar.

'Time's up! They are going down, kiddo, with or without your help. They are going down!'

FORTY-THREE

I WAS TO DELIVER A message to my foes: give yourselves up or hole up until the militia arrived.

CIA spooks instructed me on the details of my mission. I was given a smartwatch with a camera that relayed visuals in virtual reality. This would help the assault teams plan their attack.

'Strapiton!' ordered a fiery young agent.

'You will take the metro to Champs-Elysées Clemenceau,' said his sterner colleague.

'The watch will direct you from there. You walk out the building with that watch on your wrist, you accept our terms and conditions.'

He looked me straight in the eye.

They came to me outside on the street. Was the offer of a trial genuine? They weren't just going to hand themselves in, so what happened next? How did I get out of the HQ? Was it true that she was alive and waiting for me?

'For you are in Elysium and you are already dead.'

I wasn't sure where this came from – *Gladiator*, I think. I sighed deeply and walked past the metro station. This told them that I was still mulling over the offer and that my obedience couldn't be bought so easily.

I took one last look at the hotel Lutetia and longed to be a guest there. The sun hid behind dark clouds and the Boulevard

Raspail went eerily quiet. I had always thought of Paris as a city of the living dead. I was one of them now, a mortal living his final hours.

I noticed the tail a few yards down the street.

'For pity's sake, piss off!' I yelled.

He obeyed. I set a new course, walking along the narrow Rue de Varenne. I wondered if this was named after the town of Louis XVI's failed escape. He had another year and a half to wait before meeting his end. My coup de grâce was coming sooner.

Further down the road, I passed a motorbike with the key still in the ignition. I walked on past. I turned left onto Rue de Grenelle. A group of chic youths stood outside a Science Po having a lively debate. I wanted to know what they were talking about. Little did they know that today would shape their futures. Should I tell them?

I skirted Les Invalides, home to Napoleon's remains. Would the Emperor have been on my side? No, he would have been one of *them*. I headed up the Rue Constantine, past the British Council and the London University Institute in Paris. This was my last chance to get help. I didn't take it.

They would expect me to head towards the river and cross the Pont Alexandre III. I turned right onto the imposing Rue de l'Université. They had allowed my deviations so far, but the sudden change of direction would set alarm bells ringing and it was only a matter of time before I was stopped. I quickened the pace.

The larger police presence meant I was nearing my target. I told myself I had nothing to lose and that I was going to go through with it, come what may. My heart began beating faster all the same. I crossed the cobbled street to get a better view. The Assemblée Nationale stood aloof, watched over by a lone sentry guard.

It was now or never. I darted into an imposing courtyard that separated me from the parliament. One hundred yards, eighty, sixty. Two gendarmes emerged from nowhere. They took aim without saying a word – they meant business. I spun around and sprinted back towards the Rue de l'Université. The guard did not stop me from leaving.

Mission aborted. I didn't stop running until I had crossed the bridge and reached the Champs-Elysées. Had the gendarmes known I was coming?

'Comply,' said an electronic voice.

'Fine,' I panted.

I meant it – I would evade no more.

It was sad that my last watch was this invasive piece of junk. The screen alternated between a map with my route and a counter.

59:42, 59:41, 59:40.

The ESIS compound was halfway up the Champs-Elysées. It was strange that it was in such a public place. A mistake? How could foreign militia raid it without shutting down half the city?

The endpoint was less than ten minutes away, so I had close to an hour to kill. I could eat, get drunk or go to a sex parlour – but my appetites were gone.

I passed the Franklin D. Roosevelt metro station.

51:11, 51:10, 51:09.

A little boy was playing in a fountain near the crossroads.

'It's not safe!' I yelled.

The virtual map on the watch pointed to the Citroën C42 showroom on the other side of the avenue as my final destination. I zoomed in to be sure there was no error.

47:35, 47:34, 47:33.

I walked past the target towards the Arc de Triomphe – my last act of defiance. The watch vibrated and gave off a high-pitched alarm.

'Turn around!' it ordered.

The cacophony was awful. Passers-by were staring at me. On a whim I ripped the watch from my wrist and flung it against a wall – bits and pieces hit astonished patrons at a street café.

Now I was truly alone. I slumped to the ground, drained of life. The avenue's symmetry was lost from street level and the buildings looked as if they were about to topple. I wanted nothing more. Nobody tendered me a hand. I staggered to my feet and crossed over to the other side of the avenue, getting stuck on the traffic island.

I caught sight of something from out of the corner of my eye that gave me a jolt. A group of tourists blocked my view.

Two familiar heads disappeared into the crowd.

FORTY-FOUR

THERE WAS NO TRACE OF the two heads by the time I crossed over to the road. To the left, there was a side street and an old cinema, to the right a Disney store and a fashion boutique.

'Did you see them? A man and a woman?'

The Chinese tourist shrugged. I went into the clothes store and spotted two pairs of shoes under the changing room curtain – one black and one silver with heels. I pulled back the curtain to find an elderly lady being fitted for a bra.

I stormed outside onto the street, ignoring the protests, and peered inside the Disney store. A grey-haired man and a brunette stood behind the Cinderella Castle and a banner that read 'where dreams come true.'

I went to enter but felt a firm grip on my shoulder.

'*Ce n'est pas possible, Monsieur.*'

The security guard radioed a message – the word 'police' was spoken. A baby who had stolen a toy came to my rescue and I pulled away sharply, hiding behind an erotic perfume billboard.

I found myself opposite 42 Avenue des Champs-Elysées, site of the rendezvous. The 'C Chic' building towered before me like a glass inferno, its postmodern façade at odds with the avenue's classical architecture. A plaque posted outside told the building's history:

Citroën has always embraced modern architecture to create

unique spaces for its products. The original glass-fronted show-room was designed by M.-J. Ravazé in 1932. It was overhauled in 1984 and rebranded as the 'Hippo-Citroën.' The look for the current building, known as C42, was conceived by architect Manuelle Gautrand, winner of international design competitions...

I entered the building. On first glance nothing indicated I was in the right place – two technicians were busy preparing for a new exhibition. There was no sign of Lutetia mafia. I had somehow misread the map and had no idea where to go.

A classic 2CV 'Deux Chevaux' had pride of place in the lobby. I circled it aimlessly. As I exited the building, I saw a poster for a new expo – 'The Citroën Revolution, A Euro Revelation.' The ESIS emblem was emblazoned on it next to the EU flag. So I *was* in the right place and the grand finale, whatever that meant, was about to begin.

Adrenaline surged through my veins. I eyed the technicians more closely. One of them was speaking into a radio. He beckoned me to come towards him and directed me over rope barring entry to the new exposition. I had no way of communicating with my CIA protectors or relaying the visuals. They were sure to be pissed at me. To the point of calling off our deal?

The interior of the C42 was hollow with a futuristic stair-way lining the walls, like a space-age helter-skelter. Seven large circular platforms, each one housing an exhibit, filled the empty space. The Champs-Elysées could be seen at every level through crimson tinted glass making it look like some faraway galaxy.

A second 2CV stood on the ground floor platform – this one a modern four-door saloon with plastic trimmings. It was bright blue with twelve golden stars in a circle on the bonnet. It was a prototype of 'Citroën Europa Gen Y,' an affordable electric car available shortly thanks to ESIS subsidies.

A fleet of 2CVs sat on the second level, each one sporting funky Euro flags. Luxury convertible sports cars that ran on the latest hybrid energy technology occupied the third and fourth platforms. All were painted in blue and golden Euro motifs and subsidised by ESIS loans.

A Citroën DS19 from 1956 sat on the sixth and penultimate level. Mercifully it had not been painted blue or decorated with the Euro flag.

La déesse – or goddess – was, in its day, the world's most technically advanced automobile. The dream car of tomorrow is now on the road again! DS Lutetia is equipped with the latest computer, biometric and remote-access capabilities. It will be standard issue for ESIS employees…

The exhibition was propaganda to introduce ESIS to Europeans after they came to the fore. It was the usual mix of fantasy and the absurd.

The lights dimmed as we climbed a spiral staircase and I readied myself for a fight. I took the steps one by one, as if to delay the inevitable. On the last stair, my legs nearly gave way. At the top, the technician left me alone to stare into a white void as light streamed in through a rooftop window.

Three silhouettes came into focus. Dr Europa, Mickie and Roper were seated around a large table, looking sinister and in control. Roper looked every bit a Gestapo officer and Michel was holding a pistol. Europa coughed. I was a lone protestor in front of tanks. Same old Lutetia tactics.

Nothing happened for a long minute.

I saw a different picture once my eyes fully adjusted. Europa's brow was creased, his mane less silvery – he even had a bald patch. Roper, as pale as ever, was looking around restlessly and Mickie was stomping his feet.

'Pathetic!'

It was involuntary, an epiphany. They were comic book Nazis who would be spending the rest of their lives in prison.

They were going down.

This didn't take the danger out of the situation. Mickie had finished toying with the gun and was pointing it at me.

'Top of the morning to you too.'

'Yer guts ganna be spread over dis fookin' floor.'

'I come here with an offer from Frank,' I said to Roper and Europa. 'Will you hear me out?'

The words reverberated around the C42 complex, boosting my confidence. Mickie stood up, knocking over his chair.

'Shot the fock op, ya Bratish pisa of shite.'

'It's over – it's been over for a long time,' I said, continuing to ignore Mickie. 'Hand yourselves in to the CIA and agree to be extradited to the United States. You get immunity from prosecution in exchange for your testimony and cooperation.'

Roper reached out to touch Mickie, who brushed him off angrily.

'They only want the big fry,' I added.

'Ellis,' said Roper affecting a calm tone. 'No need for melodrama. Come over here, take a seat at the table, let's chat.'

They were on the back foot and I had every intention of keeping them there. Mickie was irate at being ignored.

'Don't be naïve about our American cousins,' Europa chimed in. 'There was a time that their word was their bond, but no more. We've taught them too well – they outdo us! Advice you may take or leave.'

'I'll leave it.'

'For once, make life simple for yourself. Come – come join us. We'll start over. Tabula Rasa. We'll overlook your, err, our diff-, difficulties,' he stumbled.

His charisma and confidence were fading fast. Roper, more ashen-faced than ever, whispered to Europa, who nodded.

'Only we can give you *her*,' Roper shrieked. 'If Frank told you otherwise, he lied. That's right, she's all yours! Downstairs for that matter. With your nearest and dearest.'

'What the FOCK?' yelled Mickie.

Mickie whipped Roper across the chest with the pistol, knocking him to the floor. He then walked backwards towards the ledge, aiming the gun at me once again. His hands were shaking with rage.

'Madeleine?' he bellowed.

I understood it all in a split second. He hadn't known that Madeleine was below and was furious at being left in the lurch. But more than that – he was in love with her too.

He unlocked the safety on the pistol.

'Gud fokin' bye!' he yelled at me.

But he stopped to peer over the ledge to see if Madeleine was below. I knew what to do. I ran at him fast, landing a blow to his back and a kick to his legs. The gun flew out of his hands as he swung around. I struck him hard in the upper chest and again in the stomach. He doubled over, winded and limp.

I hauled his body onto the platform's ledge. He spat at me like a mad dog. Maybe he was going to ask for mercy? I wasn't going to find out. I pushed.

His body landed with a thud on top of the DS19.

Roper dashed to the ledge.

'Mickie, my love!'

It only took a nudge to send him flying. Bump. He lay still at the bottom on the lower platform.

I picked up the gun and faced Europa.

'We mean it Ellis,' he gushed. 'You and Madeleine... together. You'll have an important role in our organisation. It was... the plan.'

'And live for a thousand years in blissful happiness? Screw you.'

The words echoed around the C42. I was no longer afraid. His destiny lay in my hands and I was not inclined to forgive.

Loud shouting came from below. Three men and a woman scampered across the floor. The woman was being dragged against her will, kicking and screaming.

'Help!'

Europa rushed to the top of the viewing platform. I was already halfway down the stairs. More shouting and door slamming. On the third level, a colossal crash shock the building, making me fall to the floor.

There was nobody there by the time I got to the ground floor. A giant pane of glass had shattered, spilling shards of glass onto the Champs-Elysées.

The Citroën 2CV Europa Gen Y had left its platform.

FORTY-FIVE

I STRODE THROUGH THE HOLE into the middle of the Champs-Elysées, gun in hand.

The traffic was held up on both sides of the road. A solitary car, the blue electric Citroën 2CV, was limping towards the Place de la Concorde. It had almost reached the Franklin Roosevelt metro station, a few hundred feet away.

She had called for me. She knew I was there! She needed help. I started to run.

One, two, buckle my shoe.

I had seen her long flowing hair, fleetingly from above in the Citroën showroom.

Three, four, knock at the door.

What if the girl was Judy? I didn't believe so but there was only one way to be sure. I would not let that car get away.

The madness of the situation wasn't lost on me – a lone gunman chasing a getaway car down the most famous avenue in the world, just me and them. With a huge effort, I matched the car's speed and gained ground. It helped that the car was slowing down. It was now no more than seventy feet away.

Five, six, pick up sticks.

There were two passengers in the back seat. I strained my eyes to see them better but there was too much movement.

Were they Foxtrot and Capitaine? Was that father at the wheel? Anger surged through my veins.

You'll pay for this and for everything you've done.

The Citroën stopped dead in its tracks. I couldn't believe it. I was closing in fast – sixty feet, fifty feet. I could see four people struggling inside the car, then the front passenger door opened and Foxtrot stepped out. He looked in my direction – he also had a gun.

Forty feet. I was waving Mickie's gun in the air.

A bang. I crashed to the ground.

'This is how it ends,' I thought.

I opened my eyes. I was lying in the middle of the Champs-Elysées. Still no traffic. I had tripped and fired a round.

I watched Foxtrot haul a stout man onto the street – it was Capitaine. He was walking in my direction, his hands reaching out towards me. Two shots rang out and he slumped to the ground. I covered my face.

Thud. The car door slammed and the Citroën was back on the road. Foxtrot was slinking away down a side street.

'Get up!' whispered a voice in my head.

I picked up the gun and started to walk.

'You must not enter a state of shock. This is how soldiers get killed. You must keep moving, look out for danger and get to safety.'

I would not let this car escape.

Seven, eight, lay them straight.

Two hundred feet. I had once again found the superhuman strength needed to chase a motor vehicle. Did Eagle have surveillance? Now, Eagle. Now was the time to come good on our deal.

I was nearing the Grand Palais and hyperventilating like a maniac. Tourists turned away fearing I was a terrorist. A man stood by the roadside filming me with a phone. The statue of General de Gaulle looked at me severely as the Place de la Concorde loomed closer. The Citroën must not get that far.

I was only half-aware of the sirens. The car was in trouble again, swerving from side to side as it tore across the road divider. It took a second sharp turn to the right onto a grass verge and hurtled towards a café with a glass dome. It smashed through a barrier – the crash was seconds away.

The car veered too sharply to the left, hit a tree and upended on one side. A front tyre blew out as it landed with a thud. I sprinted as fast as possible, sure to catch father before he escaped on foot.

The Citroën was crippled, but stop it did not. It reversed then lurched forward and started off faster than before. It picked up speed, weaving and ducking through the trees until it found its way onto the northbound side street. I tried to keep up with it but was lagging by forty feet, then fifty.

I clenched my teeth to fight the pain. The British Embassy was less than a mile away. Was it the destination? They must not reach it. The Citroën would slow down and stall – the laws of physics demanded it.

I was nauseous and my head was spinning. I tried to get a sense of what lay at the end of the road but could only see iron gates. The car was now limping at fifteen miles an hour, but still fifty feet away. A cop retreated into a sentry box. He must have seen the Citroën and me. *Something was about to happen.*

A green van was parked conspicuously on the pavement. It happened in a flash. A dozen police officers in army combats, armed with riot shields and machine guns, deployed out of the van onto the street. The Citroën faltered and ground to a halt twenty feet from the police line. I slowed to a trot then stopped.

At last, I could see inside the stationary Citroën. A young woman was waving her hands, struggling with the driver. It was father and Madeleine.

An officer spoke through a muffled loudspeaker, instructing father to exit the vehicle. I braced myself for the shock of seeing him – but nothing happened. The officer repeated the instruction. Still nothing. The third message sounded more urgent. He was following a protocol that must end in violence.

A single shot. It rang out like a judge's gavel. The bullet struck the window on the driver's side. It took a moment for me to realise that it came from within the car. Madeleine's porcelain cheeks were pressed up against the passenger window as she fought father and scrambled for the gun.

The officer spoke and the Citroën was pounded with bullets. It crushed like a tin can – the rear windows smashed, the roof caved in and doors buckled. I lost sight of father and Madeleine. I rushed towards the police line with no thought of the danger. Madeleine needed help and now.

The officer shouted into his megaphone and the troops turned to face me. The top of father's head came back into view. The police turned towards the car but held their fire.

The Citroën – against all the odds – started up its engine and lurched forward. Nobody moved. The passenger door swung open and Madeleine was ejected from the vehicle. Father stepped out with a gun to her head. She was his hostage.

He looked through the police line and straight at me.

'Screwed up huh, son?' he mouthed.

He took a step backwards, his gun still pointed at Madeleine's head, and looked over his shoulder to his left and right. He was looking for someone.

Take him out, take him out!

Ten paces. Nobody moved.

Twenty paces.

He stopped at the street curb.

It unfolded in slow motion. I saw him release the safety of the gun. I saw him pull the trigger. I saw the bullet leaving the barrel and hurtle through the air. I saw Madeleine's body infected with the energy from the bullet and fly gracefully through the air.

'FUCK OFF TO HELL!' father screamed.

I dived headlong into the fray and the police opened fire again. Bullets crashed and banged around me, like fireworks feting my heroism. One hurtled past my ears and another in front of my eyes.

And then one didn't hurtle past me, or in front of me, but took me down. It didn't hurt. I felt relief. The fight was over.

There was still one last thing I had to do. I had fallen about five feet away from Madeleine. I felt pain in my upper body but was able to crawl towards her and prop myself up with my hands. The crimson stain on her crisp white blouse had morphed into a messy blot.

She lay still, her eyes shut and face lifeless, a doll left on a city street. A fallen angel. She was breathing softly. I rolled onto my back and lay my head on her knee so that we were both facing the sky.

She took hold of my hand.

'*C'est toi.*'

'*C'est moi.*'

I lifted my head without letting go of her hand. In the corner of my eye, I saw a man in a dark suit limping towards the iron gate of the French Ministry of the Interior.

I lay against Madeleine's body and closed my eyes. I make a wish that this moment would last an eternity. Bliss. Paradise. Nirvana. Shangri-La.

Sirens. Ambulance. Stretchers. Oxygen masks.

A third hand tries to prise ours apart. We hold on until we can no longer.

FORTY-SIX

It is all quite easy.

I make it to a port in Normandy, pass myself off as a dock-hand and board a freight ship bound for South America. I make a bed out of grain sacks in between giant bulk containers and bunker down. I figure that so long as we are at sea when I'm found, I'll make it to safety.

The ship's engine roars into action and the lights turn off, but it is not long before they find me. I am encircled by a cacophony of alarmed voices in Spanish and Portuguese. They demand to know how I got aboard, and things are tense for a moment. They debate what to do with me and I'm taken away for interrogation.

A saltwater breeze stings my face on the deck. I see ES-marked on the side of a lifeboat. I look back as I'm led through a narrow door, but don't need to – I know that I've walked headfirst into a trap. On the bridge, I am tied to a chair by ship hands while the senior crew is alerted.

'A sucker for punishment if ever I saw one!'

'Always knew he would get his comeuppance.'

'Gonna fix t'e b'stard gud 'n propa.'

The voices belong to Europa, Roper and Mickie. I'm thrown to the floor and battered with kicks before my captors leave me to 'decide my fate.'

I ponder this latest turn of events. How did it come about? Who betrayed me? I'm taken to a holding cell, about ten square feet with no window, toilet or ventilation. The door is bolted from outside. I peel a rusty iron bar off the inside wall and bash it against the door until it crumbles in my hand.

I clasp my ears to block out the deafening roar of the ship's engine. The cabin is going up and down as the ship cuts through rough Atlantic waves – each rise and fall more turbulent than the last, like an endless fairground ride. I crouch down to be sick and want to die, such is the pain.

An hour goes by and the swings become ever more violent until the cabin turns fully on its side. I count to twenty, waiting for the boat to level itself – but it stays put. I hear rushing water outside and know the ship is in serious trouble. I pound on the door, but no one heeds my call.

Water is seeping through cracks and is already up to waist level. I will drown unless someone comes to my aid. I shout at the top of my voice, to no avail. At the point of giving up, the ship is rocked by a huge explosion. The door opens and I wade through the corridors to the upper deck.

The storm is so violent I want to go back inside the hull. I see that the boat is sinking – the stern is underwater and the bow is pointing up at forty degrees. A man slips and is swept fifty feet across the deck and blown overboard, screaming for his life. I cling on to an iron rail while I desperately figure out what to do.

I try to reach the port side where men are making for a lifeboat and inch my way across the deck, buffeted by the hurricane gales. Roper, Mickie and Europa are among the passengers. They clamber aboard the lifeboat, pushing and shoving everyone in their way. Two men in raincoats stand behind them next to one of the ship's officers.

The officer is the last one to board. He is a portly man and has great difficulty battling the winds. As he tries to bridge the gap at the top of the ladder, he loses his balance. It looks like he is going to make it when a hand emerges from below and yanks at his foot, pushing him overboard.

'*Merde!*' screams Capitaine as he falls overboard.

A man in a rubber mackintosh is watching the scene unfold. He is well equipped for the storm and doesn't try to board the lifeboat. Rather he grabs an axe from the deck and slashes the ropes securing it. The first snaps quickly and the boat veers to one side, ejecting three men into the ocean.

The man begins work on the other rope as the sailors scramble to climb out. But they are too late. He wields the axe again and the lifeboat nosedives into the sea. I rush to the edge but there are no survivors. The boat is flooded and everyone overboard – all except the two men in raincoats.

They struggle to their feet and clamber onto the only part not submerged. They are drenched and bloodied but in no mood for giving up the fight. One of them raises his hand at me with a raised middle finger. It is Foxtrot. The other eyes me with sheer loathing. It is father. A large wave catapults them out of view.

A gust of wind lowers the axeman's hood.

'I told you so!' Eagle yells.

He smiles at me and points at the starboard side. I battle with the wind and rain to find a second lifeboat deployed. There are two women aboard. They appear to be identical and are tilting oars at each other like lances.

They are Judy and Madeleine. One strikes the other across her back, then her stomach. She doubles over but manages to drag her opponent towards her. They fight savagely with their fists and nails. It is hard to see in the mêlée, but one of the women seems to get the upper hand.

A huge wave rocks the boat, pushing the women to one side. The twin who was losing the fight picks up an oar and jabs. The stronger woman leans back to avoid the blow, loses her balance and totters. Her face reveals sadistic pleasure as she looks upon her watery grave. She hurls herself into the ocean.

I strain to see the lone survivor, but the boat is too far away. The ship is sinking fast and I look around for Eagle, but he is gone.

A fierce gust of wind knocks me over. I hit my head and black out. I am vaguely aware of the freezing water soaking my body.

'Do nothing and you will die,' says a voice.

'I'll be together with her!'

'You will die,' it repeats.

I grab a plank of wood seconds before I am swept into the ocean and pulled underwater. Blank. Nothingness. No dark tunnels with light at the end. No out-of-body experience. My last thought is that it is the end.

An island. I am enjoying the warm sun beating down on my face. There are coconuts, crabs and seashells. I lie still and admire the tranquil sea. A naked girl with long loose hair and pear-shaped breasts is perched on a faraway rock, a perfect mirage. As she swims through the water towards me, I see it is Madeleine. It is all too perfect, too cliché. But when she is on top of me, her hair covering my face, her breasts caressing my chest, tears streaming down our faces and our mouths locked, I believe that it is true.

FORTY-SEVEN

'You lucky son of a bitch!'

I was in a room full of medical equipment. I didn't feel lucky. My chest was aching and my vision was blurry.

'Plastic bullets. The French are goddamn pussies! Put you in a coma for a few hours though.'

Flashbacks. Madeleine being lifted into an ambulance. The Faubourg Saint-Honoré. The American Hospital.

'Got ya out in the nick of time, huh?' Eagle boasted. 'It's debrief time so listen up. You did good. You kept your end, more or less, so we're keeping ours. Neat work on Michael and Roper by the way. Overzealous, perhaps – dumb assholes are in intensive care. That Europa fella pissed his pants when we came for him!'

He laughed heartily.

'EUCO got wind of our friends' demise moments before the President was about to tell the world about ESIS. They cobbled together a package of half measures to save face, intelligence sharing, joint training, etc. ESIS never saw the light of day.

'The UK voted for Brexit, by the way. Poor bastards. 51.9% to 48.1%. How about that? The shock on the Continent was palpable – the riots stopped as Brexit became the new crisis. The EU heads of state put on a unified front against the new bad boy.

'You guys are in one hellova hole! But on the bright side, ESIS is overcome!'

Eagle read me an article from *The Guardian*. It was a calamity. Britain had shown itself to be isolationist and xenophobic. An MP had died in vain. We had deprived our children of privileges that we had taken for granted. The UK had turned its back on stability and prosperity, it was an act of war, etc.

'It ain't so bad. If you guys play your cards right, you'll strike a trade deal or two. Medicare can take over your NHS…'

The vote had only one implication for me. There was no need for me to have set foot in the C42 building. This could have ended differently.

'This wraps up operation EUROFOE for yours truly. Off to pastures green!'

I shut my eyes and wished him away.

'I see you're in a bad way. You wanna know about your pa, huh?'

He drew a deep breath to signal bad news was coming.

'Yeah, he got away. He was rescued and given safe passage to the British Embassy by his last remaining friends in the DGSE, then helicoptered to a private hospital on the island of Jersey. The FSB was waiting for him and he got on a private jet to Kaliningrad a few days ago.

'Our people are on the case. Man is he screwed! Up the creek without a paddle! Leagues out of his depth! Finished! Basta! There's a prison jumpsuit with his number on it. Nobody wants a loser political has-been, not even the Ruskies. Played with fire and got his fingers scorched.'

'Burned,' I tried to say.

'The Brits have hardly noticed he's AWOL. His office issued

269

a statement to say he was resigning as Foreign Secretary and an MP. A few papers ran career obituaries. The fall from on high, the man who snatched defeat from the jaws of victory etc. The story got lost, truth be told, in the seismic shockwaves of the Leave victory.

'The papers are revelling in the chaos of a national cockup. What a goddamn mess! Leave-supporting Tories can't believe their luck. The Prime Minister has resigned, and the usual suspects are getting down and dirty to replace him. Let slip the dogs of war!

'But what do you care? You're coming with us, Ellis. You 'n me. To Langley, Virginia. You're one of us now. Green card, new identity, the works. You won the lottery of life, amigo!'

He reeled off the usual catalogue of promises.

'Madeleine?' I blurted.

'Meeting adjourned old boy. You'll be needin' all your strength.'

FORTY-EIGHT

PLEASE ACCEPT MY APOLOGIES. I'M out of line. You kept your end of the bargain. You're the good guys. You did everything promised. I had the nerve to object to being detained in an underground prison cell. How ungrateful! As you say, I'm a major league limey asshole.

You keep asking me how I'm doing. Like you care. What do you honestly expect me to say? Oh, I get it – you *want* to hear about my pain and distress. I've long since understood that Americans are not just a group of naïve, friendly dimwits. The world is figuring this out too.

I will give you this pleasure. It's bad. Bad air. Bad food. Bad days. Bad dreams. Bad times. It's hell on earth. I am a 'voluntary detainee' – what the hell does that mean? Not that I can leave at any rate. You could've had the decency to make me a regular prisoner. I would have a lawyer and a trial. A sentence would entail a release date.

I haven't seen the light of day since I got here. Looks like someone forgot to give me the behind-the-scenes guided tour. I only have your word for it that I am in Langley, Virginia. I'm at Guantanamo Bay for I know. Why detain people at your own HQ? It's not a good idea to shit in your backyard.

There are no books, no television, no internet, no banter with the guards. The other voluntary detainees wail and scream at night. You probably expect me to whisper down the drain or scribble notes on toilet paper telling my story. Sorry buddy, not going to happen. My secrets are safely locked inside me.

There are no clocks, so no way to know what time it is. The fluorescent tubes are always on, like in a frozen meat truck or a mortuary, and the wardens set their watches to different times to screw with me. Clever. Yeah, you don't need to tell me the Geneva Convention counts for jack.

I was docile as sweet Jesus when I got here. But you know that – you pumped me with sedatives. I slept for a few hours and woke to go to the toilet and eat slop. Repeat and repeat and repeat. I say sleep, but I never really slept. Then you took away the meds and I woke up to the horrors of my reality.

I stopped eating the slop in protest. You said you'd force-feed me, but instead you watched me thrash about like a lunatic. The hunger was terrible beyond words, but it was worth fighting through the pain barrier because at the end were lavish illusions. The more starved I was, the grander the dreams. It was a way for me to be with Madeleine.

You fed me a good breakfast of eggs, pancakes, fresh toast and ground coffee. I loathed myself for eating it. I knew it meant you needed me. Sure enough, later that day, you called me in for the first interview.

'There's no such thing as a free lunch,' Eagle used to say.

No kidding.

I didn't play ball. I insisted on speaking to Eagle – to Frank, whatever the hell his name is. You told me there was no such person. I laughed in your faces, spat on the floor and refused to say another word. And that was that. I tried to recall your faces back in the cell but could only see brown stains.

The next day you told me Eagle was on an undercover mission. I told you there were ways of getting in touch with people away on business. You had lots of questions that demanded lots of answers. I wanted an answer to a single question and refused to talk until I got it. It was a standoff.

You bribed me with luxuries and threatened me with worse conditions. It didn't work. As far as I was concerned, you had reneged on the only fucking part of the bargain that meant anything to me and there was nothing else to talk about. You told me it was 'bad form' to get hung up on details. We were at square one.

You changed tracks. You told me that, as a matter of fact, it might be possible to see Eagle if I wrote a full account of my dealings with ESIS. I agreed to write after speaking with Eagle. You said it didn't work like that.

'Write the goddamn A to Zee of ESIS or never again see the light of day.'

I stood my ground. An audience with Eagle or nada. What the hell – with no one was waiting for me on the outside, I could hold out for decades.

A few weeks later my slop was served with an electronic tablet. A set of wily eyes came into view.

'What do you want? I debriefed you at the hospital,' Eagle said impatiently.

I instantly regretted asking for this interview and was at a loss for words.

'Let me tell you one last story,' he said with a sadistic smile. 'A brief recap. Grandpa Schneider had the dubious honour of being one of Nazi Germany's best young genetic scientists. During the war, he was given a mission to make test-tube Aryan babies to populate the Third Reich with übermensch. He failed and was sent to die on the Eastern Front.

'He was captured by the Soviets and sent to East Berlin. Luckily Uncle Sam came to the rescue, brought him to the Land of the Free and put him on payroll. Officially as a mid-level government researcher. In reality, he was top dog at a secret biogenetic research centre in Washington DC.

'The bad guys had picked up from where the Nazis had left off and Uncle Sam couldn't be caught with his pants down. It so happened the hub of operations was the lab where Grandpa S had been chief geneticist during the war.'

I raised an eyebrow. Grandpa S had been handpicked by the Americans for exactly this reason.

'You don't buy it. So what?' Eagle growled. 'These are historical facts. After the borders were redrawn, the lab found itself in Basel, Switzerland. It's still there and owned by Syngentrix International.'

He cleared his throat noisily.

'The Swiss rebooted the lab and staffed it with Europe's biggest brains. In 1949, word spread among the intelligence community that they'd engineered supermen and women – *überspezies*, or *spezies* for short. The Soviets and the Americans duly sent their people to investigate. Grandpa S oversaw the American delegation.

'It turned out to be a hoax – the scientists had gathered up young Aryans and pumped them with steroids. It was a publicity coup to persuade the superpowers to finance the lab. The Russians were furious at the decadent capitalist's bad joke and went home to carry on with their own eugenics experiments.

'Franz agreed to look at the research data. He believed they were close to achieving the real thing – implanting enhanced embryos into surrogate wombs to make supermen. He secured sizeable US funding for the project and sure enough, a breakthrough in the late 1950s led to the first *spezies* being born.

'It was a huge step forwards – but it wasn't plain sailing and there were endless problems with the prototypes. The scientists had no idea how to raise the children or look after them. They were Apollos and Venuses in their early years, but their health failed as soon as they reached adolescence. None lived to fifteen.

'The next batch was more resilient and got to adulthood, but by now the buyers were sceptical. It wasn't just the faulty genes. The *spezies* had bonded during their early years, showed extreme loyalty to one another and a total distrust of outsiders, which made them pretty goddamn useless spies.

'The Americans went ahead with their orders, but none made it into the CIA. They were used as cops to patrol the no-go zones of NYC and Miami and as border agents in Texas. This second generation of *spezies* also aged badly. The ones that weren't gunned down by the cartels died of natural causes in a few years.

'The lab shut down in 1978. Officially. But ex-Nazi scientists are stubborn bastards and a team of geneticists clandestinely carried on the operation. Grandpa S retired that year and bought a lodge in Switzerland. Coincidence, huh? We didn't see him so often back home after that.

'In 1979 they made a breakthrough that fixed – in fact slowed down – the ageing process. The next gen were twins, physically identical in every way. But the DNA coding affecting emotions was modified, giving them opposite character traits. In brief, they were engineered to hate each other. End of loyalty problem.

'This was biogenetic engineering worthy of a Nobel Prize! But on the cusp of glory, they hit a roadblock. The merchandise was ready in the late 1990s, just as the two major buyers were no longer in the game. The Russians couldn't afford beans on toast and the US was too busy pissing on the grave of communism. No sales without a market, old boy.

'There were a dozen remaining *spezies* for sale in 1992. The scientists lowered their price and did a brisk trade with African governments. Now you'll recall that our mutual friends, Capitaine and Foxtrot, were prowling for post-Cold War basement bargains right around this time. By the time they arrived at the negotiating table, there were only two females left.

'Sensing that the duo was desperate to get their hands on them, the scientists drove a hard bargain – ten million apiece. That's a fair few diamonds. And unbeknown to our mutual friends, the final pair of *spezies* suffered from psychiatric disorders – one was bipolar, the other psychotic.

'One twin was so violent she had tried to murder her sister. The scientists had decided to terminate her.'

Eagle paused to study my reaction.

'Madeleine and Judy – ten years old, were acquired in 1993. Madeleine went to live with Capitaine as Luc's half-sister.'

'Judy was sent to London. Foxtrot despised the idea of fatherhood so his friend and ally, John Goodman, adopted her. Judy is your half-sister.'

I laughed out loud. Eagle's story was insane nonsense – I'd been played for a fool for the last time.

'Enough!' I interrupted. 'I acquiesce! You'll get your goddamn account. Where is she now?'

'Judy is in a secure location.'

'Madeleine.'

'Escaped from hospital and got on a plane to Dallas. She was last seen at LAX.'

FORTY-NINE

You told me to write three pages a day.

You gave me a laptop, a desk, plant and clock. I got a bagel for breakfast, a sandwich for lunch and meat or fish for dinner. The lights came on at 8 a.m. and went off at 10 p.m. The air was fresher, and I was taken to an indoor fitness court for an hour a day. The wardens even spoke to me.

But I didn't write anything. I slept between meals and sat on the bed naked and played with myself. I tried to hack the computer. I stood on the desk, recited Shakespeare and made speeches to imaginary crowds. I made obscene gestures at the surveillance camera and typed pages of gibberish.

The food went back to slop and the exercise stopped. I didn't want to suffer more, but I didn't care. I laughed a lot after the meeting with Eagle. The old bastard should take to the stage as Iago. I went over everything he'd said, though, and had to accept it couldn't all be fantasy. I spent hours trying to sort out the truths from the lies.

The encounter had, in any case, left me feeling depressed. I wasn't ready to write. Soon, perhaps – but not yet. I needed time to collect my thoughts and to find the inner peace and mental space to relive the recent past's traumas. On a more lucid day, I wrote a note to you about this.

'Write the report,' was your answer.

It's okay. I didn't expect you assholes to understand. I began by jotting down random thoughts, memories, jokes and stories. I tried my hand at free verse.

On Love

We all love, we all lose.

Love is loss, loss is love.

We have all been loved and we have all been lost.

Even abandoned orphans were born of love, if you care to think about it.

There is nothing new in this. It plays out ten thousand times in the act of sex. You can make love to your beloved for days, weeks and years on end, but one day you will withdraw for the last time. So in a way, each withdrawal is the end. 'La petite mort.' Just as sleep foreshadows death, we are reminded of our pitiful mortality.

I had a reoccurring dream about the MI6 test centre in London. I got the job one time and had James Bond adventures. But I didn't usually get past the death of the tramp in the underground. I saw him fall in slow motion and the remains of his charred body collected piece by piece. I wrote it down and this became a starting point for my story.

I wrote about my arrest in Brighton – after some reorganising this became the starting point of my story – then went back episode by episode. The meeting with Bigboy and Madeleine. The ESIS letter and dinner with father, mother and Debs. Work on the *Definitive Tour* promo in the grotto, the fights with my co-partner leading up to the frenzied sex bout, Gaz, the fire, the fateful party and the harrowing discovery of Angie Hammond's decapitated body.

This by far the most traumatic event and the aftermath – time in the cells and my expulsion to France – was relatively easy to narrate. I finished up the section that took place in Brighton and read it back. My style was imbued with a certain detachment that let me write the account like a novel populated with fictional characters. 'I is another,' a French poet once said.

In Paris, I'd often been under the influence of alcohol and drugs and was hazy about many events, so I made lists – of incidents, names and places – and a rough timeline to help structure my narrative. You tasked me with describing how I experienced things, not what actually happened. If you want hard facts, ask your ESIS felons.

It was often tough figuring out when exactly Madeleine and Judy had switched. I first laid eyes on Madeleine at Bigboy's flat. I was with Judy in the grotto, but the sex was with Madeleine. I'd sighted Madeleine in the metro in Paris and she was my writing partner and lover. I travelled to Cannes with her but met Judy at the station.

It should be fairly obvious, even to you knuckleheads. But there were a few moments I wasn't a hundred per cent sure about, so for the sake of simplicity, I refer to Judy in the UK and Madeleine in France – even at times when it patently was not Madeleine. It lends a certain unreliability to my narrative I feel sure you'll appreciate.

I was able to write four or five pages a day. Living conditions improved again, though I barely noticed. At night I speculated about what had happened to each of my foes – Mickie, Roper, Dr Europa, Capitaine and Foxtrot. I tried hard not to think about him, father – that most toxic of poisons. But he crept into my head like a cancer. Villain, what hast thou done?

Finishing was the hardest part. It felt as if I was cutting ties with Madeleine and going back on my promise to be with her.

I wrote a story where I rescued her – we escaped to Italy by boat, evading capture at every turn. But it only made the final episodes more painful to describe.

All in all, it took six months to complete my report. It's what you've just read. Reading it back, I studied my reflection in the laptop screen. All traces of youth had vanished from my face.

'I am not what I am,' I muttered to myself.

You took it without ceremony. A week later you told me it was 'BS from start to finish, one hellova fantasy.' I would be spending the rest of my days in jail, etc. But when you asked me about loose ends, I knew you were bluffing.

One day I woke up to find I was free.

EPILOGUE

'We suffer because we desire.' (Buddha)

*'Life. We are born. We screw. We die. There are great times.
There are fucking terrible times. That's about it.'*

(Billy, Sage of Venice Beach)

I WAS GIVEN A CHOICE of five cities to relocate to – New York, Seattle, Boston, Miami and Los Angeles. I chose LA without thinking about it. I've been here for six months. I live in a condo downtown and drive a Mustang. It's better than the Langley dungeon.

It's strange how when trials are over, the memory of the ordeal is but a shadow of the suffering itself. All that we feel – pain, pleasure, despair – we experience in the now. I'm writing this for an essay on Nietzsche's 'pure present' for a class at UCLA. I don't go often but it was included in my 'deal.' I also got membership to an exclusive gym, a pass to a Hollywood club and a discount card at Starbucks.

America is the free-market economy of love, and LA its capital. Everyone is about getting the best they can for their credit, on credit. I belong to five internet dating sites and spend most of my time in chat rooms. All the girls write the same dumb crap but I read it all the same. I'm currently in a virtual relationship with an actress from Encino – Maggie is blonde, spiritual and dreams of living in Paris.

I see a therapist. I tell her I don't know who I am and she agrees that I'm in a 'bad place' right now. I flirt with the gay guys in the gym changing room and let them eye me up, I'm used to it now. I roll up my DNKY tee-shirt and am horrified to see a pound of loose flesh around my waist. I vow to get my six-pack back – this will give me some purpose.

The first thing you learn in LA is that you are nobody without a car. I bought the Mustang on a whim from the dealership two blocks from my house because I'd been drinking all afternoon and it looked so fucking cool. I've been driving without a licence or papers safe in the knowledge that the police never stop white people. I have a number anyways that makes my troubles go away.

One day I have fuck all to do, I go to the Department of Motor Vehicles, which is the shittiest place on earth. I eavesdrop on the man and woman sitting behind me. From their voices, I imagine that they are young and hip but when I turn round I see an old junkie and a crack whore. The woman who serves me at the counter weighs three hundred pounds. She asks me if I had come for a sex licence and I say yes. I am a little off-balance.

I barely eat these days, just drink. I wake up feeling rough, although I've learned to deal with the hangover by drinking neat tequila. You crash out, sleep lightly, wake early, but retain the alertness and the perspicacity of the night before. No impaired mobility, none of the fatigue and cloudiness that beer brings. On the downside, I am given to anxiety attacks, amnesia and blackouts.

I turn on Fox News then mute the sound as soon as people start talking. Some TV star has been tweeting about Mexican rapists, illegals, shithole countries, Islam, using nukes and fake news, and it turns out he is the President of the United States. Everyone agrees he's a racist asshole, but no one is too bothered because it's like a reality show and so entertaining. Elsewhere there's trouble in the bubble, and pain at the pump, and things move so freaking fast here, it's overwhelming.

I drive around to pass the time. It's mostly just garages everywhere – some dialysis centres and more garages. The air is lurid with gas and carbon, and the cars just keep crashing and polluting all over town. Even the goddamn papers get delivered by car here. Everyone is freaking out today as it's so freaking hot, and the religious fanatics in Korea Town are out in force, begging infidels not to go to hell, 'prease.' And on Vermont, Toni is standing with his sign for the Little Caesar's five-dollar pizza with cheese or pepperoni, and he's always there, night and day, and I wonder if he even works for Little Caesar.

At the downtown Rite Aid, the black security guard who works sixteen-hour shifts is on his cigarette break outside and I stand in line behind a bum in garish silk pyjamas who tells me that he produced the *Rolling Stones* back in the day and I believe him. In the endless checkout line, I browse the magazines which are full of stories about this month's hot couple who are either so getting married or so splitting up, a dead porn star and a rock star in rehab who strangled her children.

There are even more arrests than when I last went out a few weeks ago. On my way home I see a pretty Asian girl being handcuffed and escorted out of a luxury hotel, and I feel sorry for her and the two Hispanic kids with their hands above their heads on the edge of gangland. And at the traffic lights, a bum is tapping on my windscreen and apologizing to me for being a junkie, and I don't know what to say other than it was cool, it was cool.

I'm home again and back on the dating sites and a girl named Mary suggests drinks tonight. Her profile picture shows only the top of her legs and I spend a long time deciding whether to reply. It's too hot inside even with the AC on, so I head off to the gym and slide into the Jacuzzi where some hot college students are bitching about their girlfriends. To drown out the noise, I tune into the TV and listen to a report about a schoolteacher who became a polygamist cult leader and mass murderer.

It's evening now, although it never really gets dark, and people are parking and hanging on the boardwalks in Venice and Santa Monica and Hollywood and Silverlake in the warm Pacific dusk. The air is still thick with smoke from the fire four nights ago in Griffith Park when, for a few hours, the whole of the East side looked apocalyptic, like it was Armageddon. There was a buzz of excitement in the air with helicopters flying overhead all night and news teams capturing some scenes of genuine panic.

I sit on my balcony sipping a cool vodka tonic and I read my scribblings from last night, about the curve – the rate at which feelings of love and passion die exponentially and pursue a downward path towards nothingness. And sex and break-ups mirror your own demise – you wake up with a jolt to discover that it is the afterlife and you are already dead. But I wrote all this down when I was drunk and I have no idea what it means.

And I look in the mirror and I admit to myself that I am still waiting for her and that I will go on the date tonight because, however improbable, she may have found me. I look out from my balcony, across the pool and the sirens and the mansions and the sweatshops, across the city towers and the sea of red and yellow coming from the ten freeway leading to the Pacific Ocean and the Santa Monica Mountains, and I know that I will see Madeleine again. It is just a matter of time.